THE LIBRARY
UNIVERSITY OF
WINCHESTER

KA 0287421 0

Women Writing Modern Fiction

Also by Janice Rossen:

THE WORLD OF BARBARA PYM

PHILIP LARKIN: *His Life's Work*

THE UNIVERSITY IN MODERN FICTION: *When Power is Academic*

INDEPENDENT WOMEN (*editor*)

WRITERS OF THE OLD SCHOOL: *British Novelists of the 1930s* (*co-editor, with Rosemary M. Colt*)

AGING AND GENDER IN LITERATURE: *Studies in Creativity* (*co-editor, with Anne M. Wyatt-Brown*)

Women Writing Modern Fiction

A Passion for Ideas

Janice Rossen

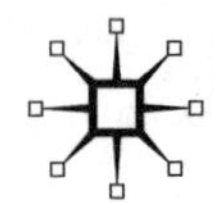

© Janice Rossen 2003

All rights reserved. No reproduction, copy or transmission of this publication may be made without written permission.

No paragraph of this publication may be reproduced, copied or transmitted save with written permission or in accordance with the provisions of the Copyright, Designs and Patents Act 1988, or under the terms of any licence permitting limited copying issued by the Copyright Licensing Agency, 90 Tottenham Court Road, London W1T 4LP.

Any person who does any unauthorised act in relation to this publication may be liable to criminal prosecution and civil claims for damages.

The author has asserted her right to be identified as the author of this work in accordance with the Copyright Designs and Patents Act 1988.

First published 2003 by
PALGRAVE MACMILLAN
Houndmills, Basingstoke, Hampshire RG21 6XS and
175 Fifth Avenue, New York, N.Y. 10010
Companies and representatives throughout the world

PALGRAVE MACMILLAN is the global academic imprint of the Palgrave Macmillan division of St. Martin's Press, LLC and of Palgrave Macmillan Ltd. Macmillan® is a registered trademark in the United States, United Kingdom and other countries. Palgrave is a registered trademark in the European Union and other countries.

ISBN 0–333–61420–8

This book is printed on paper suitable for recycling and made from fully managed and sustained forest sources.

A catalogue record for this book is available from the British Library.

Library of Congress Cataloging-in-Publication Data
Rossen, Janice, 1955–
Women writing modern fiction : a passion for ideas / Janice Rossen.
p. cm.
Includes bibliographical references (p.) and index.
ISBN 0–333–61420–8
1. English fiction – Women authors – History and criticism. 2. Women and literature – Great Britain – History – 20th century. 3. English fiction – 20th century – History and criticism. 4. Modernism (Literature) – Great Britain. I. Title.

PR888.W6R67 2003
823′.91099287–dc21

2003045690

10 9 8 7 6 5 4 3 2 1
12 11 10 09 08 07 06 05 04 03

Printed and bound in Great Britain by
Antony Rowe Ltd, Chippenham and Eastbourne

KING ALFRED'S COLLEGE
WINCHESTER

02874210 | 823.9109 ROS

for Jane, Joan, Peggy, Jo C., Mary, and Michelle

Contents

Preface

The novels which appear in the following chapters share one quality: they are exciting to read. Some are extravagantly emotional; others are enthusiastic in pursuing tortuous intellectual paradigms; but this intensity also makes them endearing. If viewed together, these novels offer a map of twentieth-century thought, showing several ways in which women were influenced by the opportunity to embrace a much wider range of experience – including entrance into the university, which significantly affected their views of academe. They were also drawn to the unfolding discipline of psychology. For women novelists who had a natural penchant for analytical modes of thought, it was an exhilarating time in which to be writing. Human passions remain the same in any age – but the increasingly self-conscious way in which women began to think and write about the workings of the mind stimulated their imaginations, whether in the gothic novels of Susan Howatch or the detective fiction of Dorothy L. Sayers.

The writers whose works I have gathered here include a wide range of British women authors, from the early part of the twentieth century up to the present time, including Elizabeth Bowen, Dorothy L. Sayers, Molly Keane, Susan Howatch, Barbara Pym, Stella Gibbons, Georgette Heyer, Iris Murdoch, and A.S. Byatt. They were fascinated by the individual thought processes of their characters, and rewrote the Victorian novel in stylish modern dress. They dramatize darkness in wartime, gothic terror, madness, and romantic betrayal, yet celebrate the triumph of rationality and the 'Higher Common Sense.' With irony, detachment, wit, and high intelligence, they bring us acrobatic tales of the mind.

Janice Rossen

Acknowledgements

I am in high danger of turning sentimental, when attempting to thank all of my companions along the way – however, it must be said at once that a great many friends have had to enter into a great deal of discussion on points related to the following study. That made it at once a much better book (for which I thank them) and also much more fun to write.

Peter Firchow first set me on the Path to Scholarship. J.J. Cilliers was my Ideal Reader; Emily Rosser, my Ideal Editor. Thys Botha was simply Ideal.

Several colleagues contributed to this book in various discussions, and I thank warmly Rosemary M. Colt, Jerome Meckier, James Booth, Max Egremont, Lesley Hall, Beth Hedrick, Tom Cable, Elizabeth Gifford, John Augustine, Charles Romney, Tim Rogers and Frank Moorhouse. Hemali Shah and Lauren Downey were cheerful research assistants. Martyn Hitchcock provided invaluable copy-editing advice.

The friends to whom I dedicate this book are a constant delight. Joan Morgan and Jane Ferson spent countless hours reading *Middlemarch* aloud with me. Peggy Weiss opened many new doors out in the world for me. Jo C. Hall saw ways around every problem, and reminded me of how much I love reading and writing. Mary McKay Duncan lights up everything around her with *joie de vivre*, and Michelle Cardenas makes me laugh continually.

My thanks also go to Tony Howe, who provided a constant stream of *New York Review of Books* issues, and to Patrick Wildgust, who poured out his extraordinary range of artistic knowledge for me to draw on. Larry Lake remained bracingly skeptical. Tony Kaufman combined pride with prejudice, pity with sorrow, and ham with eggs, to counteract Over-Seriousness and Desperate Melodrama. Simon Jenner saw the background landscape of literary history. Brian Thompson always believed that It Could Be Done. And John Carey reminded me that a writer most needs to be Passionate About An Idea.

Manchester was a crucial part of the writing of this book, and I thank my friends there, especially Mary and Tony Berry, Philip Parr, Raymond Lau, and Steve Pilling. The John Rylands University Library of Manchester kindly gave me a beautiful study in which to work, and Sam's Chop House – in its anachronistic Victorian glory – a place in which to celebrate small creative victories. My thanks as ever to the Bodleian Library and the Department of Western Manuscripts, especially to Colin Harris and the staff in Room 132.

Yet again, I express deep gratitude and affection to my husband, William Rossen, whose chosen role of Benedick the Married Man he has played with spirit and generosity. He has shared his computer, his resourcefulness, his travel budget, his culinary finesse, and his academic expertise, with a whole heart. *'Bid me do anything for thee.'*

Introduction

Two forces in the early part of the twentieth century impacted women writers for the rest of the century: feminism and literary modernism. These movements later came to be seen as having been centered on the figure of Virginia Woolf, whose influence has been felt either directly or indirectly by the British novelists who followed her. In her fiction, she experimented with 'stream-of-consciousness' techniques and pondered the human mind's powers of perception; in her essays, she called for a 'Room of One's Own' and for a renunciation of the subservient Victorian 'Angel in the House' model for womanhood. The combination of modernism and feminism which Woolf represented came to be by-passed, however, by a number of twentieth-century women writers for various reasons – often not so much in a spirit of reaction against these ideals as from the fact that they derived inspiration from elsewhere, and felt drawn to anachronistic literary styles. For 'popular' writers such as Baroness Orczy, Georgette Heyer, Stella Gibbons and Susan Howatch, the Victorian novel form called for a well-defined plot and fairly stock characters. It had the advantage of providing what their audience enjoyed and was used to reading. Similarly, the detective story genre in which Dorothy L. Sayers worked in the 1930s also demanded the sort of logical progression and resolution which were associated with Victorian writing, rather than with open-ended modernism. For more 'serious' novelists, such as Molly Keane, Olivia Manning and Barbara Pym, a tradition of realism suited their ironic tone, in which heroines observed the world around them with wry detachment. Elizabeth Bowen was perhaps more directly influenced by modernist ideals, though she none the less tended to write in a conservative style. And for novelists with scholarly backgrounds, such as Iris Murdoch and A.S. Byatt, their choice of literary style seems to have been, in part, a self-conscious turning away from the experimentation of a modernist mode, and towards more deliberately ordered fiction. A.S. Byatt observed of her own writing that she felt instinctively 'resistant to the idea that the world hits us as a series of random impressions (V. Woolf) and that memory operates in a random manner.'[1]

Still, all of these authors are extremely interested in individual thought processes, and especially in the conscious application of reason to a character's choices. Taking for granted the greatly increased freedom for women in the twentieth century, these authors bring forward the Victorian concern with reason and morality into the modern world of uncertainty and flux. They are fascinated with the human mind – how it perceives things, whether its own filtering belief system adversely affects its ability to be rational, and whether it can actually have any power over the way things are in the world. Belief in the power of reason seems to underlie the work of many of these novelists, who often write about highly intelligent heroines. At the same time, the mind, as portrayed in these novels, is potentially treacherous – a character can be fundamentally wrong in her perceptions, or can lapse into compulsiveness, or can even go mad. In other contexts, though, the mind can focus will and reason into a tremendous power for good. This underlying idea links these modern novels with the Victorian interest in questions of morality – whether characters can choose to be good, and whether they can (like George Eliot's Dorothea Brooke) be mistaken yet virtuous in their beliefs and actions. The advent of psychology in the twentieth century made contemporary authors all the more self-conscious about describing the thought processes of their characters, and they employed an increasingly ironic tone in their novels as the century went on, to express this uneasiness.

The authors whom I have included in this study did not, for the most part, determine deliberately to ignore the literary innovations of the modernists; to them, it seemed a natural progression to carry forward a nineteenth-century style into the twentieth century, adapting it to suit their own purposes, and altering it to act as a filter for contemporary ideas and problems.

The influence of feminism affected them in a much more complex way. The achievements wrought for women by feminists made it possible for these writers virtually to side-step this as an issue. This is especially notable in relation to the university; many of these authors had strong academic connections. Dorothy L. Sayers was among the first women to earn a degree at Oxford University, and eventually – following her fiction-writing career – produced an impressive scholarly translation of Dante's *Divine Comedy*. While Elizabeth Bowen did not attend the university, she had many friends who were notable academics, such as Sir Maurice Bowra, or who were highly respected men of letters, such as Cyril Connolly and Philip Toynbee. She wrote critical pieces about the art of fiction, and was a well-known figure in the London literary world of her era. Barbara Pym earned an Oxford degree, as did Iris Murdoch, who, as a philosopher, became a Fellow of St. Anne's College. A.S. Byatt attended Newnham College, Cambridge, and taught literature courses for several years, in addition to writing works of literary criticism on such figures as Wordsworth and Coleridge, as well as on Iris Murdoch. Susan Howatch is in many ways the most impressive of all, since she is an autodidact: her extensive research into twentieth-century religious and philosophical history underlies her complex saga of ideas related to the Anglican Church.

To some extent, writers such as Bowen, Sayers, Pym, Murdoch, and Byatt were able to avoid many of the limitations of being women in twentieth-century Britain because of their social class, their relative wealth and freedom, and their access to the academic world. The university was – at least in principle – a place where women could prove their merit on an individual basis (thus lessening the need for preoccupation with feminist goals), and their presence there made it more possible to follow their natural inclinations towards thinking about abstract ideas. This is not to say that they did not also cherish ambitions for romance and adventurous living, or that intellectual interests consumed them. Their presence at university constituted, in some ways, a difficult transition, as is evidenced by the internal struggles of Dorothy L. Sayers' passionate heroine in *Gaudy Night*. Writing later in the century, A.S. Byatt conflates these ideas by evoking irony about the firm faith that her heroine has in her own merit, based on both academic achievement and on her relationship to the opposite sex. In *Babel Tower*, Frederica Potter reflects, years after graduating, about Cambridge women and their relations with male undergraduates, 'We thought we were special and we were only scarce.'[2] Both were in fact true, but the recognition of this conundrum was at times uncomfortable.

The relative indifference to specifically feminist concerns on the part of many of these authors was also felt and expressed in another way, having to do with their aims in writing fiction (a profession about which all of them were fiercely serious). As A.S. Byatt described her own creative process, she wrote from a viewpoint that was not specifically feminine, but which was intended to extend beyond what Byatt experienced as the 'limits' of being female.[3] It is not that these writers undervalued either their experience or their identities as women; as John Carey has wittily observed about Elizabeth Bowen, '[she] is female to her fingernails, and knows things men do not. Perhaps that is why men tend not to read her. It is also why they should.'[4] Still, their natural artistic bents seem to have found an outlet in being modern without modernist, and feminine without being feminist.

At the same time, since these writers were building on a nineteenth-century literary tradition, they were also affected by the intrinsic feminist energy which gave many of the great works of that century such power. The feminist criticism of Ellen Moers' *Literary Women* and of Sandra Gilbert and Susan Gubar's *The Madwoman in the Attic* – to refer to only the most seminal scholarly works in this field – amply demonstrates the emotional frustration which burned white hot for such novelists as Charlotte and Emily Brontë and many others. This covert connection has also been explored in several scholarly works which consider more traditional novels by twentieth-century women, in particular in Nicola Beauman's wonderful *A Very Great Profession: The Woman's Novel 1914–1939*, Anthea Trodd's excellent *Women's Writing in English: Britain 1900–1945*, and Nicola Humble's intriguing *The Feminine Middle-Brow Novel 1920–1950*, which discover for us threads between novels of domesticity and professionalism, describing novels about women's private lives and secret trials. Feminist literary history has been charted in twentieth-century women's novels by many scholars, and I also want to mention here especially those studies which take the seminal historical period of World Wars I and II as a focus for discussion about the interrelation between national, political events and women's choices, including Jenny Hartley's *Millions Like Us: British Women's Fiction of the Second World War*, Alison Light's *Forever England: Femininity, Literature and Conservatism between the Wars*, Gill Plain's *Women's Fiction of the Second World War: Gender, Power and Resistance*, and Sandra Gilbert and Susan Gubar's *No Man's Land*.

The descriptive and historical work which many of these studies have offered us is also complemented by several more purely theoretical feminist approaches; Ruth Robbins has cogently pointed out that the development of this academic field has created a number of parallel 'feminisms.'[5] While all of these scholarly texts have created a background for the study which follows – and indeed, have made it possible – I have not made direct use of many of its tenets, since the writers whom I have grouped together fall largely outside of these concerns. They cannot be classified as women who live and write on the 'margins' of society, as did the interrelated circle of female writers who are described in Hanscombe and Smyers' *Writing for their Lives*, a group which was valiant in pursuit of modernist artistic goals.[6] Nor can their books be described as being 'girly,' in the sense which Nicola Humble uses when talking of a certain set of twentieth-century authors, or as 'women's novels,' as Nicola Beauman and others have described them.[7] The interests of writers such as Dorothy L. Sayers, Susan Howatch, Iris Murdoch and A.S. Byatt (to name only a few) are deliberately more broad-ranging, and (although this is not especially significant in itself) they write at times from a masculine point of view as well as from a feminine one. Olga Kenyon, analyzing contemporary authors in her *Women Novelists Today: A Survey of English Writing in the Seventies and Eighties*, notes of both Murdoch and Byatt that they described their own creative preoccupations as being 'androgynous.'[8] And while Byatt is clearly fascinated by language and perception, Kenyon points out that 'she is not interested in the feminists' claim that the very notion of what constitutes knowledge is male-defined.'[9]

The authors whose novels appear in this book seem to defy categorization. But they form a loosely related group whose works become increasingly interesting, the more they are read together. In this study, I have pieced together a fabric of novels by several important modern writers, including Elizabeth Bowen, Olivia Manning, Dorothy L. Sayers, Baroness Orczy, Barbara Pym, Molly Keane, Susan Howatch, Caroline Blackwood, Stella Gibbons, Georgette Heyer, Iris Murdoch and A.S. Byatt. They are a fascinating group of writers, with one particular interconnection: while not being intellectual (except in a very few cases) they have a passion for ideas, and for dramatizing the workings of the mind. They delight in showing their characters thinking, analyzing, and puzzling over everything from a straightforward detective case to a dramatic affair of the heart.

If characters are to be given free rein for individual choice, it is important that they be seen to possess this latitude. Byatt's notion of her characters as 'hypotheses let loose in the world' is representative of the aesthetic behind the work of many of the novelists whom I have mentioned here.[10] This view reflects her academic background and her wide reading in several disciplines – particularly in science, a field whose fundamental method of approach is to posit questions and to propose answers to them. And it also assumes that logic works; one can reason one's way to a conclusion, and the likely thing (given past experience and the data gathered) will most probably happen. Academic training is often seen as a positive good, in these novels, because it promotes rationality of thought. At the same time, Byatt's characters can be devastated by a horrific accident which 'ploughs a furrow' into their lives. The underlying question here is: is there free will, and is individual choice possible?

The answer for Byatt – and for similar women writers in the twentieth century with her academic bent – is provisional. The process of thinking itself can be misshapen or thwarted through the hand of fate. The devastating effects of war, the horror induced by gothic malevolence (the supernatural is real in many of these fictional worlds), and the acute pain of grieving can crush characters into numbness. Madness makes nonsense of logic and the mind's perception, and can easily lead to self-destruction. Those characters who consciously try to think rationally can be overcome by the mind's tendency to self-deception or to addictiveness; even the potentially joyous effect of falling in love can have terrible consequences for those characters who are overmastered by passion. They do not have a choice. Still worse is the pain and numbness induced by being betrayed in love, where one can be hurt through no apparent fault of one's own.

These writers possess a number of other qualities in common, sharing a tendency to darkness and fatalism – yet also an insistence on the virtues of reason, which does sometimes triumph. They chose to work in a nineteenth-century narrative mode. They shared a passion for the intellect, and often constructed complex plots, with irony and detachment, either wry and cynical or witty and playful. They were not especially feminist. In their writings, they are often passionate, yet detached; when describing pain, their narrators and characters analyze it, rather than feel it, in order to hold it at bay or to protect themselves. It can occasionally become tiresome for the reader to wade through the heavy irony which sometimes infuses these novels (especially when this is intended to heighten extravagant emotion); and these books can, at times, seem like too much 'head' at the expense of 'heart.' Nonetheless, ideas are interesting, especially when pursued with such vigor and intelligence. Further, when read in relation to each other, the works of these novelists illuminate what each of these writers observed, felt, and thought in her era.

In the chapters which follow, I have traced several themes which recur in these novels, by way of illustrating their nineteenth-century style and twentieth-century content. The structure of the book moves from dark fatalism to an increasing realm of light and of free will. This study takes in several quintessential twentieth-century preoccupations, beginning with the most extreme of pressures which affect fictional characters, and thus throw their decision-making processes into relief. I begin with the effects of war, particularly in the dark, brooding sagas of Elizabeth Bowen and Olivia Manning. But even under these circumstances, if a writer is willing to don a more Victorian, sentimental mode, the possibilities for heroism can be shown, as in Orczy's *The Scarlet Pimpernel*. Chapter 2 takes up another impossible foe to combat: the supernatural. Writers such as Susan Howatch, Elizabeth Bowen and A.S. Byatt use a gothic tradition to challenge their characters' thoughts and beliefs about the powers of reason, all the while contrasting it with a popularized view of Freudian psychoanalysis. At the same time, a writer such as Mary Stewart can use the supernatural dimension to create a manifestly romantic novel. Chapter 3 completes the section on darkness in the mind, looking at the relation between grieving and madness, particularly in Iris Murdoch's *Nuns and Soldiers*. A.S. Byatt takes this inquiry a step further, by satirizing clinical psychologists' analyses of their patients' manias in *A Whistling Woman*, and also by examining the collective insanity of a religious cult. Her novel *The Game*, in addition to books by Elizabeth Bowen and Caroline Blackwood, depict characters whose despair drives them to suicide. At the same time, the British tradition of charming eccentricity can still be upheld, in novels such as Molly Keane's *Treasure Hunt*, where the escape into complete fantasy of a character such as Aunt Anna Rose is deeply (and protectively) respected by her family.

Part II of this book extends the theme of intellectual analysis to an unlikely situation: sexual passion. In Elizabeth Bowen's view – as well as that of many of these novelists – romance is a kind of madness, and skews her characters' ability to see the world rationally. Her genius as a writer is particularly apparent in the progression of her early novels, which show successive variations on the social pressure which afflicts her heroines in contemporary novels published in the 1920s and 30s. Not every depiction of romance is stark, of course; Dorothy L. Sayers' lavish romance between her detective figure, Lord Peter Wimsey, and the novelist Harriet Vane is ebulliently consummated. And A.S. Byatt draws a sympathetic portrait of courtship and marriage between Stephanie and Daniel Orton in the first two volumes of her tetralogy. The following chapter, 'Betrayal,' considers the darker side of sexual politics in the numerous depictions of female rivalry, from Molly Keane's *Taking Chances* to Elizabeth Bowen's *The House in Paris*. Iris Murdoch's *The Sacred and Profane Love Machine* and *A Severed Head* show the complexity and potential devastation of betrayal within marriage; yet it can also be turned to creative use, as is done by the character of Prudence Bates in Barbara Pym's *Jane and Prudence*. In each of these chapters, I discuss several ways in which characters try to think clearly, yet cannot, due to various pressures. Nonetheless, the implicit belief in the power of reason and free will still exists, if only to intensify the drama of choice.

Part III considers several instances where reason and logic can be seen to effect change for the better: most notably, in academic and detective novels. Dorothy L. Sayers' *Gaudy Night* and A.S. Byatt's many discussions of university life, from *Still Life* to *Possession* to *A Whistling Woman*, show various ways of employing logic as a defense against the chaos of the world. Part of the irony of passion in the context of academic characters' lives is the fact that they exalt the powers of rationality, yet can be driven by emotional forces as well. In the conventions of detective fiction, it is a given that deductive reasoning will produce – at the least – the apprehension of the criminal by the detective. While this may only be a partial gain, and a reaction against something evil rather than a creation of some positive good, it is nonetheless crucial to society. A fascinating corollary to novels which exalt the power of reason are Georgette Heyer's historical romances, which present a world of 'supersanity,' in Byatt's description of it.[11]

In the final chapter, I discuss novels which exalt the use of rationality – yet which do so with humor. In Stella Gibbons' brilliant *Cold Comfort Farm*, positive change is effected through what Gibbons' heroine calls 'the Higher Common Sense,' which succeeds as much by fulfilling the characters' deepest desires as it does by persuading them into holding more rational beliefs. This novel brings light to bear on seemingly intractable situations, and manages to combine warmth of heart with keenness of mind.

It is my hope that everyone who browses through this book might find a novel or two which seems intriguing. Above all, it is the sheer pleasure of reading which animates these novelists, who have pursued their craft with such commitment and zest. They have opened doors onto many new worlds for us, and there are many journeys of the mind still to undertake in their company.

Part I
Darkness in the Mind

Authors such as Bowen, Manning, Murdoch and Byatt are interested in the ways in which the human mind works, particularly when it is under extreme emotional duress. They describe the dissociation that arises from intense suffering, and the process of grieving – both of which cause a temporary loss of self, self that must be reacquired or else relinquished entirely in suicide. In addition, they surround human experience with a supernatural dimension (which may in fact be purely psychological, a projection of the brain's tortuous inner workings). From war to gothic terror to grieving and madness, they chart the valiant efforts of their heroines to reason their way out of crushing dilemmas.

1
The World Gone Mad in Wartime

Wartime – as the background setting for a novel – creates a dramatic situation by its very nature. And for those novelists, such as Elizabeth Bowen and Olivia Manning, who are writing melodramatic stories while maintaining ironic distance, it provides a useful way of depicting suffering without suggesting that it is extraordinary. This is not to say that the harrowing context in which the characters are forced to endure is not challenging; their heroines are placed in life-and-death situations repeatedly, and must show their nonchalance and bravery in the effort merely to keep going. What is striking about these novels, however, is the contrast between the gripping drama of these trials and the cool, detached way in which the characters seem to regard them. It is almost as though a determined effort is made by the novelists to strike a sophisticated tone, in order to ward off any suspicion of Victorian sentimentality. In twentieth-century fiction, one cannot admit to asking whether a heroine is courageous. The novelists do not even hint that this is a question.

Both Stella Rodney in Bowen's *The Heat of the Day* and Harriet Pringle in Manning's series of World War II novels take their own intrepidity for granted. Stella has decided to stay in London during the Blitz, and continues there, engaged in war work. In Manning's *The Great Fortune*, Harriet has married a young university lecturer at the outbreak of the war and travels with him to Romania. Through successive novels, she goes to Egypt and Greece, eventually traveling on her own through the Middle East. She has self-consciously chosen a life of adventure, by agreeing to marry Guy Pringle; and yet many of the events of Manning's novels seem to happen to her as part of the miseries of war which affect everyone in a time of universal trauma. Moreover, a great deal of Harriet's suffering seems to come from being neglected by her husband, of whom she realizes, in despair, that he 'was a man who could never be present when needed.'[1] Manning's novels are stories of intensely personal romantic sufferings, set in the larger context of wartime; Elizabeth Bowen's *The Heat of the Day* has much of the same focus.[2] The world around them has gone mad, leaving the heroines to face the challenge of thinking clearly in a crushing situation – though abandonment or betrayal by their lovers causes the most pain.

Part of the effect of wartime, however, is that thinking is not something that one expects to be able to do, in a situation where everything seems fatalistic for everyone. This throws it into relief as a startling occupation. Both Harriet and Stella are affected by the relentless, grinding pressure of the war, which serves to highlight their stoicism. The inherent irony is that it is not a time for grand gestures, and yet it is; it is a time when all personal ambitions or hopes must be put aside, and yet it is not. This intensifies the drama of the choices that characters make, since the pressure that wartime has imposed upon them seems to have suspended independent free will. Bowen describes an atmosphere of paralysis, which overwhelms any sense of individual choice or thought. Caught in World War II London, characters in her fiction cannot be expected to do anything except turn their energies towards surviving enemy onslaught: 'To work or think was to ache,' the narrator says in *The Heat of the Day*.[3] The war embodies quintessential fatefulness, in the heroine's own view of her era: 'in these last twenty of its and her own years she had had to watch in it what she felt in her – a clear-sightedly helpless progress towards disaster. The fateful course of her fatalistic century seemed more and more her own: together had she and it arrived at the testing extremities of their noonday.'[4] War preempts a sense of personal choice or destiny; it also becomes an analogue of darkness in the mind, with its attendant depression, loneliness, destruction, and loss.

The isolation of both heroines is intensified by the fact that beyond surviving the war itself, a central drama for each of them consists of dealing with immediate crises connected with their estranged or threatened lovers. This shifts the focus yet again. The novels become brooding studies of women who are trying to discover and interpret what their lovers think or feel. They are forced into a position where they must think and act for themselves, as they ponder the possibility of betrayal or deceitfulness (or merely indifference) in the men they love. While they cannot be expected to exercise free will in a terrible and numbing situation, nonetheless they are forced to do so. This is a peculiar dynamic, because it is not feminist in the sense of promoting independence – they remain riveted to their lovers and thus fixated on men. And yet it does reveal them in a heroic light, since they undertake such a huge effort in order to keep a significant relationship intact. Further, wartime heightens the perceived value of each individual life, since danger is immediate and present; death is starkly possible, which renders close relationships still more romantic.

In a convoluted way, Bowen and Manning minimize essential differences of gender, evading the latter as a question of importance in itself. Harriet Pringle and Stella Rodney are not so much type-cast as women in wartime as they are portrayed as individual people caught in larger-than-life dilemmas. While they are independent women coping with difficulties in long-term romantic relationships, they are, at the same time, experiencing many of the same trials as their lovers: both men are noncombatants, and are engaged either in a desk job (Bowen's Robert Kelway) or in a university teaching job abroad (Manning's Guy Pringle). Even as civilians, they are all subjected to attack. Stella is bombed in London, Harriet runs away from the enemy. They are women facing problems, but their femininity is not a critical issue in the kinds of danger they face. Moreover, they show no self-doubt, but rather enormous poise and competence. Their bravery is taken for granted; yet the weight of their trials is nonetheless palpable.

In this chapter, I want to follow this particular synthesis of war-induced numbness with thinking and the pursuit of cool, objective reason by the heroines. I want to focus on Bowen's *The Heat of the Day*, but to glance also at her earlier novel set during the Troubles in Ireland, *The Last September*, as it is here that she begins to work out many of her ideas about wartime and its corrosive effect on the lives of civilians. I go on to consider Manning's two war trilogies, *The Balkan Trilogy* and *The Levant Trilogy*, which follow the progress of her heroine, Harriet Pringle. These dark novels are then contrasted with an unabashedly melodramatic tale, Baroness Orczy's *The Scarlet Pimpernel*, a historical novel about English aristocrats at the time of the French Revolution. This setting distances the theme of national crisis to the other side of the Channel, where the characters are being killed because of a principle which invites a heroic response from the English and their belief in *noblesse oblige*.[5] Everything that can possibly be weighted towards ardent heroism and gender differentiation is here given full rein. Orczy does in a simple and cheerful way the same kind of thing that Bowen and Manning do with elegance and finesse, but then reverses it. Her resolution is stunningly happy, and her use of irony (while directed to many of the same sorts of issues – analyzing how a man thinks and feels) is intended to heighten romance and emotion, rather than to reveal it by indirection. She plays up her heroine's femininity and passion in order to intensify the plight of her relative helplessness in a man's world, and also to highlight her courage.

In each of these novels, the heroines make a determined effort to try to see clearly, in order to gain power over their situations, or over their tormentors; both Stella in Bowen's novel and Lady Blakeney in *The Scarlet Pimpernel* are being blackmailed by villains. (I am conscious that this juxtaposition will seem incongruous, as the novels are so vastly different in tone; but I ask the reader to keep in mind that what I am trying to reveal here is the similarity of the strategies, rather than similarites between the novels as wholes.) The characteristic which marks the situations of these two heroines is the fact that they are trapped in seemingly impossible situations, yet must think or act. In the heavily ironic novels by Bowen and Manning, the heroines are – and feel themselves to be – impeccably right; a great deal of the drama consists of their puzzling over others' betrayals. In Orczy's flamboyant novel, the heroine is found to have been wrong; she herself has been a betrayer of others. In a flight of pure fantasy, however, she is completely forgiven, and also is allowed to go on a dashing adventure, herself, rather than sit around thinking. (Beauty trumps brains, every time, an accepted truth that many women writers invoke, if only by self-consciously reversing it.) The supreme irony in *The Scarlet Pimpernel* is also the most romantic one imaginable: Lady Blakeney, who has been utterly estranged from her husband, discovers that he is the very man with whom she has been secretly in love.

The tendency we might feel to laugh at Orczy's dramatic tale leads us to see more clearly why Bowen and Manning wrote as they did. Depending on how far we identify with her, it can be annoying to see Lady Blakeney, the 'cleverest' (and also the most beautiful) woman in Europe, triumph so dazzlingly.[6] On the other hand, it can also become tiresome to hear Manning's Harriet Pringle complain endlessly of her husband's chronic inattentiveness. And Bowen's elaborate spy plot never seems quite convincing, though the novel as a whole is a remarkable evocation of wartime London. These three authors use the setting of wartime to dramatize a certain way in which their heroines think. In what is perforce a dark time for all of them, the novelists ask, for their characters,how much hope do they have for the future (even if they do keep their heads)? And how much does being a woman affect this thought process? Bowen, Manning and Orczy use wartime in a way which they feel will lend automatic weight to the emotional components of their novels.

In *The Heat of the Day*, Bowen evokes a specific ambience, in showing the effect of the war on London. The Blitz has created an atmosphere of danger and daring, and it has even created a specific kind of person to inhabit it: 'These were campers in rooms of draughty dismantled houses, in corners of fled-from flats – it could be established, roughly, that the wicked had stayed and the good had gone.' She captures the edginess of this nomadic existence, which lends itself to reckless action because of its omnipresent reminders of death. Living for the moment prevails in such an atmosphere, as her narrator points out:

> The very temper of pleasures lay in their chanciness, in the canvaslike impermanence of their settings, in their being off-time – to and fro between bars and grills, clubs and each other's places moved the little shoal through the noisy nights. Faces came and went.

The transitoriness of the cast of characters leads to prodigal emotion (as seen, at least, by the disapproving moralists): 'There was a diffused gallantry in the atmosphere, an unmarriedness: it came to be rumoured about the country, among the self-banished, the uneasy, the put-upon and the safe, that everybody in London was in love. . . .'[7]

This background is a crucial context for the relationship between the three main characters, a subject to which I shall return later in the chapter. What I would like to note here is the obviousness of the impending danger which all of the characters in London face. They refuse to think, insofar as possible, by distracting themselves. Bowen's early novel, *The Last September*, invokes a situation where the threat of violence is submerged. *The Last September* describes Ireland in 1922 in a mode of denial, even though violence is seething there. The Naylors, who are the owners of a large Anglo-Irish country house, attempt to carry on with their summer program of hosting visitors, giving dinner-parties, playing tennis and arranging outdoor teas – all the while being threatened by Irish rebels who, in the end, burn the house to the ground (an act depicted on the last page of the novel – the resulting devastation of its owners is completely understood by the reader by this point). This novel dramatizes the effort involved in steadfastly refusing to acknowledge the threat of real violence.

The Irish characters are self-conscious about the presence of an English garrison in the neighborhood, which feels itself to be an 'army of occupation' that has been prevented from doing anything significant. In a conversation with two young ladies at an afternoon tea-party, the young hero, Gerald Lesworth, pours scorn on his beleaguered position, saying sarcastically that the soldiers will be leaving 'As soon as we've lost this jolly old war.' The instinctive response from the local Anglo-Irish residents is: 'Oh, but one wouldn't call it a *war*.' At the same time, the potential drama of talking socially to an attractive soldier appeals to the young ladies: 'They thought how daring it was of Mr. Lesworth to come so far to a party at all, and only hoped he would not be shot on the way home; though they couldn't help thinking how, if he should be, they would both feel so interesting afterwards.'[8] The view of the professional soldiers in such a situation is clear: '"If they'd just let us out for a week –" felt the young men,' who are eager for revenge on behalf of an army barracks which had been recently attacked and in which men had been killed. To the Irish guests assembled at the party, this event represents 'unpleasantness' that is unnerving, yet against which they feel doubtful about taking action. Discussion of the event is clothed in general terms: 'It was this they had all been discussing at tea, between tennis: "the horrible thing."'[9] Paralysis grips the bewildered party guests, as war still seems an unreality to them.

In the same way, Bowen shows the indirect effects of violence on the lives of her heroines, both Lois, who is young and naïve, and Marda, who at twenty-nine is fully adult and also determinedly cynical. The undercurrent of potential violence is felt by Lois, who longs to avoid it, and confides to Marda her fantasies about traveling abroad: 'She wanted to go wherever the War hadn't. She wanted to go somewhere nonchalant where politics bored them, where bands played out of doors in the hot nights and nobody wished to sleep.' Marda has more actively sought to escape the hovering presence of war by fleeing to England. When she visits the Naylors, mid-way through the novel, she is engaged to a severe Englishman named, appropriately, Leslie Lawe, whom Lois imagines as being 'one of those keen square people,' and who has clearly been chosen by Marda as a potential life-raft for herself. Once married, she will no longer have to make her own choices. In one sense, this novel is a straightforward drama for young women – when Lois repeats her piteous refrain of 'I must marry Gerald,' it is expressed in the hope of finding a settled course of life for herself, in the same way that Marda has accepted Leslie Lawe. However, Marda offers a problematic example of someone who has had much more freedom than Lois has been granted, and who also possesses enormous vivacity and spirit. Yet she admits a kind of defeat in her attempts to find satisfying adventure, telling Lois, 'I don't know for myself what is worth while. I'm sick of all this trial and error.'[10]

The war continues to intrude on characters' lives, as it cannot be held away indefinitely as an abstraction. Real, individual people are lost.

When Lois' suitor Gerald is shot, it is felt as a direct blow to the Naylors – they know him personally, and he cannot be accounted a mere cipher. Yet nothing can be done to change the essential situation, as Bowen makes clear in the reaction of Lois' uncle, when the news is brought: 'Sir Richard had slipped away quietly; he was an old man, really, outside all this, and did not know what to do. He was wondering also, about the Connors. Peter Connor's friends: they knew everything, they were persistent: it did not do to imagine. . . .' This exemplifies the muddiness of the situation in which the Anglo-Irish are living – they know the people involved in ambushes and violence – or they know people who know them. They do not want to think – to 'wonder' or to 'imagine.'[11] Bowen is both wry about this, and sympathetic to their plight, and their feeling of helplessness.

Still more insidious than Sir Richard's flight into willed ignorance is the patronizing tone of his wife, Lady Naylor, who writes her condolences to Gerald's mother: 'he was the life and soul of everything,' she asserts, assuming that her praise of him is a fully adequate reward for his life's having been sacrificed in such a way. Gerald's mother feels differently, as her reply indicates, and to Lady Naylor's evident surprise: 'And she wrote back – I did not think tactfully, but of course she would be distressed – that it was her first consolation to think he died in so noble a cause.'[12]

For people who are actively participating in the war, or emotionally invested in it in some way, the pain of defeat or loss is acute. But for those who strive not to pay attention to it, it can seem tastelessly melodramatic, and expressions of defiant patriotism rather embarrassing. Part of Bowen's point in *The Last September*, however, is that regardless of what the characters think or feel in response to it, its power can be devastating. The Naylors' house is burned down nonetheless. The war which is steadfastly seen *not* to be a war in this novel still affects the characters deeply, whether they consciously reflect on its impact or not. Although ordinary life goes on during wartime, it is also affected by it, and can be shockingly changed. Characters are shot; Marda suffers the loss of 'a few pieces of skin' in her accidental encounter with the rebel in the abandoned mill, which she deliberately makes light of.[13] But Gerald loses his life, and Lois her 'young man.'

This early novel of Bowen's demonstrates something of the peril of *not* thinking, when imminent violence threatens – not that it is made clear what families such as the Naylors could have done to prevent the loss of their house and, more acutely painful, the loss of their way of life. As for the drama of World War II, as depicted in *The Heat of the*

Day, its effects cannot be ignored. Bowen does not minimize the immediate horrors of the bombing which rends the city; rather, she uses it for dramatic effect, suggesting that it can be – in certain circumstances – romantic, and can even give city-dwellers license to not care about consequences or about the future. Hence the 'shoals' of pleasure-seekers, who move through the night-time streets of London.

At the same time, war is crushing in its emotional devastation, and affects the heroine's ability to think or to feel. Stella Rodney's response to the erosion of Europe is one of complete desolation: 'after the fall of France, more loss had not seemed possible.' The idea of France's occupation by the enemy is made tangible by the actual, physical onslaught of the Blitz, as the narrator describes it:

> On through the rest of that summer in which she had not rallied from the psychological blow, and forward into this autumn of the attack on London, she had been the onlooker with nothing more to lose – out of feeling as one can be out of breath. She had had the sensation of being on furlough from her own life.

This detachment from life creates the context for the beginning of Stella's love affair with Robert Kelway. The two lovers meet in the present moment, without reference to past or context: 'life-stories were shed as so much superfluous weight,' and they plunge into an emotional attachment.[14] They choose a suspension of thought in favor of passion.

Stella has been Robert Kelway's lover for several months when Harrison shows up, uninvited, on her doorstep. This one encounter is the catalyst which forces her into thinking – furiously – for the rest of the novel. His purpose in visiting her is to tell her that Robert is a traitor, and that she ought not to associate with him: 'you should be careful whom you know,' he tells her. The oddness of Harrison's approach is still more strange because it occurs in the context of an absolutely ordinary situation. It is obvious that he has hoped to seduce her or to impinge upon her life in some other emotional way – an ambition for which she holds him in contempt. Her manner of treating him shows that she has definitively refused his advances already: 'After what I said to you last time – detestable things I should not have been forced to say – only you could have insisted on coming back!' she tells him. Yet this very passion marks the encounter as a power struggle which Stella is losing. The choice has been hers, to allow him to return.[15]

The question here is: why she has agreed to talk to him again, and moreover, why she has allowed him to come alone to her flat? This gesture is almost a mockery of her expectations of him, as though she expected to ward off the possibility of sexual assault or entreaty by making it seem ridiculous. At the same time, when she attempts to analyze the real reason for speaking to him again, she half senses a genuine threat which reveals a real fear. She tries to diminish the assault made by his renewed approach by seeing it entirely in terms of seduction:

> Had he hinted and threatened his way in, his way back, for nothing more than one final bid at self-salesmanship, one last attempt to 'interest' her? But then – this was itself a point – how had he known she had melodramatic fears? How had he guessed her to be a woman with whom the unspecified threat would work?

Part of her fear stems from fear itself: 'To point out that he had forced this meeting by an implied threat would be to admit that in her life *any* threat could have force or context at all.'[16]

On one level, the tension between them stems from a difference of temperament related to class: she is cool and sophisticated, while he is, in his own words, 'not [her] sort.' Stella had taken him at first for a private detective (he is, in fact, a government agent), and later he acknowledges that his 'sort' is empowered by the war: 'War, if you come to think of it, hasn't started anything that wasn't there already – what it does is, put the other lot of us in the right.' Stella, in his view, has had the luxury of living by means of 'fine feelings' and with the view that love is important (which for Harrison is not the case – he experiences it as 'a spanner in the works').[17] The point of the war is, for Harrison, that he now has leverage to force her to take him seriously. 'I can't help feeling "This is where I come in,"' he tells her, suggesting that he make continued visits to the flat. He wants the polish of her social class, and the connection that he desires with Stella herself. When she asks what he wants, he replies promptly: 'Me to come here, be here, in and out of here . . . To be in your life. . . .'[18]

This one scene places all of the sexual politics neatly on the table. Bowen draws a love triangle where Harrison hopes to take Stella away from her lover. The heroine is alone with a blackmailer, doubly so because he threatens someone whom she loves (and herself, by implication), and he isolates her still further by telling her that to share this information with Robert would damage Robert irrevocably. The novel as a whole is more an evocation of a wartime ambience than an actual

KING ALFRED'S COLLEGE
LIBRARY

story; the plot is laid out in this scene between the two of them, and there is nothing left to discover, once Harrison's charge has been made. In one sense, Bowen creates pure, sustained tension without resolution – and without much suspense. Events fall out as Harrison predicts: once Stella tells Robert that he is suspected by a government agent, he gives evidence of being watched, and is to be arrested. His initial motivation for becoming a traitor to his country is difficult to discern, in retrospect, even when he tries to explain to Stella at the end of the novel why he has chosen to give information to the enemy. It is neither a compelling nor a logical argument, and explains little of his feelings. Stella's own motivations are equally murky – this, however, is what makes the novel interesting. One can think and ponder endlessly, as Stella does, and yet not reach any sort of satisfying conclusion. Her thought process itself becomes the drama, which she does eventually resolve by making two key decisions: to tell Robert of Harrison's threat, and eventually to agree to sleep with Harrison in an effort to protect Robert for as long as might be possible.

Still, we do not know why. It is understandable that she tells Robert of Harrison's charge against him; she is worn down by bearing this burden alone, and either does not believe it or wants to force the issue. Her attempts to analyze Harrison's claim and its implications have been fruitless. But the very earnestness of the attempts makes its own statement about their tortuous and sinister nature. When she does finally bring up the subject with Robert, the first focus of their discussion is her thought process: he immediately latches onto her hesitation over the question: 'You say, two months ago? There's certainly nothing like thinking a thing over. Or did it simply happen to slip your memory till tonight?' This is, of course, defensiveness on his part, since she has hit upon a dangerous truth for him. At the same time, though, he is also angry with her, in an unreasonable but hurtful way: 'Whatever did you think? – that I might take umbrage?' He responds with fury, sputtering in denial of her suggestion. Her hesitation has proven that it was a dilemma which required a great deal of consideration – and also dramatizes the isolation and loneliness which she has felt. Her response brings the question of gender into the equation: 'One can live in the shadow of an idea without grasping it. Nothing *is* really unthinkable; really you do know that. But the more one thinks, the less there's any outside reality – at least, that's so with a woman: we have no scale.'[19]

What Bowen does in this conversation is to blend the personal aspects of war with the political. Robert observes, during this exchange, 'you do not seem to have shown any very great patriotic fervour,' attempting to make light of her reaction.[20] This suggests that although a woman might not (in Stella's view) have concepts of scale with which to measure things, it is none the less possible that she cares passionately about what happens between herself and her lover, rather than about passively assisting in betraying her country in wartime.

The darkness of mind which Stella experiences in this novel is in many ways similar to that of the ordinary kind of romantic entanglement which goes awry. It does not require a war to make two lovers quarrel, and when she does confront him with Harrison's claim, his anger produces a purely emotional response from her: 'This is breaking my heart,' she says of his bitterness. The two things are closely related, as Robert senses – love and spying (in the sense of feigning or pretending). His most terrible charge is: 'You keep up the appearance of love so beautifully.' This is punishing because it is an effective counter-attack: it turns the charge of treason onto her. Her own instinctive response to Robert's charge is the cry of a wounded and disillusioned lover: 'I thought it had all been perfect.'[21]

The interesting point here is that the blame for a searing lovers' quarrel can be shifted onto a third party (Harrison), and remotely – beyond him – onto the ideological conflict which the war has brought into stark relief. Stella herself has desired to remain loyal to Robert. Harrison is to blame, for upsetting things. She tells him, mid-way through the novel, 'You've succeeded in making a spy out of me.' This sense of personal degradation helps to account for her ultimate decision to offer herself to Harrison – she wants to stop thinking, and to act. (And, by implication, she finally acknowledges that his claim is correct, and that Robert is a traitor.) Stella sums it all up when she throws herself at Harrison, intending to 'buy out Robert, for a bit longer?' – and he rejects her. Her moral for Louie, a minor yet important female character who appears in this scene, has to do with this sense of sudden disillusionment: 'At any time it may be your hour or mine – you or I may be learning some terrible human lesson which is to undo everything we had thought we had. It's that, not death, that we ought to live prepared for.' Nothing can be done to save Robert from the consequences of his decision to align himself with the enemy – a delaying action is all that can be hoped for, and even that is impossible when Stella tries to accept Harrison's offer.[22]

At the end of the novel, nothing has changed from Harrison's initial assessment of the situation, or the inevitability of its end: Robert is shortly to be arrested, and he falls or leaps to his death from the roof of Stella's building after he leaves her apartment. This is melodramatic, yet also a practical solution to a problem. But what has changed radically is Stella's own view of this emotional triangle. What she now thinks is: 'It was Robert who was the Harrison.'[23] This is a stunning reversal of feeling on her part. It alters the whole shape of Stella and Robert's relationship, in retrospect. The war has irrevocably affected them. When the narrator describes the progress of their affair, she says: 'their time sat in the third place at the table.'[24] This is true both in the sense that chronological time is running out (Robert will eventually be unmasked and be forced to leave her) and that their times have conspired against them by forcing a choice of political allegiances. *The Heat of the Day* is intended as a novel which incorporates political forces, but is not in itself political. Bowen's interest is invariably in private lives and feelings, in what she often refers to (yet never in a sentimental sense) as 'the heart.' Emotional tangles are difficult; one copes with one's own powerful emotions, and with betrayal on a personal or on a national level as best one can. War, as an unwelcome outside force, causes darkness to descend upon the two lovers, who have been otherwise so comfortable with each other. And the literal darkness demanded by the black-outs also manifests itself in the heroine's mind, which is numbed. Pressured by the threats of men such as Harrison (and, indirectly by Robert, who has 'become' Harrison), she is forced to think. But, as John Coates points out, the private and the political are one and the same, in Stella's growing distrust of her lover. Rather than challenging her feelings, Harrison points to something which she half intuits already:

> By his persistent nagging, his constant awakening of suspicion about Robert, he prompts doubts which Stella has herself suppressed about her lover. Harrison's strength here is not his secret information but his instinct for the point of real weakness in Stella's and Robert's relationship.[25]

Olivia Manning's Balkan and Levant trilogies are very different from Bowen's interior drama. They set out to give a panoramic view of the war, both of military and of British expatriate life. The terrifying significance of political events is never far away for Harriet Pringle and other characters. At the same time, much of the heroine's emotion is channeled into a reassessment of her husband's character, followed by a series of adjustments calculated to make the best of her marriage. Her dissatisfaction with Guy in his role as a husband often becomes a subject of discussion between them, in addition to one of continual meditation for her. When Harriet learns that one of Guy's Romanian students had tried to persuade him to marry her, in order to obtain British citizenship, she explodes: 'If anyone had asked me before I married, I would have said I was marrying the rock of ages. Now I realize you are capable of absolute lunacy.' His response echoes a kind of British nonchalance: '"Oh, come, darling," Guy protested. "I didn't want to marry Sophie, but one has to be polite. What would you have done under the circumstances?"' Harriet's reply is peremptory: 'Said "No" straight away. One doesn't complicate one's life unnecessarily.' Yet the real point of this exchange is that Harriet herself is intended to be seen as both wise and firm in all matters of principle: 'But she would never have tried it on with me. Knowing I was not susceptible, she disliked me on sight. With you, of course, she thinks she can get away with anything.'[26]

This conversation between the two spouses early in their marriage constructs a pattern from which they seldom deviate for the remainder of the novel series. Guy is, in actual fact, well able to avoid any emotional entanglements that bore him (even including the relationship with his wife). Harriet continues to criticize him, both in public and in private, though it is clear that he will never fundamentally change. Talking the matter over yet again with a colleague of Guy's, later in the novel, she admits that she cannot envision that the proposed marriage with Sophie could actually have occurred: 'He *thought* of it. But I doubt if he would ever have done it.' This leads to further bitter remarks, which express not only her own disillusionment but her sense of outrage: 'No, when it came to marriage, he chose someone he thought would not make too many demands. Perhaps the trouble is, I make too few.' She goes on to tell Clarence, her confidant on this occasion, 'I'm not strong. I suppose I'm intolerant – a bad fault. I have no patience with people. Sophie told Guy he had married a monster.' Her final, defiant denunciation of herself begs for sympathy: 'I sometimes think I shall end up a lonely, ragged, mad old woman trailing along the gutter.'[27]

Remarks of this kind do not entirely dominate Harriet's conversations with other characters, but they do form a steady stream of resentment which is seldom allayed. The problem – as she states it to herself – is one of personal as opposed to general allegiance. When Clarence observes, 'You've got Guy. I suppose you'll always have Guy,' she retorts, 'And he'll always have the rest of the world.'[28] This is a crucial theme in these novels, since the immediacy of the war makes the fate of the world at large one of pressing importance. It also forms one of the perplexing problems of this story: it is difficult for a reader to feel compassion for someone who speaks as self-pityingly and sarcastically as Harriet does. It is not that she does not suffer heartache; but she speaks of it with the kind of ironic detachment which repels sympathy as much as it invites it. In the Pringles' private marriage relationship, Manning expects the pathos of the wronged wife to speak for itself; moreover, she extends this to the drama of wartime which haunts everyone in the novels. Emotional intensity is assumed to rage rampantly, given the inherent drama of the situation. At the same time, no one is allowed – to put it in the most bald terms – to simply break down and cry.

The main problem with Harriet's predicament is that she never allows herself to admit that she has been wrong. The possible suspicion that she has made a mistake in marrying this extrovert and attractive young man is never allowed to cross her mind, except in oblique reflections such as this: 'Her feeling was that she had been taken in, and too easily' by Guy's apparent friendliness. More to the point, she admits to herself that 'Being unsuccessful in the world herself, she had to find someone who would be successful for her.'[29] At the same time, this irritation does not lead to a cessation of complaints – in spite of her covert pride in his energy and success. While still feeling neglected, later in the series, she secretly rejoices in her resolute conviction that Guy will someday be recognized by society as a Great Man (with herself as his consort).[30] What is particularly interesting, I think, is that the larger drama of wartime meshes with Harriet's private self-defensiveness – even her self-righteousness. In a terrible battle against Fascism, there can be no question in the minds of the British expatriate characters that their side is entirely right. (Some characters, such as the egotistical Pinkrose, are portrayed as being too stupid to be sensitive to the early signs of enemy oppression; yet he is suitably punished for this obtuseness by being assassinated later on, while standing up to deliver a lecture on English literature.) This sense of rightness and purpose lends extra energy to the characters' actions and thoughts.

Furthermore, Manning takes some trouble to link personal, emotional needs with larger political convictions – particularly in the case of Guy, who is the most absorbed in continual discussions on the subject of political philosophy. Harriet describes his Marxist convictions to Clarence, in a later discussion (though with a suspiciously patronizing tone): 'I think it's the need to put his faith into something. His father was an old-fashioned radical. Guy was brought up as a free thinker, but he has a religious temperament. So he believes in Russia. That's another home for little children above the bright blue sky.' When Clarence gives the stereotypical Freudian interpretation of these events – 'he's simply what the psychologists call "a rebel son of a rebel father"' – he associates Guy's political convictions with tangible events as well. Harriet also reflects upon this influence: 'When Guy was growing up the mills and mines were idle. The majority of the men he knew, his own father among them, had been on the dole. He had watched his father, a skilled man, highly intelligent, decline and become, through despair and the illness brought by despair, unemployable.' As a result, she concludes, Guy had 'resented this waste of human energy and become absorbed in the politics of the wasteland and the welfare of the wasted.'[31]

This horror at 'waste' of energy, talent, and interest is perhaps an even greater spur to passion for the novels' main characters – more, even, than the devastating effects of war itself. In fact this is another of the terrible effects of political conflict. One problem which confronts Harriet and others is the seeming purposelessness of what everyone in civilian life does. She works, at one point, for an American press agency in Cairo; but her experience is also numbing in its tediousness. Guy Pringle's enormous energies have no outlet after he is ordered out of Romania, and he goes to Cairo and later to Alexandria in search of work as a university lecturer. Harriet is furious at his isolated situation in Egypt: 'She felt rage that he should be wasting his learning on this wretched place.'[32] It is evident, however, that he has tremendous energies and abilities as a lecturer, and employs them in and out of season. He throws himself into his teaching, even using all of his vacation time to prepare lectures on twentieth-century literature, although Harriet thinks that this is virtually useless, since it is doubtful whether he will be allowed to give them.

The main point of contention between the couple synthesizes all of these themes. Harriet is angry at Guy's devotion to his political convictions (which she does not share), wondering at 'Guy's vigour and determination in the pursuit of his political interests. Why could he not bring as much to the furtherance of his own career?' In the way that she never admits to her own jealousy of the dreaded Sophie (which constitutes, among other things, straightforward female rivalry, since she had attempted to marry Guy), Harriet also refuses to admit to herself her ambition on Guy's behalf – and her desperate desire for him to succeed in order to justify her. This seems to her a profound betrayal, as she thinks back over the course of their relationship: 'When she first met him, she had imagined he needed nothing but opportunity; now she began to suspect he did not want opportunity.' The crux of their conflict is the question of who is right:

> He wanted amusement [she concludes]. He also wanted his own way, and, to get it, could be as selfish as the next man. But he was always justified. Yes, he was always justified. If he had no other justification he could always fall back on some morality of his own.

Her final condemnation turns his own judgement of 'waste' of potential back upon Guy himself: '[she began] to fear that he was a man who in the end would achieve little. He would simply waste himself.'[33]

Guy is not unaware of this possibility, though it strikes him from a different angle. The true test of his purpose in life – and his achievements as a young man – comes when he thinks about his profession, late in the war, and reflects on what he has done:

> Now, no longer challenged by the nearness of war, he could see the futility of his reserved occupation. Lecturing on English literature, teaching the English language, he had been peddling the idea of empire to a country that only wanted one thing; to be rid of the British for good and all. And, to add to the absurdity of the situation, he himself had no belief in empire.[34]

Upon those characters who have been deprived of meaningful work and self-expression, such as the English actor Aidan Pratt, war inflicts a particular torment. Aidan is disappointed that – as he perceives it – his acting career has been destroyed by the war; in fact, its effects on him have been more far-ranging even than this. Harriet asks if his sense of emotional desolation has to do with the war, to which he replies, categorically, 'The war has destroyed my life.'[35] Two books later in the series, Aidan is still talking about having lost his career as an actor. He reminisces to Guy about his first major theatre role, now years in the past: 'On the first night, I said to myself, "Now it's all beginning," and less than three months later, it had ended.' The sheer bleakness of wartime also afflicts Aidan as well, however – loneliness and isolation afflicts those characters who do not wish to glory in political action. Like Harriet, Aidan feels despair about ever gaining attention from Guy (with whom he is in love, and to whom he is addicted). Begging for time with Guy, Aidan is met with the curt rebuff: 'No, I haven't time for holidays.' He personalizes this immediately: 'Or for me?'[36] Aidan feels so betrayed by Guy's indifference to him that he proves this point by shooting himself in despair.

The key relationship in these novels remains Guy and Harriet Pringle's marriage, and its problematic dynamics are focused in a dramatic incident which unites the crises of wartime and the grating difficulties of domestic unhappiness. Harriet leaves Guy – at his express wish – in order to board a ship destined for England. Yet she decides at the last minute not to board it. When the ship is sunk, Guy believes she is dead, and she wanders around in the Middle East by herself, unaware that she is missed in Cairo. Guy goes through a whole process of grieving that includes an improbable repentance for his former treatment of her. The narrator sums up his thoughts on the matter, in which he realizes that 'Harriet must have spent many nights on her own and he had never asked her what she did with herself.' Part of the reason for this is that he himself had been satisfied with his own circumstances: 'Loneliness was something outside his experience.' In a failure of compassion, or of perception, he has overlooked her needs: 'He had his work and his friends, and he had sacrificed Harriet to both.' He then moralizes this personal abandonment into a larger statement about his times: 'The truth was, the war had given his work too much importance. Work had condoned his civilian status. Its demands had left him no time for his wife and he had instigated her return on the doomed ship.'[37]

This is an odd (and, perhaps, unconvincing) twist to these novels; at the least, it is an ironic reversal, since Harriet has spent endless time in trying to discern what Guy feels; and now he is analyzing himself in relation to her. What wartime does is to dramatize vividly the potential hazard of neglecting people: they could die. The young British soldier Simon Boulderstone must cope with this during his first few weeks in the army:

> He had two friends on board, Trench and Codley, who had been his family, his intimates, the people nearest to him in the world. The sense of belonging together had been deeper than love – then, at Suez, a terrible thing had happened. He had lost them.

This plunges him into a state of being 'numb with solitude.'[38] More pervasively, he must bear the burden of the death of his brother, Hugo, for whom his parents grieve, and which loads him with still more responsibility. But also, as for Harriet and for Aidan in their loneliness, it is possible for any of the characters – even civilians – to slip away and be lost forever. Moreover, no definitive moral lesson can really be drawn, even when terrible consequences are miraculously reversed. A melodramatic reunion scene ensues when Harriet returns to Cairo and to Guy. But he goes out again the same evening, abandoning her as usual.

His behavior does not change, despite the insight into her predicament which he might have been expected to gain.

In these novels, wartime creates an extraordinary kind of emotional distancing – and also, a particular kind of deprivation. Guy Pringle expresses to Aidan his belief that, in war, 'what is lost stays lost – you don't get it back again.'[39] Part of the strangeness of this grieving and numbness is that Manning's characters do not seem to have a good way to think or to talk about it. They sound inevitably banal when they deal with such subjects. Harriet replies, for instance, to Aidan's claim that the war has destroyed his life, with the flat statement: 'It hasn't done any of us much good.' Aidan has particular reasons for despair: 'When it's over – if it ever is over – I'll be verging on middle-age. Just another not so young actor looking for work. In fact, a displaced person.' Harriet sounds governessy in response: 'We're all displaced persons these days. Guy and I have accumulated more memories of loss and flight in two years than we could in a whole lifetime of peace. And, as you say, it's not over yet. But we're seeing the world. We might as well try and enjoy it.'[40]

The irritating thing about this response is that Harriet is trying to make her story into an adventure; this does not quite work, however, since no one ever admits to being scared. Disappointment is all that the characters allow themselves to express. It is difficult to say anything meaningful or heartfelt about how awful the uncertainties of wartime are, and they take refuge in irony instead. When Guy and Harriet tell a friend the story of their having fled from Athens, for instance, the couple use wry understatement: 'they described their escape, making humor out of the hungry voyage, the vermin, the lice in the cabins, the passages boarded up because the freighters had been prisoner transports, the useless lifeboats, with rusted-in davits.' As has become appropriate in wartime, they acknowledge their friend's summary of the situation: '"Well, well, you're safe," he said. "That's the main thing."'[41] Yet this seems almost dismissive, and we are unable to grant Harriet and Guy the heroic stature that they seem to require and yet to repel at the same time.

Baroness Orczy, in contrast to Bowen and Manning, takes her story to the extreme of melodrama. Anthea Trodd points out that *The Scarlet Pimpernel* is a successful melding of two different genres: 'a hybrid based on the two major contesting definitions of romance of the period,' in other words, adventure fiction which was 'set in the more dangerous past or on the frontiers of empire' and the traditional female version of romantic fiction.[42] I think that it is also interesting to show it in contrast with these other, contemporary, self-consciously modern novels, because its enduring popularity shows the hunger for heroic tales which a sentimental public still holds. Yet it is escapist in a way that both distances it from and relates it to the twentieth century.

Set in 1792, the novel was published in 1905. It has a very simple plot, centering on a marriage (the couple are estranged, when the novel opens) and a crafty villain, the arch-spy for the French revolutionaries, M. de Chauvelin. By threatening the life of her brother, he blackmails Lady Blakeney into discovering for him the identity of the Scarlet Pimpernel, leader of the band of English aristocrats who are rescuing doomed French noblemen sent to the guillotine. Predictably, the Pimpernel is her husband, Sir Percy Blakeney, whom she does betray; but Chauvelin's plan is altogether foiled, as the two lovers escape together and are reunited in perfect accord.

Both main characters are lavishly idealized figures. Before her marriage, Lady Blakeney, née Marguerite St. Just, was a young Parisian actress described as being 'lavishly gifted with beauty and talent,' and able to gather around her in her Parisian flat 'a côterie which was as brilliant as it was exclusive.' Superlatives abound in the narrator's description of her position as hostess of a salon:

> Clever men, distinguished men, and even men of exalted station formed a perpetual and brilliant court round the fascinating young actress of the Comédie Française, and she glided through republican, revolutionary, bloodthirsty Paris like a shining comet with a trail behind her of all that was most distinguished, most interesting in intellectual Europe.

Not only is Marguerite able to command admiration from the most discerning, she is herself exalted with the title of 'the cleverest woman in Europe.'[43]

Because of the extreme political tenor of the times – and the shocking and violent behavior of some of the French aristocracy she is in contact with – she betrays two different men at two different times. First, she denounces St. Cyr, a nobleman who has caused her brother to be harmed ('thrashed like a dog within an inch of his life,' for daring to write a love sonnet to St. Cyr's daughter).[44] Second, she betrays the identity of the masked Pimpernel to Chauvelin, this time to protect rather than to avenge her brother. The narrator goes to great lengths to explain the background of the various pressures brought to bear upon Lady Blakeney, and the many sources of her unhappiness, so that we will not condemn her, but acquit her – at least, to some extent. Further, she is shown to be penitent for her denunciation of St. Cyr, and is punished (indirectly) for this error by the withdrawal of her husband's love. This isolates her in her plight, alone with her blackmailer.

As for Sir Percy Blakeney, Orczy goes to the same trouble to give an elaborate explanation of the complex forces which affect his emotional state. It cannot be claimed that she is consciously trying to give a psychological profile of him, but she does allow the reader to delve to the roots of her character's motivations by way of his childhood history. This, in its way, is as melodramatic as the dazzling career of Marguerite. Sir Percy's mother has been utterly unable to tend to her son's needs, as she had

> become hopelessly insane after two years of happy married life. Percy had just been born when the late Lady Blakeney fell a prey to the terrible malady which in those days was looked upon as hopelessly incurable and nothing short of a curse of God on the entire family.

Percy has spent his youth abroad, by his father's arrangement, where he 'grew up between an imbecile mother and a distracted father.'[45]

Since the romantic reconciliation of the two main characters forms a major part of the plot, it is important to know why and how their estrangement has occurred. The civil violence in France is a vital background to this, as it provides the pretext for a fundamental misunderstanding between the two spouses: Sir Percy cannot trust his wife with the secret of his aid to the threatened aristocrats, as he believes she is in sympathy with the Jacobins. And this problem derives from another, more basic, one, which is that the two are hiding their essential characters from each other. Sir Percy affects nonchalance and even stupidity, to preserve his secret; but this underscores the fact that he is a master of disguise. Her exposure of him to Chauvelin is ironic, since in his Sir Percy persona she dislikes him, while she admires the Scarlet Pimpernel identity which he has constructed.

To the extent that this is a romantic novel, the great drama is her reconciliation with her husband, and this involves three things: thinking and detective work on her part, penance and forgiveness, and active adventure. Once she has handed Chauvelin the vital piece of information about the secret band of rescuers, this sparks the departure of Sir Percy for France, and she begins to notice clues in the house around her which point to her husband's secret identity. Looking at his private study, which bespeaks the authority with which he administers a vast family estate, she goes through a rapid intuitive thought process which first divines the fact that he is hiding his abilities:

> this obvious proof of her husband's strong business capacities did not cause her more than a passing thought of wonder. But it also strengthened her in the now certain knowledge that with his worldly inanities, his foppish ways, and foolish talk, he was not only wearing a mask, but was playing a deliberate and studied part.

This leads to a chain of intuitive reasoning, where she assumes the role of detective: 'At what particular moment the strange doubt first crept into Marguerite's mind, she could not herself afterward have said.'[46] Yet it is a tribute to her much acclaimed brilliance and cleverness that she does reach the correct conclusion, and takes immediate action.

The novel then becomes pure adventure story, as she sets off in pursuit of her wronged husband, collecting a minor character along the way to escort her to France. This constitutes the active penance, as she suffers physical discomfort and anxiety on the journey, and she formalizes this by asking Sir Percy's forgiveness. Her explanation of the urgency of her quest to Sir Andrew, Percy's associate in his small band of heroes, expresses passionate regret: '"I *must* get to him! I *must*," she repeated with savage energy, "to warn him that that man [Chauvelin] is on his track!"' Her penance also includes her determination to perish with him, if necessary: 'Can't you see – can't you see that I *must* get to him . . . even . . . even if it be too late to save him . . . at least . . . to be by his side . . . at the last.'[47]

The extreme cleverness of Orczy's plot, however, lies in the fact that the novelist brings about the total defeat (through audacity and deception) of the villain – at the same time that Lady Blakeney becomes heroic. Lady Blakeney remains suitably feminine – in one sense entirely passive, as she must look on helplessly at what she believes to be the inevitable demise of Sir Percy. When he appears at the French farmhouse where Chauvelin has expected him, she realizes that her proposed warning or aid would be useless: 'The trap was closing in, and Marguerite could do nothing but watch and wonder.' None the less, her determination emphasizes her penance, as she decides – should Percy be surrounded by soldiers, as she expects – to 'rush down and help Percy to sell his life dearly.'[48]

Percy's confrontation with Chauvelin, and Marguerite's covert observation of it, brings together both of Percy's roles in his wife's perception, as she 'indulged in the luxury, dear to every tender woman's heart, of looking at the man she loved.' For her own perception has now been sufficiently sharpened that she can easily pierce his assumed disguise:

> She looked through the tattered curtain across at the handsome face of her husband, in whose lazy blue eyes and behind whose inane smile she could now so plainly see the strength, energy, and resourcefulness which had caused the Scarlet Pimpernel to be reverenced and trusted by his followers.[49]

This reflection brings the reader back to recalling the civil violence which first caused the Pimpernel to don his mask – a mask which he must wear with humility (as the rest of the world believes him to be a fool), yet also with secret pride at the cleverness of deception. Wartime, in this novel, serves to highlight the dashing heroism of its major characters – especially when it is conveniently located in another country, from which they themselves can escape. (Sir Percy's yacht, used for these purposes, is named – probably without irony – the *Day Dream*.)

As a heroine, Marguerite retains old-fashioned ideals of femininity, in the novel's climactic crisis. Nonetheless, despite her enforced passivity as an onlooker, she plays a heroic role, in the sense that she is an active presence in the final drama. Since women are not expected to participate in such affairs, in this historical context, Lady Blakeney has all the glory of being heroic in an unlikely setting. She can also be allowed to be traditionally feminine, in that she is passionately devoted to her husband; and she achieves a happy ending. She does prove herself to be self-consciously brave, and Orczy emphasizes this, unlike Bowen and Manning, whose heroines are invariably seen to be deliberately cool and calm.

For all three authors, it is crucial that it be seen by the readers that the *world* has gone mad – not the heroines themselves. It is a way of justifying their actions, or their moral characters, to insist that *they* are all thinking rationally – or at least attempting to do this – under the most trying of circumstances. With the exception of the stereotypically passionate Lady Blakeney, all of the other heroines are cool and detached, even when in the proximity of physical and emotional violence and danger. Bowen's and Manning's heroines all keep their heads, though it is hardly a matter of pleasure. Facing down their grim, sadistic blackmailers, or puzzling over the inexplicable behavior of their lovers, they bring their minds to bear upon difficult problems, and under the most wearisome of circumstances. Wartime poses a special challenge to purely personal dilemmas because it polarizes beliefs and also intensifies powerlessness in individuals. As Bowen's Harrison aptly puts it, war causes everyone to be on 'one side or the other.' Accordingly, it can become a matter of life and death to determine which side one's friends and lovers are, in fact, on. Reason is portrayed as a high value, in each of these novels, as it aids in discernment. To be the 'cleverest woman in Europe' is no mean advantage to Lady Blakeney. Yet it is not this which renders her, at the close of the novel, 'the most beautiful woman' present at the society wedding which rounds out the amazing adventures of the Scarlet Pimpernel and his adoring consort.

2
Gothic and Fabulist Tales

For twentieth-century authors whose emphasis is on rationality and intellectual sophistication, the use of supernatural phenomena in their fiction marks a significant choice. In the modern age we have collectively moved away from a belief in ghosts, in the sense that each individual may now choose whether or not to believe in God and in the doctrines of the Anglican Church, or indeed in the existence of a spiritual realm at all. Agnosticism has become accepted as a tenable worldview. But this prevalence of skepticism makes fabulism all the more appealing. It becomes a daring artistic choice. At the same time, the gothic convention also has a long literary history from which to draw, stretching from Walpole's *Castle of Otranto* through Charlotte Brontë's *Jane Eyre*. The temptation is to travesty it; the figure of a lone, endangered woman in a dark and sinister mansion has become a cliché.

But this is precisely the reason why such a subject can be used by twentieth-century writers with such powerful results: no one even affects to believe in such superstitious nonsense any more. Like Jane Austen in *Northanger Abbey*, these authors satirize the gothic literary traditions from which they draw. At the same time, they go beyond this pronounced skepticism to suggest that there is, in fact, a possibility that – after all – danger lurks in a supernatural dimension. Moreover, the self-conscious link which many of these writers make between psychology, scientific research into paranormal phenomena, and the appearance of ghostly presences as a force in these stories means that they can have it both ways. The supernatural is contrasted with a seemingly rational framework.

This in itself is not a new argument. As John Sutherland has pointed out in *Is Heathcliff a Murderer?*, Victorian explorations of spiritism tried to find a rational, scientific basis upon which to rest their beliefs about such subjects as mental telepathy. Sutherland observes that the scene in *Jane Eyre* during which the heroine hears Mr. Rochester's voice is written in a style which would convey to contemporary readers the trance-like state which such experiments in hypnosis used as their basis.[1] In a similar way, twentieth-century authors draw upon a popularization of Freud's psychoanalysis in order to explain that a seemingly supernatural manifestation might spring from a part of the unconscious.

This is even more frightening as a prospect. By allowing for the fact that the mind might be split in such a way that it could not integrate thoughts within itself, a person might (theoretically) act in an evil yet unconscious way. This is a key theme in Dorothy L. Sayers' *Gaudy Night*, in which a 'poltergeist' or 'poison pen' terrorizes a fictional women's college in 1930s Oxford. First of all, the naming of the villain by her victims is crucial: while she is termed a 'poltergeist,' which suggests a creature who exists in a purely spiritual dimension, it is clear that everyone in the college believes there to be an actual woman who is causing havoc. The attacks are physical and direct: she overturns shelves and breaks pictures in the newly built college library, she piles gowns in the quadrangle and sets fire to them, she runs through the college at night turning off the electricity by pulling fuses, and so on. When Harriet Vane, a former college student who is now a novelist living in London, is asked to stay in college in order to expose the prankster, she becomes a version of the gothic heroine. She walks through the empty corridors at night with a flashlight, seeking to catch the culprit, who gains power from her corporeality, yet also from her apparent alliance with a purely supernatural realm.

At the same time, Sayers incorporates a distinctly psychological dimension into the conflict. Everyone believes the 'poltergeist' to be an actual person, though with much of the power of a supernatural agent because she is irrational, or mad, and in what the college fellows imagine to be a quite specific way. When Harriet first learns of the threat to the college's reputation, she muses on the fearful possibility that women are, after all, unfit for learning, a cliché which constitutes part of the argument which had kept them barred from Oxbridge for so many centuries. She imagines the following accusations against academic women, made by the outside world:

> 'Soured virginity' – 'unnatural life' – 'semi-demented spinsters' – 'starved appetites and suppressed impulses' – 'unwholesome atmosphere' – she could think of whole sets of epithets, ready-minted for circulation. Was this what lived in the tower set on the hill?[2]

On the one hand, this way of putting it emphasizes that this is simply a straightforward hunt for a predatory monster, a vicious, hidden presence that lurks in the tower of learning and must be exorcized. On the other, it sets the heroine a fascinating problem, since she has personally chosen celibacy (at this point in the novel series), yet she is tempted to assume that her failure to express sexuality properly will indeed damage her – hence the string of accusatory epithets which spring to mind. This goes straight to the heart of the matter: if she is to begin engaging in self-doubt, there is no end to her torture. How can she know, herself, if she is insane? If she were, she would be unable to discern the fact.

The senior members of the college also feel this threat to their self-confidence. One common assumption among them is, as the Dean articulates to Harriet:

> 'I suppose it might even be one of ourselves. That's what's so horrible. Yes, I know – elderly virgins, and all that. It's awful to know that at any minute one may be sitting cheek by jowl with somebody who feels like that. Do you think the poor creature knows that she does it herself?'

This comment leads the Dean to do as Harriet has done, which is to wonder if she should apply the possible blame to herself: 'I've been waking up with nightmares, wondering whether I didn't perhaps prowl round in my sleep, spitting at people.'[3] Since this is primarily a detective novel, it is clear from the start that the identity of the 'poltergeist' will be unmasked eventually. But it is also important to note the extreme discomfort that accrues among the college members in the meantime. The question then becomes: does psychology (which attempts to offer a rational explanation for irrational human behavior) give characters superior insight? That is what makes all of these novels and short stories so interesting. The assumption is that to understand motivations and causes is to be able to take logical, rational steps to lessen one's sufferings. But these writers are also willing to assign moral culpability to their characters, as well as acknowledging the psychological influences which affect them – which adds yet another dimension to the danger which threatens Sayers' fictional Oxford college, or the Anglican characters in Susan Howatch's novels about the fictional cathedral in Starbridge. Though it can seem predetermined and inevitable for obsessed or misguided characters who harm others to lash out, they could (theoretically) exercise free will to act in a moral and good way.

That is why thought processes – especially those which can seem logical but are not – are examined so closely in these books. It offers novelists another way to to pit passion against reason. And the description of supernatural phenomena is a useful way of dramatizing strong emotions. This dialectic comes full circle when – in some of these fictions – supernatural events can be interpeted as projections of the human mind, thus fulfilling psychology's prediction that this diseased perception accounts for seemingly surreal events.

In a way, it does not matter whether supernatural phenomena (whatever they might be, and however a novelist might describe them) are active in the matter or not. If ghosts are 'real,' characters can either try to exorcize them or to avoid them. If they are not real, but rather the projections of a raging unconscious, the effect is the same – except that it is intensified by the fact that one cannot easily escape one's own thought processes. Rationality in one sense is no help, since one cannot reason with a ghost; nor can one reason effectively with the subconscious, either with a demented human 'poltergeist' who is attacking the Oxford college in Sayers' novel or with one's own self-doubts. None the less, reason is crucially important for the characters who are threatened, either by potential madness lurking in their own psyches, or by the action of an outside, evil agent. They must discern, as best they can, what will next threaten them, in order to protect themselves.

The use of supernatural terminology to describe seemingly inexplicable events in these novels is another way of urging the reader to see all human beings as fundamentally mysterious. When the heroine in Dorothy L. Sayers' *Gaudy Night* first looks around her at the junior college members gathered together at dinner, her eyes are drawn to the unusual women first, and then to those who appear to be ordinary on the surface:

> The rest [of the group] were nondescript, as yet undifferentiated – yet nondescripts, thought Harriet, were the most difficult of all human beings to analyze. You scarcely knew they were there, until – bang! Something quite unexpected blew up like a depth charge and left you marvelling, to collect strange floating débris.[4]

This ability to blend in with the crowd is important for a crafty villain, who seeks anonymity. And part of what gives the 'poltergeist' such power over the college members is that they begin to suspect each other of eccentricity or worse; in effect, they try to 'analyze' each other, which leads to suspicion and rancor. But that is what is fascinating about the unpredictability of the human mind: its ultimate opacity. No one can know for certain what another character is thinking or feeling.

The surreal cannot be seen in a twentieth-century context without relating some of its power to psychology, and to an effort to stare down irrational behaviour by logical reasoning about a complex yet partly comprehensible mystery: the human mind. The supernatural – as a vague, malevolent realm or as a specific, localized force – poses a challenge to rationality in the same way that the workings of the mind do. Writers deal with this interface between the supernatural and reason in various ways. Elizabeth Bowen satirizes those arrogant characters who believe that they can overcome supernatural hauntings by the use of psychological distancing. Susan Howatch affirms this approach, suggesting that supernatural forces can only be met by other supernatural powers; in the context of her Anglican psychological thrillers, satanic powers can only be exorcised by Christ (although a token spiritual director invariably appears to interpret the psychological intricacies which also occur). At the same time, she uses this as a background to dramatize the actions of characters who believe that their own powers of reasoning enable them to think their way out of dangerous situations. Her main interest lies in the ways in which characters deceive themselves, by believing the false perceptions of their own minds. A.S. Byatt is interested in the relation of ghosts to human grieving, or to unresolved emotional dilemmas – though she also indulges in pure fabulism, in her stylized tale, 'The Djinn in the Nightingale's Eye,' in which an exotic djinn appears to a startled heroine and grants her the ritual three wishes. Iris Murdoch also leans towards heavy irony, in at least one of her uses of supernatural encounters, when her character Anne Cavidge has a religious vision of Christ in *Nuns and Soldiers*, a meeting which represents a variation on yet another stereotype of spiritual events.

The thread that I want to pursue here is the way in which characters think about supernatural phenomena. These are by definition irrational and therefore beyond reasoning with, yet this makes the workings of characters' minds all the more compelling, since their persistence in this course argues a profound belief in the powers of reason. This is an important idea in these novels and short stories because it allows the authors to do two things at once: to show the sinister nature of a mind which itself is in darkness (either consciously or not), and to show the arrogance of people who think that they can exorcise ghosts by flaunting psychological theories. Feminist critics have concentrated, in ground-breaking studies such as Gilbert and Gubar's *The Madwoman in the Attic*, on the energy in gothic fiction which stems from anger at oppression. Many of the twentieth-century authors just mentioned, while choosing to work in a gothic tradition, have yet self-consciously attempted to bring gender questions into the problem in a new and unusual way. Gender is less of a defining issue in these works, since logic and perception are what tend to fascinate these writers. In this context, the constant, covert presence of popularized psychological theories pits logic against irrationality; characters try to think their way out of emotional dramas or pain. But the fact of supernatural presence means that they are contending with something beyond themselves. They face an enemy with superior powers, which gives the reader a requisite *frisson* of terror, and also provides the characters with arresting challenges.

Elizabeth Bowen's satirical short story 'The Cat Jumps' is the most direct expression of the connection between the supernatural and the popularization of twentieth-century psychology. The couple who choose to buy the house in the country in which a *crime passionel* has been committed pride themselves upon being rational: 'They had light, bright, shadowless, thoroughly disinfected minds. They believed that they disbelieved in most things but were unprejudiced; they enjoyed frank discussions.' This description makes it evident from the first that they are being set up for a fall; such smugness must be challenged.[5] The Harold Wright family refuses to identify with the Harold Bentley family who formerly owned the house. This proclaims their arrogance; nothing like this could happen to them because they choose not only to be rational, but to confront the irrational with combative psychological texts and with 'frank discussions.' Moreover, they accept the house's associations as a direct challenge to their views: 'In their practical way,' the narrator says, 'the Wrights now set out to expel, live out, live down, almost (had the word had place in their vocabulary) to "lay" the Bentleys.'[6] Thus the story is clearly a ghost story, although the protagonists do not know this. Predictably, the party of five friends who have been asked down from London for the weekend become increasingly affected by the malevolent atmosphere of the house, and everyone begins to quarrel.

Jocelyn, the owner of the house, is eventually overcome as well, vividly imagining the death by dismemberment of the victim (who was also a wife, and who was killed by her husband, also named Harold). In a moment of pure terror, she thinks: 'There was no comfort: death (now at every turn and instant claiming her) was, in its every possible manifestation, violent death: ultimately, she was to be given up to terror.' Her fear is irrational yet based on a practical fact at the same time (another character has locked Jocelyn's bedroom door, so that she cannot run to others for protection), in addition to verging into the supernatural realm. When Harold, her husband, enters the room, he has 'assumed the entire burden of Harold Bentley. Forces he did not know of assembling darkly, he had faced for untold ages the imperturbable door to his wife's room.' At the same time that Bowen crafts a kind of supernatural imposition of one spirit over another, she casts Harold's feelings in a psychological, misogynist mode. He thinks: 'She would be there, densely, smotheringly there. She lay like a great cat, always, over the mouth of his life.' Though he does not carry through the actions of the murderer, he feels his same feelings, and for a moment the two 'Harolds [are] superimposed on each other.' Jocelyn imitates the actions of Mrs. Bentley: she 'went down heavily' – although she has fainted rather than been struck.[7]

This is brilliantly chilling writing – and it gains power from the contrast with a weird kind of rationality and cunning which infuses the story. Muriel, the character who has locked all of the house's bedroom doors from the outside, is seeking to prevent Edward Cartaret (whom she fears) from attacking her. In her attempt to prevent him from leaving his room, she locks everyone's door: 'Muriel was a woman who took no chances,' as the story concludes, and in this she is markedly different from the Harold Wrights, who have taken an extremely daring chance, in buying the house, and in believing that they could 'lay' the ghost of the Bentleys by means of talking about it dismissively. This is indeed a ghost story, with the characters becoming successively possessed by the malign spirit who committed a cold-blooded crime. And yet it gains in terror and in satire as well, because of the ironic references to Krafft-Ebing (who has made a study of madness, and therefore figuratively laid its power), and also to 'Freud, Weiniger and the heterosexual volume of Havelock Ellis,' which the house guests have all been consulting in the course of their discussions.[8] (The fact that they avoid the homosexual volumes constitutes another jab of irony at the characters, who are brave enough to pursue information on one course, but not on another which might be less socially acceptable.) That is, psychology can perhaps explain irrational phenomena, but talking does not ultimately hold emotion at bay. Psychology and the supernatural reinforce each other here, all the more so as the lines are blurred between unconscious projection or imagination and the recurring acting out of the drama of a murder.

Bowen's most well-known ghost story, 'The Demon Lover,' ventures still further into the supernatural realm, by having its heroine whisked away at the end by a former suitor who has now returned to claim her.

It takes place in London during World War II, when the heroine, Kathleen, arrives from the country to see her empty London house: 'She had been anxious to see how the house was . . . .' The war itself is an overwhelming force which she cannot hold at bay, except by escaping to the country, although this is a despairing gesture: 'There were some cracks in the structure, left by the last bombing, on which she was anxious to keep an eye. Not that one could do anything. . . .' In the same way, she cannot do anything to escape the inexorable progress of the 'demon lover' who is coming to claim her. She finds a letter in the house which announces 'You will not have forgotten that today is our anniversary, and the day we said.'[9]

The narrator then reconstructs the background for the inevitable meeting. The heroine recollects that she had been briefly engaged to a soldier during the previous war, and upon his departure, 'she already felt that unnatural promise drive down between her and the rest of all human kind. No other way of having given herself could have made her feel so apart, lost and forsworn.' The narrator adds that 'She could not have plighted a more sinister troth.' When she lets herself out of the London house in order to escape, she flags down a taxi, and when she has entered it is flung forward in her seat: 'Through the aperture driver and passenger, not six inches between them, remained for an eternity eye to eye. Mrs. Drover's mouth hung open for some seconds before she could issue her first scream.' She has been abducted: 'After that she continued to scream freely and to beat with her gloved hands on the glass all round as the taxi, accelerating without mercy, made off with her into the hinterland of deserted streets.'[10] While this story is – like 'The Cat Jumps' – in the genre of a stylized ghost tale, it also has elements of realism in it which render it still more terrifying. The heroine's recollections of a conversation with the departing soldier in 1916 have surreal overtones, and yet they also express the kind of ordinary romantic line which a suitor might offer: '"I shall be with you," he said, "sooner or later. You won't forget that. You need do nothing but wait."' She does imagine 'spectral glitters' in his eyes, and he is painted as slightly sadistic – he presses her hand against a sharp button on his coat 'without very much kindness.'[11] But the progress of the plot is also prosaic in a time of universal war and destruction: the soldier returns to France from his leave, and is later reported missing in action. His return will not be that of a soldier; the title of the story announces that we should understand his unexpected reappearance literally – though the 'Demon Lover' in this case is not one for whom the heroine yearns.

Part of the appeal of these short stories is *Schadenfreude* – which is perhaps a large ingredient in the enjoyment of the gothic literary conventions. Bowen, in particular, paints the Wrights in 'The Cat Jumps' as being so obnoxious and arrogant that it becomes a pleasure to see them receive their just deserts. Kathleen in 'The Demon Lover' is more problematic, as she merely seems dim, and the prey of gratuitous, sadistic evil. Since the genre of short fiction allows the author to exit the story quickly, she can create characters who are stick figures; thus, when they come to grief, the reader will not be overcome by sympathy on their behalf, and moreover, can be confident that she would never get into such a stupid situation herself. This is part of the genre's appeal. It seems a kind of talisman to ward off evil, if we wish to believe that all the bad things in the world happen to other people.

A.S. Byatt uses something of the same formula in some of her short stories, though they strike a balance between poignancy and irony. Ghosts in these fictions tend to assume their traditional roles of the dead appearing to the sight or hearing of the living. This direct connection to their recent life on earth makes them seem the more plausible as active agents – just out of reach of the main characters, for good or ill. This intangible presence extends the temporal and physical boundaries of a story. One important point about ghosts – besides their presence as a possible projection of the psyche – is that they connect specifically to places. Both Bowen and Byatt draw on a convention of the genius loci in their works. The main character in Byatt's 'July Ghost' becomes involved with the ghost when he talks to a sympathetic woman whom he has just met at a party, and says he must leave his flat: 'One could not, he said, go on in a place where one had once been blissfully happy, and was now miserable, however convenient the place.' His reason for doing so is grief at losing a lover, as the woman he has been living with has moved out.[12] The two characters intuitively understand the physical pain of grieving, as connected to their immediate surroundings.

Both of them have lost loved ones – the woman's young son has been killed in an accident, and it is this child whom the lodger sees, first sitting in a tree, and later on in the garden. The story dramatizes a séance which has missed its step; it is she who passionately longs to see her son – begging the lodger for descriptions of him – but who cannot do so. 'The only thing I want, the only thing I want at all in this world, is to see that boy,' she tells him.[13]

The presence of the ghost is made still more visual and concrete because the lodger is able to describe the boy's clothing, which the mother recalls from the past: 'I must be seeing your memories, he told her, and she nodded fiercely, compressing her lips, agreeing that this was likely, adding, "I am too rational to go mad, so I am putting it on you."' This draws a definitive connection between psychology and the supernatural, which the grieving mother combines. She agrees that the lodger is seeing something tangible – her memories – yet in a ghostly way (irrational) which is also rational (bearing out her idea of herself as being sensible). She attempts to go on being 'rational,' though the ghost story is definitely a ghost story in the sense that the supernatural being has a will which it imposes on the living. When the lodger tries to pack his suitcases and leave, at the end of the story, the boy appears: 'Do you want me to stay?' the man asks, upon which 'the boy turned on him again the brilliant, open, confiding, beautiful desired smile.'[14]

At the same time, the boy's apparent request for the man to comfort the mother is irrational. As the man argues with him, about the pointlessness of his intervention, 'I can't get through.' The mother grieves endlessly, and his attempts to console her sexually prove futile. She tells him, 'Sex and death don't go.'[15] This is part of the ghost's impact on the living – to demand something which seems hopeless to the living character. At the same time, he proves a sort of effective medium between the two of them, since she literally cannot see her son, except through his interpretation and description. Everything is left unresolved, because no real resolution is possible. The child's presence and the lodger's presence both combine to reveal or externalize the thought processes of the grieving mother.

Byatt's story 'The Next Room' deals with similar themes of a dead family member who still haunts a place, although this time the person who has died is the aged mother of a middle-aged woman. Joanna Hope, the heroine, has buried her mother, although 'The house, now her house, was still full of her mother's presence.' Houses in this story contain the shimmering presence of people who have left them, as when a colleague of Joanna's relates having stayed as a guest in a house in Japan: 'I had breakfast every day with the family's grandfather, who was dead. He was present at every meal – his picture, anyway, in the middle of the table – we all bowed to it, and he had his own little servings of meals.' Joanna's instinctive response to this is denial of such sentimentality: 'I'm quite sure death is the end. I'm sure one just goes nowhere, as one came from nowhere.'[16]

In the same way, she is attempting to be rational in response to her mother's death. Her friend Michael attempts to console her, and also to persuade her to acknowledge this as being part of the source of her recurrent toothache, which he sees as a physical manifestation of her grief.

He respects yet also doubts the efficacy of her desire to remain stoic, telling her: 'you can't expect not to be upset at all, Joanna.' She attempts to carry through in a reasonable manner, going at his suggestion to consult a dentist – although even there, she meets a woman who speaks at length about her Near Death Experience, and subsequent conversion to a religious cult which believes in life after death. This character enthusiastically shares her own vision of an encounter with her relations in what she takes to be heaven; she describes them as living in 'a little bungalow, ever such a lovely bungalow . . .' which exactly answers her mother's notions of the ideal.[17]

Joanna, having the opposite experience, begins to hear voices in her own mother's actual house: 'Aggrieved voices, running on in little dashes like a thwarted beck clucking against pebble-beds and rooted impediments. They had the ease of long custom and the abrasiveness of new rage.' This suggests the contrary flow of energy to that described by the woman who has had a vision of the bungalow; life continues for her parents after their death, still escalating. Her rational response to this is to decide to sell her parents' house, which brings up the possibility that the human interactions in it have affected its atmosphere. The estate agent whom she consults assures her that the house has 'good vibrations,' as opposed to those of a malevolent kind: 'He had had a client once who had had to resort to an exorcist. The property had been brimful of rage and hatred. You could feel it like a temperature change, like a damp chill, coming over the threshold.'[18]

Since this is, in fact, something like what the heroine herself is experiencing, it suggests that only she feels the chill and can access the rage and disdain of the voices in the next room. The story closes with their continued pursuit of her, even when she has gone to a new place and is staying in an impersonal hotel room. The other curious thing in this story is that these voices are not melodramatic: when she ponders them from a distance, she thinks that 'Her ghosts only grumbled, they did not threaten, nor did they bear with them any searing experience of unbearable pain. No, the truth was, they were simply *theoretically* frightening.' The possible explanations, which she resolutely names to herself in attempting to analyze her situation, are three. First, that the Academy of the Return cult is in some sense correct, and that her parents will continue to persist in the guise of their accustomed characters 'much as they had been in life.' The second possibility is that she is: 'schizophrenic and hallucinating, of course, but she believed she was not, and was by no means going to waste her valuable and abbreviated future on discussion of raised iris beds with an expensive psychiatrist.'[19] Her third hypothesis is that her parents' spiritual presences are literally linked to the house where they have lived, and that, by selling it and leaving for another place, she can leave them behind as well. The voices continue to pursue her, giving no hope of a respite from their tormenting.

In this story Byatt again shows a character who is consciously trying to be rational in the face of grief, though in this case she has cause to feel relief in escaping her mother's demands and manipulation. The voices can conceivably be seen as a projection of her own guilt, or her unresolved anger with her parents. She attempts to think out her position in a sensible way, though declining the aid of psychology; she chooses not to believe in that, much in the same way that she rejects the ideas of the Academy of the Return (a cult which is, in its own way, trying to muster more dignity by giving itself this name). Joanna Hope's ghostly voices seem to her to be '*theoretically*' frightening – they do not so much menace her directly as irritate and annoy by their presence. But that makes this story all the more interesting, because it is not one of gothic terror or outrageous threat. These ghosts externalize the sort of internal voices that anyone might hear internally. This gives Byatt the opportunity to explore from another dimension – one devoid of immediate threat – the dynamics of coping with a problem that seems entirely beyond the access of reason.

Iris Murdoch describes a religious vision in her novel *Nuns and Soldiers*, in which a Christ figure appears to Anne Cavidge, a former nun who has now left her convent and is making her way slowly back into the world. The novel follows her through this process of reentering secular life and the awakening of long-dormant romantic passion which torments her. She goes to stay with Gertrude, her friend from Cambridge undergraduate days, and in the course of deciding what to do with her life she falls in love with Peter (one of the figurative 'soldiers' of the title). His nickname, the Count, bespeaks his deep-seated melancholy – his father was Polish, and he carries with him that sensibility, even exaggerating it. He is in love with Gertrude, Anne's friend, while Anne is in love with him – a feeling which she experiences as a piercing affliction: 'Something terrible had happened to Anne. It had happened some time ago and it was going on happening. She had fallen terribly terribly in love with the Count. Of course she had told no one of this dreadful love.'[20] As typically with the most intense suffering, she is entirely isolated in her pain.

The unrequited passion which she has for Peter is strongly linked to the dream vision (and may prompt it, or represent another aspect of it) which she has of Christ. Her conversation with him takes place in the kitchen of her flat, and he circumvents all of her preconceived notions of him, that were presumably derived from long vocational devotion. Physically, his hands are not scarred, and he parries her fascination with his possible wounds: 'The point? No, though it has proved so interesting to you all!' When she asks what she must do to attain salvation, he rebuffs her again: 'You must do it all yourself, you know.' Her final plea for love is also turned aside, as he wonders at her being 'sentimental' and tells her: 'Love me if you must, my dear, but don't touch me.'[21] Her desperate lunge for his sleeve produces a searing pain, and the wound on her own hand does not heal during the rest of the novel.

While this exchange is presented as a dream, it also has a tangible, physical reality, as evidenced in the burn on her hand – manifesting in her own person the wounds which are lacking in her vision of Christ. And it also expresses some aspects of the state of her heart and mind; the unrequited love which she cherishes for the Count is similar to the careless indifference with which the Christ figure in her dream treats her. That is, Murdoch represents here an almost worse fate than the sheer gothic terror of a malevolent threat: Anne encounters casual indifference.

The supernatural elements in Byatt and Murdoch are both real and surreal at the same time. They run close to the characters' passionate desires, and therefore can be seen to spring in part from the distress of their minds. But the characters who are afflicted with these sorts of visions are markedly intellectual and rational, attempting to control their thoughts and discipline their minds. Joanna, in Byatt's 'The Next Room,' is said to be 'a believer in human ingenuity. Also in progress.'[22] Anne, in *Nuns and Soldiers*, has also been an intellectual. These short stories and novels venture out into the supernatural realm, but they remain rooted in the primacy of human thought and perception as their real basis for reality.

Susan Howatch goes still further in invoking a spiritual dimension in her six-part series of novels about the Anglican Church, which traces a chronological line of cultural beliefs about religion in the twentieth century from the 1930s to the century's end. These books are fascinating in part for the research which she undertook, as underpinning for contemporary beliefs in each of the books, but also for their decisive descriptions of paranormal phenomena – which are buttressed by highly detailed psychological explanations of the events. Each of the novels is narrated by a main character who describes the process of his or her progressive mental breakdown, which at some point leads to a determined effort to come to terms with the character's past behavior. Since these are twentieth-century sagas, a rational, logical bias underlies all of them.

I want to concentrate here on *Mystical Paths*, the fifth novel in the series, as it makes use of a number of paranormal events which are then interpreted in this way. But in addition, the novel is a quintessential example of Howatch's style, which strikes a fine comic balance between off-handed familiarity with the spiritual world and prosaic daily affairs. The novel opens with the narrator, Nick Darrow, engaged in domestic tasks: 'I had just returned from an exorcism and was flinging some shirts into the laundry,' he tells the reader – a wonderfully comic juxtaposition of the exotic and the mundane.[23] The telephone call for help which interrupts this scene in the kitchen turns out to be a parrying of his offer to give spiritual aid. Venetia, who has narrated her own dramatic story in the preceding novel, resists the application to herself of Nick's psychological healing powers. This is standard practice for those who are afflicted. Howatch continually insists that no one really wants to change; it is only in the throes of the most dire crisis – and at times, with the exercise of absolute authority by a spiritual figure – that the sufferer can be restrained long enough to delve for the root of the problem.

In each of her six interlocking novels she uses a different narrator, each of whom draws an extended psychological profile of some larger-than-life crisis, delving to the source of it, which necessitates immense energy.

In *Mystical Paths*, Howatch's character Nick Darrow, who comes of age in the 1960s, explains his particular spiritual gifts to the reader, though with some irony: 'Many people think it must be fun to be a psychic. Fun! When as a small child I first experienced the long slam I screamed non-stop until my father arrived to stitch up my shredded little psyche.'[24] Since his father possesses this visionary gift as well, Nick has someone who understands him and can to some extent protect him; but part of the drama of the novel derives from Nick's struggle to separate himself ultimately from his father. This is obviously a psychological angle, as any twentieth-century reader perceives immediately. Howatch's genius is to combine psychological ideas with spiritual ones – and to do so in a blatantly gothic manner. Her novels are theological thrillers, a genre which she has perfected, drawing on the whole array of fictional techniques which adorn detective novels. In *Mystical Paths*, Nick becomes intent on tracing the whereabouts of Christian Aysgarth, who is presumed to have died in a boating accident at sea.

However, his original entrance into the action begins at a party, where he describes his vision of the young and well-heeled crowd who surround him:

> Then time suddenly went out of alignment, and I knew that in that drawing-room, so civilized and elegant, a priest had been killed during the Civil War when the Roundheads had smashed up Royalist Starbridge [the cathedral town which is the setting for most of these novels].

This reference to the historical past gives momentum to the sweep of time which Nick is seeing, and it shifts from the murder to an all-encompassing vision of death: 'There was wall-to-wall blood, I couldn't see it, but it was there, I was wading in it, and all at once the Force – the psychic force – roared into top gear. . . .' What he apprehends is darkness, and the word 'DEATH' which repeats itself in the abstract, and defines the particular futures of others in the room.[25]

Nick goes on: 'Then I looked at my companions, that *jeunesse dorée*, those glamorous friends of Marina Markhampton all glittering in the Light, and I knew the Dark was closing in on them, I knew the Côterie was doomed.' He then goes on to describe particular fates of various characters – drug addiction, madness, suicide, drowning, and so on. These are actually logical outcomes of the individual courses which many of them have chosen, but the *frisson* is there nonetheless, both for the reader and for the visionary who sees the horrible consequences of a spiritually destructive path, for the group as a whole and for specific characters. He yearns to leap to the aid of his particular friend, Venetia, 'and the word that roared through my brain was DANGER, DANGER, DANGER – and I thought: I've got to save her, got to act, got to speak –' though he is deflected from his intention (both at that moment, and ultimately – no one can 'save' another).[26]

This is a brilliant way of fictionalizing the combination of emotional terror with rational thought which typifies a twentieth-century cultural value. Nick is impulsive in his actions, yet always thinking furiously. Moreover, it is both chilling and at the same time rather satisfying for the reader (should she possess any degree of *Schadenfreude*) to know that the glamorous Côterie is doomed, through its own arrogance and excess. And this is the puzzling thing about Howatch's fiction as a whole: while it is absorbing to read, it also leaves one feeling ambivalent, rather than compassionate towards her characters. The reader's sympathy with Howatch's heroes and heroines arises in part because each of the novels is narrated in the first person, which leads us to identify with the main character's point of view. And it also allows the narrator opportunities to express self-mockery and rueful hindsight. When Nick reports his attempts to console Katie, Christian's widow, he says: 'Her last words before we copulated were: "I feel forgiven now." Pathetic. I can hardly bring myself to admit this, but I still honestly believed I was healing her.' His summary of it is cast in spiritual terms, as well as personal ones: 'Game, set and match to the Devil. What a catastrophe.'[27]

Howatch's characters enjoy speaking in this way, and the reader's tolerance for such an attitude will determine how much she enjoys reading these novels. They remain fascinating in any case, not least for the skill with which the author manages to have it both ways: to write about wicked and shocking events, and yet to maintain a cool, moral tone towards them. The real test of righteousness, of course, is whether the main character does eventually experience repentance – but then, perhaps it would be boring if he or she actually did. In some sense, the crisis which hurls each character into a sort of quick fix course in psychotherapy remains simply that; he or she confronts some deeply buried psychological trauma (usually related to early childhood, and the character's parents) and as a result becomes reoriented sufficiently to go on living in a more or less functional manner. Nick Darrow of *Mystical Paths* reappears in a later novel, *The Wonder Worker*, which Howatch wrote after completing the six-volume series of 'Starbridge' books, and he behaves yet again in a reprehensible manner which causes his wife (from whom he has been long estranged) to divorce him. Part of this, however, is an efficient plot device which makes it possible for him to move towards a union with the narrator of that novel, a stout, plain young woman whom he has rescued from her own emotional crisis. The irony of this is rather neat – he has always had a passion for steamy brunettes, as opposed to fragile women (into which category his first wife falls), and this is the sort of woman whom he will eventually remarry. Although Nick does not make this point, the Freudian parallels with his mother are evident to the reader.

What Howatch excels at is showing characters who are suffering (sometimes for reasons they refuse to face themselves), and who turn to addictions of various kinds in order to escape. The fact that they keep their religious convictions at the same time as they are, for instance, committing adultery, illustrates the compartmentalizing of which the mind is capable. In *Scandalous Risks*, a clergyman writes to the narrator, a young woman with whom he is having an affair, to reassure her that he is literally split between his wife and his mistress: 'Dido [his wife] has so little, just her children and – well, yes, she has me. Or rather, she has Stephen. But she doesn't have *me*, Neville Four [his alternate self]. I belong entirely to you. . . .' His characterization of himself is par for the course, in this kind of pseudo-confessional letter: 'Well, there it is, darling – the plain, unvarnished truth at last. As you see, I'm at heart a very simple, honest person, but I admit I do sometimes have difficulty finding the words to explain myself, particularly if the explanations involve deep emotions.' And he confidently rejects psychology's ability to shed light on his character, adding: 'I suppose the earnest disciples of Freud and Jung would want to know all about my parents and my Uncle Willoughby, but I hardly feel that sort of ancient history's relevant to us now . . .' The signal that he is entirely unwilling to deal with this subject is his summary of his relatives: '[they] were all wonderful, all perfect, and they loved me just as much as I loved them.'[28]

The fact that this same character, Neville Aysgarth, has already gone through an earlier breakdown and supposed rehabilitation, in the novel *Ultimate Prizes*, suggests that such crises can leave one fundamentally unchanged. But the novels remain interesting for the ways in which characters rationalize their actions, even while they acknowledge them to be theoretically wrong. Howatch shows the possibility of a mind divided within itself, and also operating in a spiritual dimension which is in itself capable of twisting the characters' perceptions. The 'Game, set and match to the Devil' which Nick Darrow describes in *Mystical Paths* continues to intensify, and the plot also employs still more bizarre psychic phenomena. Darrow attempts a kind of séance which goes wildly astray, has a powerful vision of his father appearing in a different physical plane, and finally participates in the exorcism of a chapel where a man has just been killed.

But throughout her description of all of these supernatural events, Howatch offers rational explanations for them as well. The climax of the novel occurs when Nick and his friend Rachel encounter Perry, Christian Aysgarth's murderer, hoping to extort a confession from him. They meet in a chapel, where he does in fact confess to the crime, but intends to kill both of his witnesses. When a fourth character enters, to save them, the murderer himself dies, and the surviving characters are left to make sense of the dramatic events which have occurred. Nick struggles to explain his perceptions to Lewis Hall, the father figure and spiritual director who has come to his aid, and who gives the following explanation: 'What Perry was doing in his confession this morning was projecting his own madness onto his victim.' Nick's response is couched in spiritual language:

> 'So, he was the one who was possessed by the Devil – or by a demon implanted by the Devil. But if Christian was sane, a victim, and not an evil man infested by a demonic spirit . . .' I stopped, unable to articulate the problem.

In the end, Hall invokes more rational, psychological terms, urging:

> 'let's give the old-fashioned picture-language another rest and try a more flexible approach to this very complex truth. We can still say that Perry was possessed, . . . but we'll now say he was possessed by his grief, his guilt, his shame and his horror that he had killed the friend he loved.'[29]

The rational and the supernatural continue to mix in an uncanny combination in the initial description and later analysis of Perry's death. In literal terms, his death occurred when he threatened Nick and Rachel with a gun, and Nick distracted him, while Rachel 'lunged forward, grabbed the wooden cross from the altar and slammed it with all her strength into Perry's skull.' In Nick's perception, it is almost entirely a psychic event:

> I was blasted onto a different level of reality. The demonic spirit screamed . . . The Light exploded, pouring down upon us, and I saw the Dark disintegrate. Black blood gushed from the corpse. The demon died.

When Lewis Hall (who is Nick's adviser and also Rachel's father) arrives, the three discuss these dramatic events, and Rachel's contempt for Nick's spiritual version of the scene is evident:

> 'to suggest that Christian's soul had been annexed by the Devil and implanted with a demon which had taken over Perry – well, I mean, it's so fantastic that no one rational – no one *normal* – could possibly believe it. That sort of thing doesn't happen in real life, and if you think it does, Nicholas, you should have your head examined.'[30]

In this way, Howatch achieves a spokesperson for every angle on the subject: Nick is not 'normal' (and admits this about himself, to some degree), while Lewis Hall tempers both viewpoints by weaving together the spiritual and the physical planes. In practical terms, he decides that

KING ALFRED'S COLLEGE
LIBRARY

the young people must be rescued from their folly: 'I'm not having my daughter standing trial for manslaughter just because a young man she barely knows used her to act out a fantasy. I'm going to detach you both from this disaster.' He does this by clearing away the evidence of Perry's death and by cleverly hiding the corpse. They clean up the scene of the death literally, bringing a bucket of water to wash away the blood in the chapel, and wiping fingerprints away from all possible surfaces (a stock scene in detective fiction). Hall works out a plausible story for each of them to tell the police, if they are questioned. But he also recasts Nick's highly spiritual language into more psychological terms ('guilt' and 'projected' are his typical words for this transformation), and he goes on to effect a kind of psychic separation between Nick and his father through a ritual of prayer. Nick speaks of this in terms of rebirth – 'I took a quick journey around my new self and patted the ragged edges into place' – though he soon begins to notice psychic phenomena surrounding the event. He questions Hall about his watch having stopped ('Is it to do with an alteration in the magnetic field?') to which his mentor replies: 'You and your passion for rational analysis!'[31]

That is the peculiar combination which Howatch invokes in these novels: passion and analysis – the spiritual, psychological, and physical planes and their intersection in a series of crescendo-ing crises. In one way, she is simply recreating another mode of gothic writing, in which her characters wander ever deeper into danger, through ignorance, innocence, or the malevolent intent of others. What is perhaps most appealing about them – since we like having our wishes fulfilled – is that the characters who err so badly are always rescued. Wise father figures appear, in order to listen, command, and (sometimes) heal the sufferers.

And this brings us back to the efficacy of psychoanalysis, which promises to offer exactly such a chance. In effect, what the popularization of psychology as a field has given to novelists is the chance to observe cultural beliefs about it: its main influence on society at large seems to have been to make everyone an instant amateur analyst. The heroine in Sayers' *Gaudy Night* seizes its terms eagerly, as do several characters in Howatch's novels. But these novels all operate in the twilight area between the supernatural and the material – between concrete facts of existence, which can be perceived, and the surreal overlay of terms like 'demonic possession' and 'psyche.'

The darkness in the mind which these novelists explore seldom seems to be dispelled, though a spiritual vision might cast another perspective on it. Anne's dream vision of Christ in Murdoch's *Nuns and Soldiers* leaves her still helplessly in love with him (as well as with the Count), and her conversation with him does seem to express her own bleak views about the spiritual quest. It is all up to her, and she must do all of the work involved – as well as endure the suffering, which in her case seems pointless. Perhaps what these writers are most interested in expressing is the difficulty of achieving true healing, emotional or otherwise. The symbolic wound on Anne's hand will never heal, just as her unfulfilled longings for love will continue. It is a difficult realm to describe with credibility, especially when writing, as these authors are, in an age of marked religious skepticism. But that is why it succeeds so well, as melodrama. It is sentimental yet embedded in it is a hard core of exhilarating cynicism.

In their encounters with the supernatural realm, their characters are nearly always bested – they can be abducted, as in Bowen's 'Demon Lover,' or simply disappointed, as in Murdoch's *Nuns and Soldiers*. Or they can call upon the power of Christ to aid them, as Nick Darrow does, in the chapel scene in *Mystical Paths*, when he reports, 'I knew I had to stop that demon-infested spirit moving side-ways out of Perry into someone else . . .' Part of the resolution to this scene occurs not only in the physical washing away of Perry's blood, but in the ritual of 'exorcism' which Lewis Hall performs afterwards, heartily assuring Nick, 'I promise you we'll heave out the demon's carcase and mop up his black blood as efficiently as we wiped out all the evidence of Perry's murder.'[32]

In one way, these ventures into the supernatural are less convincing for trying to explain and account for these phenomena in terms of psychological and spiritual terminology. Shakespeare's ghost in *Hamlet* is never anything but real, because no one even tries to account for his presence – people merely verify repeatedly that he appears. By contrast, the passion for rational analysis which Howatch's characters show seems to shift the emphasis away from the actual impact of psychic phenomena.

But these writers are interested in how their characters think, as well as in how they feel, and each individual mind interprets events in a unique way. Rationality is important in these novels because it tempers what might seem to the reader to be an excessive display of emotion. As Lewis Hall does in his analysis of the chapel scene in Howatch's *Mystical Paths*, it is possible to explain supernatural phenomena and bring them into the realm of something characters can deal with, and so not be left terrified at their mercy. Artistically, this contrast between melodramatic fear and dry, objective analysis helps to create the illusion of a 'realistic' story. The rational explanation is more real or believable than the psychic one (although both are alleged to be true perceptions of the events recorded from Nick Darrow's perspective), and thus the novel gains in force.

The supernatural dimension may also be brought into the narrative in a fabulist, mystical way. In A.S. Byatt's 'The Djinn in the Nightingale's Eye,' she announces the story as a magical one by its conventional fairy-tale opening line: 'Once upon a time, . . . there was a woman who was largely irrelevant, and therefore happy.' Immediately, we see that the business of the story will be to make the woman unhappy – rather, to educate her in some way that will deepen her engagement with life. While it is obviously a fabulist tale – a real genie pops out of a bottle – the story also plays on a highly ironic contrast with the academic mindset, which seeks to analyze everything. The heroine, Gillian Perholt, is an academic who specializes in 'narratology,' or 'storytelling,' and this activity is defamiliarized by the narrator into a strange pursuit: her 'days were spent hunched in great libraries scrying, interpreting, decoding the fairy-tales of childhood and the vodka-posters of the grown-up world, the unending romances of golden coffee-drinkers, and the impeded couplings of doctors and nurses, dukes and poor maidens, horsewomen and musicians.' Still more exotically, 'Sometimes, also, she flew.' This matches the opening description of an era 'when men and women hurtled through the air on metal wings,' which in this context actually means flying on modern airplanes – thus not so strange to modern sensibilities after all.[33] This parallel track, coupling dry, objective description with wild and magical phenomena, continues throughout the story, as glamor is slyly undercut with either irony or practical common sense.

When the mysterious Djinn offers Gillian three wishes, for instance, her instinctive first request is to ask for physical restoration of her body to a time when 'I last really *liked* it, if you can do that.' The resulting transformation leaves her still essentially herself, and not idealized beyond recognition; she sees herself in the mirror as 'a solid and unexceptionable thirty-five-year-old woman,' and she congratulates herself on the practicality of her request in terms of self-satisfaction. 'I shall *feel* better, I shall like myself more,' she concludes. 'That was an *intelligent* wish, I shall not regret it.'[34] Even at the center of a bizarrely fabulous situation, the heroine strives to think rationally and to keep her head – and the clever irony here is that her studies in fairy-tales of this kind have prepared her for just such a chance. As an academic, she does not request glamor; she avoids the potential pitfalls of a Faustian figure.

The Djinn himself suits her admirably, offering her both a selection of tales of his former mistresses and a detailed description of his long and varied life; he also provides a courteous audience to the narration of her own life story. He becomes a brilliant lover – her second request – and her final wish sets him free from vassalage to a human, and releases him into the universe. The mystical adventures which she has with him, both intellectually and sexually, all bear the stamp of concrete reality, while at the same time he remains an utterly surreal figure, adorned with 'a green silk tunic,' while 'Behind him was a great expanse of shimmering many-coloured feathers . . . which appeared to be part of a cloak that appeared to be part of him, but was not wings that sprouted in any conventional way from shoulder-blade or spine.'[35] He is a shape-shifter, in the sense of being able to change size, appearance, and costume at will.

In retrospect, Gillian Perholt contrasts the startling intrusion of the surreal into her life with her easy acceptance of it:

> She was later to wonder how she could be so matter-of-fact about the presence of a gracefully lounging Oriental daimon in a hotel room. At the time, she unquestioningly accepted his reality and his remarks as she would have done if she had met him in a dream. . . .[36]

The dream-state is a useful standard of reference for the author to compare the ability of her heroine to acknowledge the existence of strange phenomena with normalcy. This suggests that – to some extent – we are used to the idea of strangeness. The contrast of objective, academic reason and wild fabulism make the presence of both seem at the same time more bizarre yet more real.

The heroine is still happy in her 'irrelevance' at the end of the story, though with a new poignance born of exotic experience and the loss of high romantic sexuality in hotel rooms. More than this, she proves herself to be virtuous and generous, by granting the Djinn his independence.

One final example of twentieth-century use of psychic phenomena is Mary Stewart's *Touch Not the Cat*, which combines three genres: historical fiction, romance and detective fiction. Unlike the fiction of writers like Bowen, Murdoch and Byatt, Stewart's work is unabashedly romantic, and it makes an interesting contrast with the arch irony of those authors to see one way in which psychic connection can be used in a novel. The heroine, Bryony Ashley, has possessed what she knows to be a strong psychic connection with her father (who dies when the novel opens), but also with an unidentified, younger male member of her family. In the course of investigating a mystery at her ancestral home, and avenging the death of her father at the hands of a member of his own family, she must discern which of the young men holds the other end of the connection.

The psychic gift becomes a crucial part of the plot, as the twenty-two-year-old heroine must become a detective and exercise discernment. It also becomes crucial for the reader to understand the exact terms of the advantage which this gives her, and she attempts to explain her experience of it as follows:

> That is hard to describe, if not downright impossible. It comes through neither in words nor in pictures, but – I can't put it any better – in sudden blocks of intelligence that are thrust into one's mind and slotted and locked there, the way a printer locks lines into place, and there is the page with all its meanings for you to read.

The connection with her lover is highly romantic, as he is both known and mysterious as a childhood lover: 'I had known him all my twenty-two years.'[37]

Stewart further makes the possession and exercise of such gifts authenticated by tracing it to historical roots. The heroine says:

> I knew he must be someone close to me, and it was a safe bet that he was one of my Ashley cousins.... It's a gift that goes in families, and there were records that it ran in ours: ever since the Elizabeth Ashley who was burned at the stake in 1623, there had been a record, necessarily secret, of strange 'seeings' and thought transference between members of the family.

The twentieth-century story is paralleled by a historical, tragic romance of 1835, to reinforce this connection – and this offers, moreover, a wonderfully gothic plot twist of a secret marriage which produces an unknown yet legitimate heir to the Ashley title. The detective part of the plot involves the complexity of hidden identities, as Bryony attempts to discover which of the possible young men in her family circle is, in fact, her long-time psychic sweetheart – misreading the signals, to her peril. However, once she discovers his identity, they have the benefit of their deep, mutual understanding, which makes them 'as settled and placid as if we had been married for years.' Discussing the current between them, Bryony calls it 'A gift we share,' and characterizes it as 'special and magic,' and this reinforces the high romance of his tacit proposal of marriage. The heroine tells him, 'you read my very thoughts. . . .'[38]

Stewart's novel is a brilliant use of psychic connection to deepen a romantic attachment, and at the same time to both help and hinder a detective investigation. The possible edge that it might have given the heroine in her search is continually blunted by her preconceptions. As she tells her lover, once he is unmasked, 'I thought it had to be an Ashley. So I never looked beyond my cousins.' At the same time, the author draws an absolutely logical connection between the two psychically connected lovers, as Rob also is a member of the Ashley family – 'Straight down the wrong side of the blanket. . . .' as he tells her.[39]

Still, while Stewart's novel is wildly romantic, she follows in the tradition of other twentieth-century authors who contrast a supernatural dimension in their works with the logical and practical. Her two young lovers in *Touch Not the Cat* must continue on to solve a mystery and adventure story by using their brains, as well as their physical courage and strength; and, moreover, the dashing and psychic lover is also the prosaic figure of Rob, the garden boy (who is of lower class than Bryony, a further romanticization of the coupling).

In all of these novels and short stories, both things are present: thinking and feeling, reason and passion. The supernatural provides a code for emotional dilemmas which can then be expressed in it. The thing which is much more destructive – at least in this group of writers – is the disintegration of the mind and of logic itself. That way madness lies, and it is far more threatening than any ghost.

3
Grieving and Madness

Hamlet is the touchstone for Iris Murdoch's depiction of melancholy in *Nuns and Soldiers*, where characters meet to drink at a pub called The Prince of Denmark, and one of the heroines is a recently widowed woman named Gertrude. It is also a central background text in A.S. Byatt's *The Virgin in the Garden*, where the young Marcus Potter portrays Ophelia in the school dramatic production. Shakespeare's play combines madness with raving that none the less makes a powerful statement, as Laertes says of his sister's wild words: 'This nothing's more than matter.'[1] And this connection is also important for Murdoch and Byatt because they write with large gestures, in a way which combines passion with meaningful verbal expression of it – yet without sentimentality. Their fictional portrayals of madness dramatize a great rush of intense feeling. But the suffering evoked does not especially call for compassion. We automatically distance ourselves from madness (which is part of the reason why Hamlet feigns it), as it seems utterly strange. This theme fits in with this kind of novel: it is analytical, yet it courts melodrama at every turn. The authors seem also to be invoking the kind of madness that might be found in Russian novels, or those from some other culture more at home with expressions of raging emotion. In the English narrative tradition, it appears in the texts differently – objective curiosity (on the part of psychoanalyst characters who study it) or wry sophistication (on the part of narrators who look on with bemused indifference). And there is also a corollary with feminism: life has changed for women in the twentieth century, and also, cultural views of madness have changed. It can now be considered a state which readers are willing to see from the inside out (and not to hide it away in the attic). Moreover, everyone is an amateur psychologist, in the modern age, and this increases the tacit understanding between author and reader that we are all ironic, detached, and analytical. This distancing becomes its own convention, as the century progresses, for expressing extreme emotion – tantalizing its readers with passion, yet keeping the sufferers at a distance.

I want to follow on from Chapters 1 and 2, here, by showing a similar sort of trajectory, where Byatt, Bowen, and Murdoch, in particular, are writing about suffering in a way that uses madness as a code for gothic melodrama, which is at the same time undercut by an ironic sense of distance. In this chapter, I first look at Murdoch's *Nuns and Soldiers*, as a picture of grieving in which characters examine themselves anxiously for signs of madness – or, even believe that they are mad – although the novel shows the triumph of the grieving process. It is a version of *Hamlet* with a relatively happy ending. I go on to discuss Murdoch's *The Bell*, where madness stems from emotional dissociation. The most extreme example of derangement is suicide, and I would like to consider the choices of characters such as Emmeline in Elizabeth Bowen's *To the North*, and Max in her novel *The House in Paris*. This is followed by a discussion of several of A.S. Byatt's works, in which madness plays a significant role in showing how characters' minds work. Finally, I want to look at an example of madness portrayed as a useful escape from a traumatic event, in Molly Keane's *Treasure Hunt*.

The link that I am drawing between grieving and madness here is a specific one: for these authors, it is important to describe how their characters think. In grieving, the thought process involved is both overwhelmingly numbing, yet also more or less predictable (at least to an outside, objective viewer). It either crushes an afflicted character completely (for example, Bowen's Emmeline) or she survives it, to her own amazement (Murdoch's Gertrude). Suffering has an immediate effect of blotting out one's ability to reason – it can be paralyzing. Bowen, Byatt, and Murdoch on occasion grind their characters down to ultimate grief, despair, or insanity. The tacit assumption is that this point of departure into madness shows us a glimpse of raw, essential human nature that we would not otherwise see. *In extremis* seems to fascinate them as a way of telling the truth about life.

Iris Murdoch appeals to the inner adolescent in her readers. She offers us dramatic situations, and also dramatic plot reversals, depicting wild swings of passion in her characters. Murdoch's characters not only feel and suffer, but theorize endlessly about their emotions. They must somehow make sense for themselves of the violent feelings to which they have been subjected, and which often amaze them – and they feel that they can best deal with them by a kind of self-examination that seeks to control emotion by means of applying intellectual approaches and irony to undercut any charge of egotism. This becomes at heart a moral issue, because they want to do it right – and to be seen to be justified in their handling of themselves. Gertrude McCluskie, for instance, in *Nuns and Soldiers*, watches the slow death of her husband, Guy, from cancer. The novel follows her progress through a long period of grieving. In retrospect, she sees this process as having effected – at least temporarily – a complete displacement of her personality: 'In order to survive a terrible loss one has to become another person,' she explains to her friend Anne Cavidge, late in the novel. 'It may seem cruel. Survival itself is cruel, it means leading one's thoughts away from the one who is gone.'[2] The actual effect of this experience, however, has not been what Gertrude believes. It is not so much that she has 'become another person' in the course of letting go of her relationship with Guy, but that she has become entirely solipsistic – without, of course, realizing it. And indirectly, she is cruel to the living as well as to the dead.

Anne, in Gertrude's view, becomes the means of her salvation: 'I was possessed by a devil and you saved me,' she tells her, after she has begun to recover. Part of what Murdoch dramatizes here is that the overwhelming nature of grief shuts out every other consideration, and it is this which contributes to Gertrude's egotistical view that everyone around her exists to aid her. Absorbed in her grief, she takes her friend Anne's companionship for granted – as though she has reappeared in her life solely for this purpose. Gertrude's summary at the end of the novel credits Anne with her present happiness: 'Your coming to me like that when Guy was ill was so wonderful, so heaven-sent. You've helped me through everything, you've made it possible for me to recover.'[3]

The theme of madness also surfaces elsewhere – not only in grieving for a particular loss, but in the rush of addictive romantic passion. Unrequited love induces obsession and madness. Watching Gertrude suffer, yet also suffering himself, the Count thinks:

> I must stop being *sick* with love. Yet how can I, I don't want to stop. I cannot endure to be in company with Gertrude, and yet if I am alone with her I risk horrifying her by some outrageous breakdown, I might seize hold of her, I am dangerous, I am *mad*.[4]

Part of the irony in his plight is that if one can diagnose oneself as being mad, one is not. He is self-conscious and aware, though he is suffering in a way that cannot easily be controverted.

These two ideas are united in Gertrude's ultimate appropriation of the Count as a perpetual suitor, which demonstrates again her egotism. She chooses for a second husband the young artist, Tim Reede – contrary to the Count's hopes and to Guy's own thoughts on the matter, as expressed just before his death. When she first begins an affair with the slightly raffish Tim, her circle of family and friends is duly shocked. But their conclusion is that (in echoes of a Freudianized version of *Hamlet*), she has first married her father, figuratively speaking, and now her son, which makes it an intelligible choice to them – and also, one for which they feel they can patronize her. In this way, the resolution to Gertrude's grieving redraws *Hamlet* with a happier ending. And yet there is a sinister side to it as well. Contrary to her own views, grieving has ultimately made Gertrude selfish and self-satisfied, so much so that she takes away others' happiness. At the end of the novel, she appropriates the Count as her acknowledged troubadour, which ends any chance that Anne (who has fallen in love with him) will be able to be seen by him as a potential lover. In addition, his status as admirer is necessarily distanced – he falls short of full happiness himself, since he cannot marry Gertrude. She does seem to feel slightly guilty about this arrangement, as evidenced by the vehemence with which she counters Anne's mild objection to it, telling her friend, 'You call it little to be loved by ME?' Still, it can be interpreted as being entirely selfish on Gertrude's part. As another character observes, of this arrangement: 'She simply didn't want the Count to get away. Why should she lose a slave?'[5]

Part of the power of this novel lies in its depiction of hidden, heroic grief. That is, the characters who hold an acknowledged place in society as mourners do feel traumatized by loss; but a great deal of private suffering occurs as well, and much of it remains unresolved. What Murdoch seems to suggest in this book is that, while grieving the death of someone is disorienting, it can be equally so to that of a lover who suffers the pangs of unrequited love. It is Anne who experiences a 'dreadful' love for the Count, and the Count who feels he is '*mad*' in his passion for Gertrude. Grieving does not produce madness (as Gertrude half expects that it might), but rather, romantic love does so.

Murdoch also describes madness as a form of extreme internal dissociation in her early novel, *The Bell*, in which unbearable emotional pain causes one character to break down mentally, and another to take his own life. As in her later novel *Nuns and Soldiers*, she links extreme grief and madness to unrequited love; this book shows the dark side of obsessive thought and passion. Part of what madness consists of, here, is detachment and dissociation from rational thought. In *The Bell*, however, she distances it to the point of view of another character – who is marginally self-deluded as well – in order to offer an outside view of it. This narrative strategy has the result of repelling rather than inviting compassion.

The novel is set in a small Christian community which lives together in a large country house in Gloucestershire, and it is next door to – and tenuously affiliated with – an Anglican nunnery. One of the two leaders of the group, Michael Meade, is a former master at a boys' school, though he has been sacked for having seduced Nick Fawley, his pupil at the time. Temptation comes his way again, in the form of Toby, an eager young man about to enter Oxford as an undergraduate, and who comes to stay for the summer at the community. Madness, in one sense, is addiction: the repetition of what he knows to be a wrong and punishable action (at least, in Michael's own perception, which is reinforced by the views of his surrounding culture). In parallel to these two strong emotional attachments on Michael's part, there is that of Catherine, a young woman in the community (who is also Nick's twin sister), and who is about to enter the nearby convent. She is secretly in love with Michael (who is doubly unavailable to her, given his sexual orientation), and she breaks down emotionally during a spectacular scene when she is about to take her vows to enter the convent. The coincidence of this gender difference between the two twins is vital to the story, as it completes an asymmetrical triangle.

The Bell gives a chilling picture of Michael Meade's destructiveness – both in relationship to himself and to the two young twins, Nick and Catherine. It is they who are insane (or at least, in Nick's case, alcoholic, depressed, and eventually suicidal). Michael is therefore not marked out to be the mad person; but he becomes the catalyst for their despair and self-destruction, which links him integrally with madness in some definition. In large part, the novel reflects its setting – the late 1950s – when Michael evaluates his homosexuality in light of the church's views:

> at twenty-five [he] had already known for some while that he was what the world calls perverted. He had been seduced at his public school at the age of fourteen and had had while still at school two homosexual love affairs which remained among the most intense experiences of his life.

The madness, however, does not lie so much in the fact of his sexual desire as in his refusal to think about it as a possible force that might lead him to harm others. He does this three different times, always to younger people: Nick, Toby, and Catherine. There are three variations here, each of them more or less unconscious on Michael's part – though it is this which suggests a kind of shared hidden madness between these characters. Passion overwhelms each of them. In relation to Nick, he betrays the trust of a person who is under his authority – and he sees it in this way himself, in retrospect:

> He had been guilty of that worst of offences, corrupting the young: an offence so grievous that Christ Himself had said that it were better for a man to have a millstone hanged about his neck and be drowned in the depths of the sea.

At the same time, this describes Michael's abandonment to pure addictiveness, as on the first occasion of physical contact between the two:

> Sitting now in his room, his eyes closed, his body limp, he understood that it was not in his nature to resist the lure of a delight so exquisite. What he would do or what way it would be wrong he did not permit himself to reflect.

In short, feeling overmasters thinking: 'A mist of emotion, which he did not attempt to dispel, hid from him the decision which he was taking . . .'[6]

What Murdoch is also trying to depict, however, is the complicity which Nick has with Michael's emotions, and the subtle perverseness of his denunciation of Michael's part in their relationship. It is the young boy who has repeatedly sought him out (and who '[held] the initiative' during their affair). Nick has made the first gesture, and has also turned an idealized, emotional bond into a grand passion. In confessing his relationship with the older man, Nick has (at least to Michael's view) twisted everything in telling it to the school authorities: 'The betrayal, which it was immediately evident had taken place, of something to him so utterly pure and sacred was so appalling that it was not until later that Michael troubled to think of the matter in terms of his own ruin.' More than this, he feels that it was exaggerated:

> . . . it occurred to him [later] that Nick had not given a truthful picture of what had taken place. The boy had contrived to give the impression that much more had happened than had in fact happened, and also seemed to have hinted that it was Michael who had

> led him unwillingly into an adventure which he did not understand and from which he had throughout been anxious to escape.[7]

The fact that Nick was manipulative does not, however, especially impact what Michael decides to do in assimilating his part of the story. It shows Michael's deliberate refusal to take responsibility for his own part in the ensuing emotional disaster – which moreover has immediate consequences for his career, as he is now prevented from taking up his chosen vocation as a priest.

The element of homosexuality and pederasty here is frankly sensationalist because of its overtly moral dimension. What Murdoch is indirectly asking is whether Michael himself is insane – in the sense that he is driven to what he consciously feels are wrong actions, but is unable to help himself from engaging in them. In this interpretation, it is his madness which hurts Nick, not Michael himself. As a corollary, it is Nick's madness which wounds Michael, in his exposure of the relationship to other eyes. The *Schadenfreude* inherent in this novel for the reader is further stressed by the culture views of homosexuality-as-madness which sets the traditional 1950s beliefs against the increasing liberality of viewpoint among Murdoch's readers.

The background of Michael's earlier, passionate attachment to Nick – who is now living at the community – sets up (in an almost fatalistic way) Michael's next transgression, in relation to Toby, who comes to live in the community for the summer before he is to go up to Oxford. Michael's brief sexual encounter with him is almost an instinctive, non-thinking, casual event. When Michael impulsively kisses him, 'It happened so quickly that the moment after Michael was not at all sure whether it had really happened or whether it was just another thing that he had imagined.' This suggests that he has been fantasizing about such events. But he does know that it is wrong (according to his own standard of such behavior), or, at the least, it makes him unhappy: 'Michael said, and found his voice suddenly thick and stumbling, "I'm sorry. That was an oversight."'[8]

Love, for Michael, is a form of madness in that his mind does not engage – either to warn him against giving into temptation and acting out a sexual gesture, or to push away the total fantasy of it. This is made understandable, by the narrator, in the description of its compelling nature. When he first falls in love with Nick, it is magic: 'The talk of lovers who have just declared their love is one of life's most sweet delights,' the narrator says with dulcet irony. 'Each vies with the other in humility, in amazement at being so valued.' The key to the fact that this is dangerous is that it becomes for Michael a period in which his brain switches off: 'This was a time for Michael of complete and thoughtless happiness.'[9]

As for his relationship with Catherine, later on, this constitutes a weird penance for his earlier seduction (in whatever terms this is understood) of Nick, because he neither attempts to seduce her, nor invites her to be emotionally attached to him. Her close kinship with Nick is apparent; on his first meeting her, Michael is stunned by a vision of Nick's head on his sister's body, as he thinks of it. This renders her passion for Michael a kind of poetic justice. But the supreme irony is that this time the madness of romantic desire is located in her, and directed towards him. Its extremity leads her to attempt suicide; she tries to drown herself in the lake, but is rescued, and then hurls herself at Michael. His own reaction to her display of passion is first of all one of shock: 'his face was to be seen, blank with amazement and horror.'[10] Upon reflection, Michael feels: 'That Catherine had been in love with him, was in love with him, was something in every way outside the order of nature.' The twins form a symbiotic couple who are both deranged, and both doomed. When Michael goes to find Nick, after this event, he discovers that he has shot himself, an act which is difficult even to interpret, either as a gesture of defiance or of despair.[11]

The Bell is a study of various kinds of madness, which all have lies and self-deception at their source. Murdoch shows a variety of mental states associated with grief, love, and spiritual vocation – and, especially because of the deliberately invoked religious framework, everything takes on a moral tone as well. Some sort of moral sense is satisfied in the novel, by the dreary penance which Michael will undertake in looking after Catherine in her deranged state. Yet wry irony infuses the whole situation, as it is clear that (in this context) he cannot be seen to be directly or solely to blame for any of the disasters which have occurred.

Madness and grieving in many of these novels is an extreme example of the loss of free will and of the power of logic and reason – or, at least, the impossibility of thinking one's way out of a given dilemma. Fatalism (which is the ultimate outcome of madness) proves the supreme test for whether characters can change their lives or not. If they relinquish a belief in free will, and are no longer self-conscious or in control of their actions, they do not have to exercise control or thought. It is a strange combination, since the tone of these novels is often moralistic; madness is the traditional defense against taking responsibility for one's actions. As Hamlet tells Laertes at the duel which ends the play:

> Was't Hamlet wronged Laertes? Never Hamlet!
> If Hamlet from himself be ta'en away,
> And when he's not himself does wrong Laertes,
> Then Hamlet does it not, Hamlet denies it.
> Who does it, then? His madness.[12]

Madness is potentially volatile, and therefore highly dramatic as a plot device. Elizabeth Bowen creates situations where extreme suffering causes her characters to die in such circumstances. In *To the North*, Emmeline Waters becomes involved in an affair with Markie Linkwater, a young rising London barrister who declares that he has no intention of marrying, from the beginning of their relationship. While she accepts this fact, she is nonetheless devastated when he rejects her in favor of a former girlfriend. When Emmeline's sister-in-law brings Markie and Emmeline together at the end of the novel, he realizes that he is still in love with her. As she drives him home in her car, their discussion escalates into full-scale drama, as he tries to reclaim her love:

> With some desperate idea of assault, but not daring to touch her, not daring to formulate what he could not express till she was in his arms, he moved her way in the car, shouting into the darkness between their faces invective, entreaties, reproaches, stripping the whole past and taxing her with their ruin.

This sweeping rage crushes her: 'He exposed every nerve in their feeling; nothing remained unsaid.' Emmeline's experience of Markie's passionate argument is one of 'unforeseen pain,' and this gives way to her absence from consciousness: 'His throat tightened, the roof of his mouth went dry: she was not here, he was alone.'[13] Their fatal car crash stems from her suspension of self-identity, so that she loses her sense of who she is. It is not suicide, in the sense that she plans it; but it does seem the logical outcome of a situation such as Bowen describes – and it is extremely moralistic, in the sense of meting out poetic justice to Emmeline's seducer at the same time.

In Bowen's novel *The House in Paris*, her French-Jewish character Max Ebhart is wounded through a tortuous series of events in which he betrays his fiancée, Naomi, and has an affair with a young Englishwoman, Karen Michaelis. But the real emotional force in the novel is his long-standing relationship with Naomi's mother, Mme. Fisher. At the end of the novel, he attempts to make as honorable a break with Naomi as is possible under the circumstances, telling her of his love for

Karen and ending their engagement. Mme. Fisher has been listening at the door, and walks into the room to exult over Max by belittling his grand romantic gesture with Karen as nothing more than opportunistic cunning. 'So with Karen you have already secured your position,' she taunts him. Naomi describes the ensuing scene to Karen some weeks later, and also its background: 'I saw then that Max did not belong to himself. He could do nothing that she had not expected; my mother was at the root of him.'[14] He slashes his wrist with a penknife, and escapes out into the street, in order to bleed to death before being discovered. Max's death is both the utterly impulsive act of a fanatical, impassioned lover and the culmination of a sadistic relationship that has been going on for several years. Karen surmises that she had disappeared completely from his consciousness at the moment Mme. Fisher entered the room, and this suggests that suicide was the only response he could think of to refute her accusation and to free himself absolutely from the continued exercise of her power.

Both of Bowen's descriptions of deaths in these novels are dark and melodramatic, yet with an undercurrent of strange detachment and irony. They seem utterly fated, in the sense that they are the inevitable outcome of extreme passion (and of betrayal, which induces despair) – and this increases the resulting *frisson* of terror for the reader. And yet it is distanced, calculated emotion, as well. Mental derangement occurs from too much stress having been applied to each of these characters; and it is by no means a random or whimsical event (even though Max's slash with the penknife is the work of a moment), but under-girded by years of malevolent power struggles between him and Mme. Fisher.

Different variations on the theme of suicide are also possible, leaning more towards black humor. In Caroline Blackwood's novel, *Great Granny Webster*, the narrator's dashing and highly extroverted Aunt Lavinia tries to take her life twice. After her first attempt at suicide, she gives a long and amusing explanation of her trials while hospitalized immediately afterwards, to the young narrator of the story. She does not, however, say anything about her possible motivations: 'She felt no need to give me any reasons why she had just tried to kill herself.' The narrator hazards one possible reason for this: 'All her relationships had invariably been superficial, and maybe she felt so superficially rooted to life that it seemed hardly very momentous to her whether she stayed in it or left it.' Aunt Lavinia's reticence stems from politeness; her attempt at suicide seems so disconnected from reason that she is not even making a statement of despair or pain. On the contrary, 'She gave me the sense that she felt it would only bore me if she went into explanations – that she thought she would be stating the obvious. She had a horror of being dull.'[15] Lavinia regards divulging such personal feelings as being in bad taste, and eludes both the appearance of self-pity and – still more bizarre – of insanity. It seems a logical, reasonable alternative, precisely because no real reason is ever suggested for her action.

Iris Murdoch creates another outlandish variation on the theme of suicide in *The Book and the Brotherhood*, whose eccentric cast of characters more or less expects to lead dramatic lives, as befitting their Oxford background. At the beginning of the novel, Jean Cambus runs away with David Crimond, a man with whom she has previously had an affair, announcing this to her husband at an Oxford Commem. Ball. This is first of all ironic because the characters are reliving the madness of their romantic youth, while they are now grown up and (perhaps) ought to know better. Jean's passionate declaration of love to Crimond is adolescent in its fervor, and intensified by the circumstances of their reuniting. She tells him, mid-way through the book: 'I have left a husband whom I esteem and love, and friends who will never forgive me, in order to give myself to you entirely and forever.' The amusing yet serious coda to this exaltation of love is her reply to his thoughtful objection to too much hysteria on her part: 'All right,' she replies, 'if it doesn't work we can always kill each other, as you said then!'[16]

Crimond is a secluded intellectual, living by himself and writing the book which his other Oxford friends (from long ago undergraduate days) hope will be a significant one – and which they have financially supported for several years. His existential despair, mid-way through the novel, causes him to urge Jean to make a suicide pact with him. In part, this stems from his terror of aging, and also from a romantic notion: 'Better to consummate our love in death,' he tells her. Her grasp of this is intuitive: 'Do you want to kill me?' she asks him, to which he replies, 'Only when I kill myself.' This exchange foreshadows the arrangements which Crimond makes for the two of them to drive two cars headlong into each other. Her instinctive swerve at the last instant causes Crimond to turn from her in disgust, and to reject her completely. 'You are nothing to me now,' he informs her. 'Go away, go to hell, it's finished.'[17]

This is a novel in which the characters' passions run high, and when someone like Crimond makes up his mind on any subject, his judgment is inexorable. These characters are fearless, and in consequence unafraid to be violent. A death does occur in this novel, which is a variation on suicide, since it is initiated by the fact that both men are engaged in settling a private score through a version of dueling. Crimond has proposed a game of Russian roulette with Duncan Cambus, as a means of dealing with their male rivalry about the fact that he has taken away Duncan's wife. While neither of the two combatants die, Duncan shoots their friend Jenkin Riderhood, with Crimond's gun. And while this is completely accidental – Jenkin happens to walk through the door of the flat at a particular moment, and the bullet strikes him between the eyes – it also seems fated, due to its exactness. And the fact that Crimond and Duncan are shooting at each other in Crimond's flat is the background which makes this possible, although even here it is a game of chance as much as it is of intent to kill.

Madness in many inventive guises is almost a stock in trade for Murdoch, who employs it in order to show deep passion, and also as a means of driving her plots forward to unexpected conclusions. A.S. Byatt is much more purposeful in her use of this theme, as she is consciously trying to describe various internal states of madness, each with quite specific effects which are individual to each character.

Marcus Potter, in *The Virgin in the Garden*, suffers as a young boy from a version of madness that is allied with his intellectual giftedness. As a child, he is young enough that he does not understand what is happening to him, but his perceptions of the world are frightening and strange. When he is taken to see the film *Snow White*, its images overwhelm him. He tries to distance himself from the film, by concentrating on its mechanics: 'he had tried to unmake the illusion by twisting his head to stare at the clear cone of light wavering and streaming from the high projector. But for the small boy, encompassed and whelmed by racket, reason was no protection.' His response to the excess of stimulation that the world at large provides is to hide as much as possible, and to '[court] vacancy.'[18]

Marcus' perceptions of the world as seeming to be unreal are directly linked to his intellectual gifts, and his ability to do complicated mathematical problems by an intuitive, visionary method. Here it is madness which is actually intuitiveness and creativity, as he describes his way of seeing: 'A kind of garden. And the forms, the mathematical forms, were about in the landscape and you would let the problem loose in the landscape and it would wander amongst the forms – leaving luminous trails.' Part of this is psychological, as well; when his father brings him to a math specialist, and insists that Marcus explain how his mental processes worked, the gift vanishes because he has been forced to expose it for others to analyze. 'I can't do it any more,' he explains to Lucas, one of his schoolmasters, in retrospect. 'Since I – told – someone – how it was done.' Part of this is terror of exposure; and part is the singling out of his ways of perceiving things as abnormal: 'I thought for ages anyone could do it,' he describes this later, adding 'I thought it was the normal way of seeing.'[19]

He also possesses gifts as an actor, having been cast in a school production of *Hamlet* in the role of Ophelia. Her madness becomes so perfectly expressed in his rendition of it that: 'He had heard singing and screaming and had never known if he had sung or screamed afterwards.'[20] Ophelia provides another version of insanity, in that she is also creative in her madness, as Marcus is in his.

The real danger of Marcus' position is that, because of his exceptional powers, he is laid open to the notice of Lucas Simmonds, a science master at his school. Lucas turns out to be actually insane, and ends the novel literally enacting an Ophelia-like role by standing naked in the school pond, mutilating himself, and singing. Following this disastrous intervention in Marcus' life, Marcus himself goes into shock and refuses to speak. He is pushed over into madness, by the madness of a mentor, and this dramatizes Byatt's related theme that madness can be collective, or at least interconnected with others in a family or community, as she later shows in detail in *A Whistling Woman*. At the same time, part of what Byatt dramatizes in these cases for her characters is the supreme loneliness of such an affliction. In *The Virgin in the Garden*, Stephanie Potter, Marcus' older sister, has been looking on in compassion at his plight, but has felt she can do nothing to aid him. When she sees Lucas' eager advances towards her brother, she decides that it might be preferable even for the two of them to have a sexual relationship (which is strictly forbidden in this cultural context), as this would be of some possible comfort to him.[21]

Daniel Orton, the curate whom Stephanie Potter marries in *The Virgin in the Garden*, chooses to try to alleviate the suffering induced by madness on a professional basis. He is an Anglican priest, although he sees himself primarily as a social worker. Byatt depicts extremes of dissociation in her characters who edge towards insanity, and her corresponding theme is that of compassion towards them. In *Still Life*, the following novel, Stephanie, as a curate's wife and a young mother, allows herself to be slowly surrounded by a group of social misfits who are all slightly insane. Part of what Byatt insists upon in her fiction is the fact that people roaming about at large in the world can be mad, and that one response to this is to reach out to their aid. In *Babel Tower*, Daniel works on a telephone help line in London, to try to help people who are in extreme crisis. He is fitted to do this by his own crafting of his particular vocation without glorifying himself in this role. His compassion for others fits him for this task, although it is also ironic in the sense that he is estranged from his own family. His wife, Stephanie, has died in a domestic accident, and his own inability to deal with his grief has forced him to leave his small children in the care of his mother-in-law. His instinctive response has been to try to die, himself; grief drives him temporarily insane, though his sturdiness of mind and of constitution prevent this resolution for him. Eventually taking up his responsibility to go on with life again, he engages in his earlier work, although he has become entirely estranged from his grown son, William.

This strain in Byatt's fiction is powerful: she dramatizes the sudden, unexpected blow which can carve a furrow into one's life, and send it into a completely different direction. Her thumbnail sketch of this appears in *The Virgin in the Garden*, in the figure of the school headmaster's wife, Mrs. Thone, who has lost her young son in an accident. The narrator comments on the bereft mother (expressing her views): 'Pain hardens, and great pain hardens greatly, whatever the comforters say, and suffering does not ennoble, though it may occasionally lend a certain rigid dignity of manner to the suffering frame.'[22] Life itself is inexorably changed, in these kinds of circumstances, and part of her point is that human character itself is also irrevocably altered. To go on living in the face of complete despair can be possible – as Daniel's experience also proves – but loss and grief can dominate the remainder of life.

Byatt's novels *Babel Tower* and *A Whistling Woman* present a view of collective hysteria, in Britain of the 1960s. In completing the tetralogy, they follow the fortunes of several characters in the first two novels, *A Virgin in the Garden* and *Still Life*. In *Babel Tower*, Frederica Potter, Stephanie's sister, reacts to Stephanie's death by marrying one of her suitors, Nigel Reiver. A flamboyant and forceful character herself, she becomes so stunned by grief that she allows him to subsume her into his life. The madness which dominates London culture of this era, in Byatt's dramatization, is centered on three men in the novel: Nigel, who refuses to divorce Frederica; Jude Mason, who has written a quasi-pornographic novel; and John Ottakar, Frederica's lover, whose identical twin brother pursues them both with maniacal jealousy. The first two issues are taken up in the court trials which form the last part of the book: the divorce and custody case of Frederica and Nigel, concerning their young son, Leopold, and the trial for obscenity of Jude's novel, *Babbletower*, which has sadistic elements in it. Each of the three men represents a different type of craziness. Nigel believes himself to be entirely sane, and justified in all of his actions – although he is trying to dominate Frederica and on several occasions brutally harms her. Jude represents the crazed artist figure, who is embittered and cynical, yet visionary. John is – like Frederica herself – more a victim of circumstances. She cannot separate herself entirely from her beloved and lost sister, and John is pursued intently by his mad twin brother.

In *A Whistling Woman*, Byatt also dramatizes an interconnected group of themes which constitute a *Zeitgeist* – and these consist of several different versions of madness. This technique allows her to write in grand gestures, which are excellent for shock effect. They are rooted in the English tradition of tolerance for eccentricity, yet with a fascinating spin: this is collective madness, which creates a religious cult and commune – not based on the idiosyncratic view of an individual. Eva Wijnnobel is the quintessential example of tolerance for an individual's point of view: her husband (the Vice-Chancellor of Byatt's fictional North Yorkshire University, and an earnest liberal) pleads with her not to make a public spectacle of herself, which she does by giving astrology and tarot card readings. Yet he does not forbid or restrain her from joining the nearby religious commune at Dun Vale Hall, nor from appearing on Edmund Wilkie's television program, which will expose her to the world at large. She is mad in a conventional way, having a grandiose conception of herself as being able to be in touch with Higher Powers – and yet her obsessions are also seen as being part of her era.

Other versions of madness in this novel include that of Joshua (Ramsden) Lamb, who experiences the trauma of extreme domestic violence (his father has murdered his sister and mother). He becomes the charismatic leader of the Spirit's Tigers, locked in combat for this position with Gideon Farrar. Joshua hallucinates vividly, yet pits all of his strength and resolution towards controlling his actions in order to seem normal to the outside world, as far as possible. His visions of blood which course down walls or over others' heads are carefully suppressed: 'He had never told any of them about the blood.' This leaves him free to hoard his energies: 'Like the whiff of the flame of his anger it needed to be hidden until it broke out and drowned everything.'[23]

John Ottakar, Frederica's lover, continues to ponder the terrible mystery of his twin-ness with Paul-Zag, in this novel, and effectively reasons his way into madness, by meditating continually on cloning and on scientific explanations of cell division and the origins of life. Lucas Simmonds (who had been the earlier cause of Marcus' derangement in *The Virgin in the Garden*) also reappears as part of the crowd assembled at the commune. Much more insidious are the observers of mental derangement: two psychiatrists, Elvet Gander and Kieran

Quarrell, discuss the increasingly bizarre behavior of the commune members by writing witty letters to each other. Their *forte* is objective analysis, rather than heading off possible disaster (which, predictably, occurs). This passion for observation also drives Brenda Pincher, a sociologist who writes detailed reports from her station as an insider and observer of the unfolding scene – although, ironically, her confidant and colleague, Avram Snitkin, never opens her letters. She complains of loneliness, yet is fascinated: 'The material is so *rich*,' she enthuses.[24]

A Whistling Woman is carefully constructed to show various points of view that illustrate the workings of the religious community, which works itself into an increasing frenzy of madness. Yet there is a hero, Daniel Orton, an observer who nonetheless acts with great decision when necessary. When his son, Will, disappears into the commune, Daniel demands that he be returned, and rescues him from absorption into it. But the natural progression of such mass delusion, as Byatt depicts it, is eruption into a crisis which burns down the entire structure (along with some parts of the nearby university, in protest); this massive destruction cannot, it seems, be prevented. The novel is intended as an anatomy of the spirit of the age, and it sets out in great detail the ideas which have captivated it.

In all of her novels, Byatt writes about darkness of the mind, and in the mind – that which prevents characters from seeing hope. This is the real danger, which causes characters to lose touch not only with reality, but with any conceivable purpose in their lives. When darkness takes them over wholly, they kill themselves knowingly. The most important connection in her work between the intellect and its consciously perceived disintegration nonetheless into madness is her early novel, *The Game*. In this work, which is less a social commentary than a story centered on a handful of main characters, Byatt defines the ways in which madness is felt by the sufferer. *The Game* depicts an Oxford don, Cassandra, who suffers intensely from 'nightmares and fears,' as she has described her affliction to the priest, Father Rowell. But her sharing of this distress is later felt to be mortifying, and she writes to him trying to diminish its importance: 'We are all afraid of being overwhelmed in one way or another; but I have lived with these fears for many years now and I meet them, to a certain extent, with the ease of familiarity.' Familiarity, however, does not make this easier; neither does the application of her formidable intellectual powers, which are brought to bear to try to combat her sense of panic. Emotion and the mind battle with each other, yet combine in a symbiotic way; she has made her illness the inspiration for her profession: 'She combined the mediaevalist's love of the strange with the mediaevalist's passion for precision,' and this stems from her passion for apprehending the world around her. Her scholarly research attempts to make sense of the world in its symbolic representation:

> She had elaborated, and believed, a network of symbols which made the outer world into a dazzling but comprehensible constellation of physical facts whose spiritual interrelations could be grasped and woven by the untiring intellect; suns, moons, stars, roses, cups, lances, lions and serpents, all had their place and also their meaning.[25]

Her pain has to do with perception – or with the feeling that she does not exist – and she writes a daily journal in an effort to give her world solidity by describing it:

> In moments of solitude she was increasingly obsessed by a sense that her life was weightless and meaningless; she told herself sometimes that she had made of the journal a moral compulsion to treat her life and its details as though they were real.

It becomes for her, moreover, a 'necessary means of distinguishing between what was real and what was imagined,' as though words themselves confer solidity. Since she is an academic, her means of dealing with this irrational fear is to apply logic: 'night after night she paced garden and buildings, arguing with fear.'[26] This kind of madness is peculiar, because it is juxtaposed with Cassandra's intense intellect, which seeks to circumvent it, but cannot.

The great terror of madness is encountering a lack of compassion in others, and being left alone to struggle with it. That is the heart of Julia's betrayal of her sister; she fails to enter into her anguish. Leaving Oxford, after a visit to her sister in her college, she ponders whether she can use her experiences there as the basis for a novel. Julia labels her sister 'paranoiac,' and sees immediately the risks she runs; her sister will feel exposed and attacked by a 'novel about the dangers of imbalance between imagination and reality,' but she cannot resist writing it because she feels it would be a good book. 'It would be a real novel, with a real idea behind it . . .' She intuits that it would be a means of 'coming to grips with Cassandra, but also of detaching us.'[27] This proves to be literally true.

Cassandra's suicide is a direct result of Julia's published novel, which exposes her and her colleagues to ridicule. When Julia comes to take away Cassandra's papers from her sister's college room, at the end of the novel, she must deal with both grief and guilt, having lost her reference point in the world: 'All her life Cassandra had been the mirror where she studied the effects of her actions. It was Cassandra's reactions that proved her existence; now, she had lost a space and a purpose.' Their mutual friend, Simon, points out that Julia is in shock: 'one doesn't *at first*, recognize a real blow,' he tells her, apprehending that her extravagant grief is actually a way of warding off true guilt. 'Because you think she wanted to make a murderess of you you won't admit that you are – partly – a murderess.'[28] That is part of the essence of suicide: it can be a gesture intended to punish another character. When Blanche Glover, in Byatt's novel *Possession*, kills herself, it is intended in part as a way of showing her sense of betrayal when her lesbian companion, Christine LaMotte, has had an affair with a male rival. Grieving and madness are connected, both in *Possession* and in other twentieth-century novels, because derangement signifies a logical extension of the loss of a loved person or ideal. It becomes, for some characters, a literal way of saying that life cannot go on, for them, without the person that has been lost. When Christine LaMotte tells Randolph Henry Ash, accusingly, 'You have made a murderess of me,' late in the novel, this shows that she has accepted full responsibility for her companion's demise.[29]

A coda to Byatt's grim treatment of madness occurs in her short story, 'On the Day that E.M. Forster Died.' Madness can also be traditionally seen as a version of 'divine inspiration' that would infuse the creative work of an artist. In this particular short story, this happens by means of indirection. The heroine, Mrs. Smith, is a writer living in London who learns that E.M. Forster has just died. This news saddens her, as she has admired him as a great writer; yet she also feels instinctively liberated by his absence, and the implied competition that he has represented in her own work. The epiphany which has concurrently visited her in the London Library is the recognition of her passionate desire to write a 'long and complicated novel.' In an exalted mood, full of purpose, she walks through London streets and encounters a man whom she has known from her undergraduate days at university. Her instinctive distrust of him is overcome by admiration for his devotion to music, which has caused him to leave a career in psychology and become a composer. At his urging, they enter a café together, and she suddenly realizes that he is mad: he spouts paranoid delusions, and raves that anarchists are about to take over the world. She manages to escape from her desperate companion, though not without some cost; he has scratched her face and torn her clothes in a frantic effort to detain her. Her main grief, however, is for the ideal of creativity which has now been lost; his former dedication to composing has ended in her disillusionment: 'In the mahogany ladies' room, with water from a Victorian brass tap, Mrs. Smith mopped her face and wept for the music.' And she makes a definite choice to turn away from sharing the man's delusions: 'Conrad was mad. She would not inhabit his plot of deathly music-machines and lethal umbrellas.'[30]

The good that nonetheless comes from the adventures which she has on this particular day are those stemming from a sense of *carpe diem*: she determines to focus her energies fully on the novel that she wants to write. *Memento mori* has been a reminder of the shortness of time, as illustrated by the death of Forster. Mrs. Smith meditates also on the fact that Forster had abandoned writing fiction – which was a choice that had not been imposed on him by shortness of time. Her encounter with the insane Conrad has a more complicated influence on her creative process; she must make an effort to push away his madness-as-creativity which has become so bizarre. Her violent struggle with him has the result that 'She had lost some virtue,' and must now determine to overcome her fear: 'She was a determined and practical woman and would go back to work, however her elation had been broken.'[31] The reverse effect of Conrad's madness has been not only to reinforce her determination to work, but to embrace the solidity of middle-aged reasonableness which is contrary to his paranoia. Novels, she concludes, are 'essentially a middle-aged form,' and represent for her telling a story of time which is at once long and short, full of experience and yet soon to be curtailed.[32]

In many of the novels which I have been discussing here, the authors have fused a quintessentially nineteenth-century theme, grieving, with a twentieth-century one, madness. The latter often stems from the former, in a sequential cause and effect: a character suffers great loss or shock and falls into irrationality as a way of self-protection (either chosen or not). Murdoch and Byatt in particular give a rational, detached account of madness, or of internal states of mind which are self-consciously analyzed by the characters themselves. Suicide – as the most extreme gesture of despair – is not a moral issue in the way it is in Shakespeare's plays, where the grave-digger comments on Ophelia's problematic burial rites, and Hamlet argues with himself whether to be or not to be, and whether to end suffering by extreme means. Still, suicide in these novels is intended as high-water mark of internal drama.

Loss can destroy one. Love and desire can destroy one. And a character can emotionally destroy others through his or her own despair.

The interrelated themes of darkness which I have been tracing in this first section suggest that this group of authors have a similar interest in how much free will is possible, in a world which often seems so bleak. It is difficult for their characters to think their way out of problems, or to become adventure heroines who triumph through cunning or strength or bravery. In wartime, individual action is nearly impossible, since the world has gone mad and everything seems fatalistic. In gothic fiction, the supernatural is often a malevolent force that defies rationality, and against which one cannot prevail. And in novels and short stories about emotional dissociation and madness, it is nearly impossible either to reason one's way back to sanity again, or to ward it off by thinking clearly.

Yet part of these authors' use of madness – and theories about madness – stems from their own passion for ideas, and their intellectual curiosity. Murdoch in particular delights in sending up her psychoanalyst characters. It is a cliché, but an amusing one, that they are supposed to be fixing everyone else, yet they are revealed to be just as crazy as everyone around them. A comic scene appears in *The Good Apprentice* where Harry goes to see Thomas, a psychiatrist who has been trying to help Edward Baltram, the young hero, to deal with his depression after he has killed his friend with a surreptitiously given dose of LSD. Harry has had an affair with Thomas' wife, Midge, and wants to talk about it to the wronged husband: 'Why pretend that you're surprised that I came, didn't you expect me, didn't you want some explanation, some account of it all, or did you just intend to get on with your work and ignore it?' he asks. To his amazement, Thomas throws him out, adding 'I see no need to talk to you and I don't want to see you again.' The humor of this lies in Harry's incredulous disillusionment, as the narrator states it:

> He realized how, with a double-think which now indeed seemed naïve, he had expected Thomas, while certainly upset, even angry, to be also somehow still his old self, ironical, cool, helpful, sympathetic, full of patient understanding.[33]

Murdoch also pillories the psychologist's vocation through her character Blaise Edwards, in *The Sacred and Profane Love Machine*. This novel includes the creation of a mad character, Magnus Bowles, whom Blaise claims to his wife that he must spend one night a week counseling. (This is a complete fiction, devised with the inventive aid of his neighbor, in order to give Blaise a chance to spend a night with his mistress, and to cover up a long-term affair.) When his life becomes too complicated to sustain this fabrication, he tells his wife that Magnus Bowles has committed suicide, which is ironic because he has never (in real life) existed. Even more comic is the effect of Blaise's temporary distraction from his psychiatry practice, which has a liberating effect on many of his patients: 'In fact, though Blaise never knew it, his patients had largely benefited from' the various disasters which have befallen him, during the course of the novel. 'Surviving these catastrophes, unhurt by them, increased by them, they all felt better,' and meet at a party to celebrate their superiority. This is also contrasted, however, with the deep and silent suffering of Blaise's son, Luca, by his mistress, Emily. When Luca is sent to a mental institution, Blaise takes refuge in the distancing which his profession allows: 'It was a relief to have it [his son, defined and dehumanized as a "problem"] officially *classified* as subnormal and taken away to be looked after by experts.'[34]

While these twentieth-century authors depict various states of madness with a conscious nod towards psychology (often using distancing as a means of gratifying the reader), it is also possible to use it for comic use, and to portray its self-protectiveness with compassion. Molly Keane's *Treasure Hunt* (which was first a play, subsequently turned into a novel) portrays the highly eccentric figure of the aged Miss Anna Rose, who carries out an elaborate fantasy of world travel on trains and airplanes, all the while stepping in and out of her secluded sedan chair in the living room of the Anglo-Irish family estate. Her first entrance in the novel shows her deciding to take afternoon tea in the Orient Express: 'She walked towards the sedan chair. It was the station walk, head high, looking anxiously for the platform number, for the right carriage, the empty one, the reserved corner seat with its face to the engine.' Her total conviction of the reality of the scene infects the viewers as well: 'One could almost smell the lovely smell of trains in the room.' This scheme places her entirely in another world, to which she has escaped, and from which she can control her family's access to her; instructing them that they can ring her 'on the long-distance in Budapest,' she departs definitively: 'She wound up her window finally and pulled down the blind. Indeed, she was lost to them.'[35]

The other characters in her family humor her in these delusions, and she remains respected by them. It is left to a visiting character from the outside world to pierce through her delusion, and to locate the treasure (her long-lost rubies, which she has put away 'somewhere very safe' but in a place she cannot recall), which will rescue them all financially and also unite the two deserving and worthy young lovers.[36] Aunt Anna Rose's delusions are those of purely self-protective madness – a traumatic event has perpetrated them, so there is a definite source for her fractured thought process. Still, the compassion shown to her by her family and also by Eustace, the sympathetic 'paying guest' who undertakes to locate the rubies, mitigates the painfulness.

The intellectual analyses of mental states, as portrayed in these novels, sets the characters at a great distance. And on occasion the heavy application of irony demands much of the reader, who is called upon to sympathize with characters enough to care about their sufferings, yet who is constantly shown their follies or self-deceptions, compounded by the larger, existential fatalism of exercising choice. If it is not the fault of these twentieth-century men and women, besieged and beset by world wars, by incursions from the realm of the supernatural, and by the collective madness of the late 1960s, then it is not, perhaps, the authors' intention to mete out moral blame for desperate measures. While the novelists' objectivity makes these books ironic (for fear of seeming sentimental), the passion which they portray is none the less riveting, and cunning makes these novels very like a romance, or possibly a tragicomedy, or else a whale or a weasel. Their creativity is largely intellectual and self-conscious. Yet it is brilliant as well.

KING ALFRED'S COLLEGE
LIBRARY

Part II
Passion

The stirrings of feminism in the nineteenth and early twentieth century validated heroines' desires for a professional life and emotional independence. But love and marriage remained a traditional preoccupation which held endless fascination for these characters, if only in self-conscious reaction against it. A.S. Byatt's Frederica Potter experiments in the 1950s with conducting her college love affairs in a cavalier manner, and Elizabeth Bowen's emotionally exhausted heroines still search for love and compulsively believe in the claims of the heart. They suffer acutely, despite adopting a self-protective distance. And the searing pain of betrayal or rejection remains devastating to those who have hoped for love – however tentatively – and been disappointed. These novels offer an anatomy of modern love with ironic overtones.

4
Romance

Sexual passion, as experienced by heroines in nineteenth-century novels, is seen to have a definite objective: 'I must marry somebody,' as Veronica in Elizabeth Bowen's *The Hotel* states it bluntly in the 1920s; 'You see, I must have some children.'[1] The economic imperatives are clear, and the social contract reinforces this. Most women only have one chance to marry – that is their most pressing business in the majority of Victorian novels – and in any case, sexual expression is forbidden in any other mode. This creates an automatic drama centered around whether or not a heroine will end with the right marriage partner. In the twentieth century, when women have more room to maneuver, professionally and socially, the emotional tension in a novel must come from another source – especially when authors are disinclined to provide happy or romantic endings for their characters. This leads writers like Bowen, Murdoch, and Byatt to delight in seeming ironic, wise, and knowing in their fiction; to show their heroines indulging in sexual adventures, yet being fastidiously analytical about them.

Elizabeth Bowen, in particular, is highly skilled at discerning a fulcrum point in the most melodramatic situation possible, where characters are utterly driven by fantastic passion; and yet there is an aloof and distanced tone to these affairs as well.[2] This is part of a larger narrative strategy. The heroines cannot be too emotional, or they will seem silly; they cannot be too objective, or they might appear to be calculating and cold. Bowen achieves this exquisite balance by invoking melodramatic situations and then being ironic about the role of passion: 'young girls like the excess of any quality,' the narrator asserts in *The House in Paris*. 'Without knowing, they want to suffer, to suffer they must exaggerate; they like to have loud chords struck on them.' But the contrast remains, between love of melodrama and the practical necessity for young women to seek husbands and thus eventually to learn to 'see love socially.'[3]

This inherent contrast between exaggeration and practicality accurately combines the nineteenth-century drive for fulfillment of the social contract (economic security, children) and the twentieth-century passion for individual expression – and for feminism, whose goal is to make women independent, to choose their own destinies, and not to be self-sacrificing in a masochistic way. In modern terms, it makes the heroine a heroine, yet in infinitely more complicated terms than, for example, Orczy's Lady Blakeney in *The Scarlet Pimpernel*, who remains virtuously chaste until she falls in love with her own husband, thus being vindicated in a union of both social contract and passionate sexuality. Elizabeth Bowen too vindicates her heroines, though their impossibly romantic choices are also often destructive.

At the same time, Bowen's heroines often do very dangerous things. It is difficult to grasp this fact, because she has taken such care to make them sophisticated women (the narrator cloaks them with irony) as well as smouldering and passionate. But if one can live dangerously on an emotional level – while enjoying many of the privileges of money and social class – these characters are often desperate. Sydney Warren, in *The Hotel*, for example, is extraordinary for her era in having achieved several academic distinctions. She is not, as are other young women at the expatriate holiday venue, trying to catch a husband, but is planning to return to her former life in England and 'try to pass [her] next exam.' Yet she is also highly emotional; the narrator's description of her draws a face in which

> the lines were now, as too often, strained and broken up by an expression of over-eagerness. An exaggerated attention to what was being said or suggested would arch up the eyebrows tragically, harden the eyes and draw in the mouth to a line that prefigured maturity. The forehead was broad and lovely and could have been bland.[4]

She suffers intensely from the tortuous emotional entanglements which form the substance of the novel.

Bowen's fiction is riveting because her heroines must struggle with fairly stock literary crises, but we hardly notice their melodrama because passion is so crafted with irony. As readers, we are continually being appealed to, to share in the joke of these over-wrought women; and yet, the heroines' self-mockery (Cecilia in *To the North*) or specialness (Emmeline in the same novel) or daring (Karen in *The House in Paris*) disarms our critical judgement of their having given all for love, and thus seeming stupidly reckless. It is an age of cynicism, in which an older character such as Mrs. Kerr in *The Hotel* can chide Sydney for her defensiveness by saying: 'You could be charming . . . But I daresay an indifference to one's company which doesn't comprehend the desire to please is really the safest. . . .' and where a young woman such as Veronica can announce (with obvious naïvety), 'You see, I've got absolutely no illusions.'[5]

The stern necessity in Elizabeth Bowen's novels is for her heroines (not the comic minor characters, who exist in order to form a contrast with them) to be morally justified in whatever they have done or chosen. They take their lives and feelings extremely seriously. But they cannot be perceived to do so, lest they seem egotistical. And this is what Bowen shares in common with writers such as Olivia Manning and A.S. Byatt, whose heroines also struggle to find a workable relationship with men. Heterosexual relations prove to be a particularly thorny spot for working out these issues. On the one hand, they provide one forum for female characters to express their rebellion, since sexual passion is socially regulated. To go against norms proclaims strident individuality and a disregard for convention. But it is infinitely complicated by the fact that men have their own ideas and desires, which also exert considerable force. And for these heroines, romantic desire cannot be stated in overly passionate terms, or the characters would appear foolish. Hence, for instance, Elizabeth's statement in Olivia Manning's *The Wind Changes*, when she expresses the following desire to Arion, with whom she has been having an affair: 'What I want – what I have always wanted and never had – is intimacy and understanding with someone I love and who loves me. I have never asked for more than that.' This seems eminently reasonable, in its restraint and simplicity. The man to whom she confides this, however, discerns at once its innate romanticism, replying, drily: 'You couldn't ask for more.'[6]

Writing later in the twentieth century than both Manning and Bowen, A.S. Byatt seizes her chance to write directly about women's changing perceptions of themselves, in Frederica Potter's 1960s television interview program. Frederica has always been precocious; when she first appears, as an adolescent in *The Virgin in the Garden*, she sets out on a determined, practical quest to lose her virginity, as a way of gaining knowledge and experience so that she will not seem naïve. This decision is defiantly anti-romantic, on her part; and it is also part of her sense of herself as an important person, who should experience the intensity of life. By the time she has reached the age of thirty-three, in the opening of *A Whistling Woman*, she reviews her life in these terms:

> Frederica the schoolgirl had known she would be someone, had known eyes would be on her, fame would touch her, people would know who she was when she walked down a street. She had wanted everything – love, sex, the life of the mind.[7]

For Frederica – especially given the connection in her own mind between sexuality and her undergraduate days at Cambridge – her instinctive response is to continue to be analytical in her relationships with men. When she awaits the arrival of her lover, John Ottakar, in *A Whistling Woman*, for example, she theorizes about the nature of love affairs in general:

> Endings. Frederica sat and waited for her lover, and wondered what the end of the affair would be. She had begun to think that there was always only an unreal moment's grace between the beginning of a love affair (the phrase was already old-fashioned, but she had a growing distaste for the word relationship) and this steady self-questioning about how and why and when it would end.[8]

Enamoured of theorizing, she also discusses life as a woman in the liberated 1960s. The second television interview program which she hosts is entitled 'Free Women,' in which the discussion is intended as a cunning parody of a *Koffee Klatsch*. The panel of three women considers what women want, listing (between them) 'Love, certainty, a family,' 'Sex and naughtiness too,' to which Frederica replies:

> Only sex is a long thing said Frederica. Because it leads to childbirth and all that is one long biological process. Except that now – with the Pill – women can pick and choose amongst men, and pick and choose whether to breed, or not.

The opportunities which Frederica has – along with other women in the novel, such as Jacqueline Winward, who does scientific research, and Agatha Mond, who works in the Civil Service – are many and varied. By the end of the novel, she considers with satisfaction that she is 'part of a new world of free women, women who had incomes, work they had chosen, a life of the mind, sex as they pleased. It was interesting. She preened herself.' Still, the accident of biology – she becomes pregnant at the end of the novel – forces choice upon her in relation to other people. Considering her work and her life in London, 'She had time, she thought. And now, suddenly, she had no time.'[9]

It is crucial that all of the heroines in these novels avoid looking smug or self-satisfied. They are allowed to be seen as a bit touchy and over-sensitive – Harriet Vane, in Dorothy L. Sayers' detective novels, is a case in point – though never without good reason. Harriet has been falsely accused of murdering her former lover, which explains her bitterness; Stephanie and Frederica Potter, in Byatt's *The Virgin in the Garden*, have the excuse of an overbearing father as an adverse influence on their actions. Romantic passion is an important nexus in which to work this out: if these heroines are to be seen as women of spirit and passion, they must feel great emotion. And they must also be seen to be rejecting the confines of a traditional, nineteenth-century Victorian plot, where all they are interested in is the sordid, practical effort to catch a rich husband. Livvy, the grasping young woman in Bowen's *The Last September*, is the quintessential example of such a character. This earnest effort to marry is too Victorian, and places heroines too close to echoing the Angel in the House, for the twentieth century, to be happy in the domestic scene; so these women must be shown to be unhappy, if they are confined. The situation of Frederica Potter in *Babel Tower* offers the conundrum of marriage which is sexually exciting (which fulfills one twentieth-century value) and which also combines a parody of nineteenth-century prosperity and respectability. She lives with her husband on his family property, in a castle romantically surrounded by a moat. Still, her excellence as a heroine is proven by the fact that she asserts, 'I must *work*.'[10] And her energy and intelligence is held to be formidable, as an article of faith in these novels. Moreover, she is born to be a Personality; yet when fame eventually comes to her, she realizes its distorting qualities, as well as its advantages:

> She had always supposed that it would be exciting to have a face that flashed into public consciousness. Charisma, the papers said mini-charisma, in a mini-personality. She found, rather grimly, that being a personality thinned her sense of being a person.

This consciousness suggests that she is neither shallow nor greedy. A related aspect of her character is that Frederica tries to outwit or circumvent passion by being forceful and practical; she sees things in terms of sex, rather than of love. Her passion for intellectual analysis makes her think about her fascination with men, as when she wonders why

John Ottakar holds such appeal for her. When he visits her in London, from Yorkshire (where he has moved), her sexual desire is reactivated to the extent that she feels, 'this is the *real thing*.' At the same time, she does not feel overmastered by desire: 'she was happy to live apart, to have times of sex like this, naked, total, fierce times, and times completely without it.'[11]

The corollary to Frederica's passion is the calm figure of her housemate, Agatha Mond, who is a successful civil servant who also becomes a celebrated and wealthy author. Agatha has produced a child, Saskia, but without (apparently, and by design) a man in her life: Saskia 'as good as had no father – none had been mentioned, no name, no history, nothing. Even a discovered uncle, Frederica thought, appeared to be too much for Agatha.'[12] Still, having shown both Frederica and Agatha to be passionate yet judicious, Byatt offers the reader a supremely romantic ending to her tetralogy, in the most romantic of feminine terms. The secretive Agatha Mond is discovered by Frederica to have gained an eminently worthy lover: the long-suffering university Vice-Chancellor, Wijnnobel, whose mad wife has conveniently died.[13] As for Frederica, her passion and the 1960s freedom has resulted in her having self-selected a mate, Luk Lysgaard-Peacock, who greets the news of her pregnancy (from one of their sexual encounters) with enthusiasm, which creates a little family (including Leopold) in which they can live happily ever after.

These twentieth-century heroines want work and love, passion and intelligence, fatalism and lyrical free choice. These are balanced in the novels by a Victorian cause and effect, plot and closure, irony and objectivity.[14] These authors offer sex, but no sentimentality; yet their work is not entirely unfeeling or without passion, either.

Elizabeth Bowen takes up two separate themes: the numbness or depression which her heroines feel (for which they substitute – or try to substitute – romantic love), and the dissociation of passion from reason and from social conventions. She starts with the straightforward notion that young women are deemed to be happiest when they fall in love and marry suitable partners, and in the course of her first six novels weaves several ironic and increasingly complex stories around this idea. The heroine of her first novel, Sydney Warren in *The Hotel*, is problematic in this respect from the start because she has tried to become a professional woman – and this at a time when it was not a usual or accepted thing. She possesses the intelligence to become a medical doctor (for which she has been training), yet her nerves are unequal to the task, and she has suffered an unspecified emotional 'breakdown' while taking her examinations. Her cousin Tessa has taken Sydney away to Italy, to have a holiday and recover. This in itself represents a very Victorian remedy being applied to a distinctly modern situation. The proposed rest cure attempts to counteract hysteria with calm surroundings, and Sydney is intended to do nothing except play tennis and perhaps socialize. When the novel opens, part-way through the holiday, it is clear that what Sydney has done in this situation is to fall in love with an older woman, Mrs. Kerr. While the hotel is located in Italy, the patrons are mostly English, and thus English norms prevail. The matrons who gather together for gossip every afternoon express to Tessa, who acts as a chaperone to her, their disapproval of Sydney's attachment to Mrs. Kerr. One woman refers obliquely to similar examples of 'these very violent friendships. One didn't feel *those others* were quite healthy.' This reflects in part on Mrs. Kerr herself: 'It is never the best women who have these strong influences,' another woman agrees, adding, 'I would far rather she lost her head about a man.'[15]

The main problem with this sort of attachment (which the disapproving matrons do not verbalize) is the stunning blow of rejection, should it prove to be a one-sided attachment, which this obviously is. The catalyst for Sydney's rejection is the arrival at the hotel of Mrs. Kerr's son, Ronald, who is Sydney's age (thus reinforcing the idea that Sydney needs a mother figure, and she has now been supplanted as a companion and a protégée). What the matrons want to see, and perceive as being healthy, is for Sydney to be spending her afternoons with a 'young friend,' instead of with the older Mrs. Kerr – who moreover has terrified the rest of the expatriate hotel guests by her aloofness and self-sufficiency.[16] They are reacting in envy as much as anything else, that Sydney has succeeded in attracting such an elegant and upper-class person to her own exclusive enjoyment.

When Mrs. Kerr's son Ronald arrives, it is suggested – in retrospect, and much later in the novel – that he was a potentially suitable companion for Sydney, the 'young friend' with whom she might have shared camaraderie and possibly romance. Instead, everything disintegrates for Sydney, just as the conventional matrons have predicted that it might. Shutting her out in favor of Ronald, Mrs. Kerr does not spend any more time with her, and when she takes her out to tea, late in the novel, Sydney observes bitterly that it is 'like being given tea by an aunt at the Zoo.'[17]

The assumption here, under the watchful eyes of the English community, is that marriage is the suitable fate for a young woman; and Sydney herself fulfills this convention by becoming engaged to an

English clergyman, Rev. Milton, mid-way through the book. She does not accept his proposal because she has fallen in love with him and wants to marry him (in other words, the ideal potential happy ending); her acceptance of him shows the true effect of unrequited love and of her dammed up passion for Mrs. Kerr: she might as well accept Milton as not, since nothing in life holds any meaning for her. The double irony of this is that Mrs. Kerr uses Sydney's engagement to torture Milton with doubts, telling him:

> 'for anyone else, any woman, as angry and hurt in her pride, and as disappointed as I'm afraid Sydney's been with me lately, to have taken you up with the strong position you've given her would have been the inevitable, rather sordid, perhaps, but effective complete little gesture.'[18]

While this is perhaps true on some level, it attributes depths of sadism to Sydney which she does not possess, or of which she is at least unaware. It is another variation on the emotional dynamics surrounding the search of a young woman for a suitable husband, here surrounded with endless difficulties.

This situation is contrasted with the similar situation of a minor character, Veronica, who is deciding whether or not to marry Victor Ammering, a young man whom she pronounces to be acceptable, although she moans, 'I've *kicked* Victor: what is the use of a man one can kick?' He is not exactly her ideal, but she 'must marry somebody.' The social scene here also has the background of the Great War to darken it; marriage prospects are felt to be grim, in the 1920s. Veronica's represents the straightforward dilemma of a young, well-to-do Englishwoman; she has limited chances to find a marriage partner, and once she makes this choice, she will be expected to stay with her husband. As Sydney characterizes Veronica's attitude to herself: '[she] had taken up a sound position midway between defiance and resignation and seemed likely to achieve serenity.'[19] At the same time, the relative flightiness of her temperament makes this not such an urgent problem. Sydney Warren is the more interesting charater, since she has a great deal of passion, and it is a matter of some drama whether she will find a way to express this, and use it for good. Its effect in the novel is, rather, to turn inwards into deep despair, and at the end of the book she is swept off, mute, by Tessa to yet another holiday spot – this time broken-hearted by unrequited love as well as crushed by the earlier trauma of her professional failure.

Bowen's first novel is a study in passion gone awry, and her next few books trace increasingly complex variations on the near-impossibility of conventional romance leading to satisfying marriage. It is not that she sees heterosexual romance as being essentially superior to homosexual passion – Sydney's grand passion for Mrs. Kerr founders because of individual personalities, rather than an inherent instability in lesbian relationships. (A corollary to their relationship appears in the heavily satirized figures of Miss Pym and Miss Fitzgerald, two comic spinsters who are traveling together; they quarrel bitterly, yet become reconciled in the end.) Bowen depicts a succession of things which can go dreadfully wrong, in the pursuit of love and happiness in marriage. It is prefigured by the fact that young women – in this social setting – are expected to marry, if they can. But the key thread through all of this is numbness, or the dissociation of feeling which most of her heroines experience. They struggle to cope with their own depression, and they relate to men in light of their own desperation to find meaning or stability or purpose.

Bowen's second novel, *The Last September*, focuses on the problem of emotional dissociation, as the young heroine, Lois, is looking for something to do with her life, and believes that the conventional course of engagement and marriage are all that lie open to her. Her aunt and guardian, Lady Naylor, strongly advocates that she take a course or do something which will give her an 'interest' – though it does not seem as though Lois desires to become anything professional (as does Sydney in *The Hotel*, though it is almost impossible to imagine her actually becoming a doctor). This makes the novel very much a period piece, with distinct echoes of Victorian ideals of womanhood. The proper outline for a woman's life remains marriage, though the period of waiting for this event (which Lois is experiencing with such desperate boredom) remains a blank. The immediate problem for Lois is that the available young man to whom she has formed an attachment, Gerald Lesworth, is unsuitable in her guardian's eyes. (This also is a quintessential Victorian situation.) For Lois, young and inexperienced, she believes that the best and only available alternative is for her to marry: 'I must marry Gerald,' is her constant internal refrain, intended to give her life direction. At the same time, this lack of larger purpose in life accounts for most of her desire to marry. When the older, married Francie attempts to lend Lois her support, by affirming the glory of romance, Lois replies, 'At least it may get one somewhere.' Francie, horrified, exclaims 'You seem very intellectual, Lois. Do – do you not love him?' Lois' reply is succinct, and sums up her willed intent: 'I *must*,' she tells her.[20]

Elizabeth Bowen's early novels depict the inconvenience of passion, which cannot be commanded at will. Each of them presents another variation on the same problem of romantic love for impassioned, sensitive, but somehow emotionally disconnected heroines. In her third novel, *Friends and Relations*, she describes this from yet another angle. The heroine, Janet Studdart, feels intense passion for Edward Tilney, who instead marries her sister Laurel in the opening pages of the novel. The rest of the book follows the progress of Janet's unrequited and suppressed love for Edward through the next several years, in which she is perversely vindicated by his continued emotional attachment to her. It is not indifference which has prompted Edward to choose the 'wrong' wife, but instead cowardice. This failure of nerve on his part keeps the connection between the two of them smouldering, not least because Edward must strive to justify himself (while never admitting that this is what he is doing). *Friends and Relations* is very much a period piece of the 1930s; the marriage choices have already been made, and we see the ramifications of passion being misguided into the wrong channels: both in the childish marriage of Edward and Laurel (ideally, he should have married Janet, a partner worthy of him), and in the disastrous, earlier adultery of Lady Elfrida, Edward's mother.

Passion fractures the family structure in two ways, in this novel; both instances are linked together, stemming from one seminal expression of romantic abandon. Lady Elfrida, Edward's mother, has run off years earlier with Considine, a larger-than-life figure (he is, among other attributes, a big-game hunter). Her husband has divorced her, and has separated her definitively from Edward, who was a young child at the time. The connecting line with the present which Bowen draws runs through the emotional damage which this experience has inflicted upon Edward, and his subsequent choice to marry Laurel, with whom he has 'designed, wordlessly, [to] re-live his childhood.'[21] (His mother's contemptuous summary of this failure to grow up is: 'fit for no one but little Laurel. . . .'[22])

The way in which passion goes wrong in this novel is based on an extremely conventional view: the narrator suggests that if Edward had not been frightened by his mother's early desertion of him, he would have married the more formidable of the two sisters and lived happily ever after. Conversely, now he is touchy and irritable, humoured in this excessive sensitivity by Laurel. The initial 'error' which Elfrida has made with Considine has resulted in catastrophe through two generations: the children of both Janet's and Laurel's marriages are described as having been 'begotten in error.'[23]

As she explains her own actions later, Janet has coped with her rejection by marrying Rodney, a relation of Considine. As she tells Elfrida, it would not be what she desired, but nevertheless a connection between them: 'It seemed something for me – I wanted to be related.'[24] Part of Bowen's genius is to create a plot with so much tension in it. The situation between Janet and Edward is still explosive, ten years after he has married Laurel. Elfrida and Considine meet again, at Janet and Rodney's house in the country, and Edward arrives to take away his two children, who are visiting at the house. In part, he wishes to insulate his own children from the painful memories which he himself associates with the Elfrida and Considine affair; he acts out of a Victorian, melodramatic conviction that they must not be allowed to see such wickedness. However, he is also afflicted by the passion which is expressed for Janet by Theodora, a lesbian who is staying at the house; it is she who has written to Laurel and Edward about Elfrida and Considine, and who has been hoping to stir up just such a reaction. Edward's passion for Janet is evident in his anguished jealousy of Theodora: 'Why do you let her brush your hair?' he cries. In this scene between the two of them, Edward articulates their mutual disaster: '"If you and I had fallen in love – But I didn't want that," he said clearly.' The crux of the novel lies in his reflection, after the fraught conversation he has with Janet: '"And life after all," thought Edward, hearing tea approach, the gay dance of china on the silver tray, "is an affair of charm, not an affair of passion."'[25]

This perspective, in Bowen's world, is a deliberately chosen decision. Characters can, and sometimes do, decide that the reverse is true. (Ironically, Elfrida and Considine have now lapsed into comfortable friendship, driving into town with their grandchildren for ices; what has once been passion is now charm.) But passion continues to rivet Janet and Edward to each other, and they enact a dramatic romantic confrontation alone with each other, late in the novel. They meet in a hotel room in London, only to agree that it is too late for their love to be expressed. It becomes an anticlimax that nonetheless exposes and then rends something within the family structure; instead of spending their holiday with Rodney and Janet, Laurel and Edward take the children to Brittany instead. *Friends and Relations* is Bowen's most direct exploration of conventional romance. She shows how it can go fundamentally wrong, from a source long ago in the past.

Bowen's novels are unique because she changes the formula for passion in each successive novel. These books describe the difficulties of otherwise privileged women, at least in terms of social class; yet they miss out on matters of the heart. Her next three novels, *To the North, The House in Paris*, and *The Death of the Heart*, take up further variations of love stories gone terribly wrong, and heroines who cannot – for one reason or another – feel emotion, or else who become tragic figures when it pierces through their defenses.

To the North portrays the romantic dilemmas of two heroines, Cecilia Waters and Emmeline Waters, her sister-in-law through her lately deceased husband. Cecilia is a young widow, still grieving for her husband, to whom she had been married for less than a year. She hopes to fall in love again, 'exposing her heart hopefully like a bird's nest.' Emmeline, her sister-in-law, is virginal and remote, by contrast; she is described in the text as being 'angelic,' and has had neither affairs nor the experience of marriage; she is passionately devoted to her professional life. She is the first of Bowen's heroines to have achieved a working position and complete autonomy; this is underscored by the fact that she has an automobile which she drives through London. She owns and runs a small travel agency, with a male friend (who is homosexual, and therefore not a threat to Emmeline's carefully preserved separateness from others). Emmeline is presented as being rather dissociated from her true passions, as she sends others on holiday, rather than traveling herself. She is slightly remote from everyone; she drinks only iced tea at London parties, and attends them in order to observe others, and to find prospective clients. She misses out on the right prospective husband for herself, Julian Tower, because he has drunk too much at the party where they first meet, which he recognizes but can do nothing to mitigate: 'Julian, already at some disadvantage through not feeling quite himself, wished they need not have met so far on in the evening.'[26] And she is propelled into an affair with the malign Markie because – ironically – the agency secretary, Miss Tripp, has conceived a grand passion for Emmeline, and overwhelms her with an emotional appeal. The narrator casts this appeal as ridiculous: 'all this time in Miss Tripp the juices of an unduly prolonged adolescence had violently been fermenting: now with a pop they shot out the cork from the bottle.'[27] This is the ludicrous side of passion; but part of what Bowen insists upon is that her characters do suffer. And Emmeline is pushed into the affair with Markie as part of an attempt to explore new emotional territory.

The demise of Emmeline's affair, given Markie's temperament and habitual behavior in such cases, is inevitable. He eventually rejects Emmeline, to return to an earlier mistress, Daisy, who is perceived as 'human,' in contrast to what he feels to be Emmeline's 'exalted' and uncomfortably intense nature. As the narrator says, 'he liked women lowish.'[28] This novel offers a picture of a time during which women are only partly liberated. Emmeline is able to engage in a sexual affair with Markie without specific guilt for this as a breach of accepted conduct. Yet the old conventions are still very much in place. When her meddlesome aunt, Lady Waters, learns through gossip that Emmeline is almost certainly sleeping with Markie – they have been seen together in a town some distance from London – she confronts Cecilia with the news immediately. And it is a frighteningly serious matter, as Cecilia herself recognizes: 'The fumes subsided, off went the Delphic trappings: here spoke sheer aunt, empowered by plain good sense. That voice went back through the schoolroom and to the cradle.'[29]

Furthermore, as the narrator explains, in this particular case (even with a noted flâneur such as Markie), the efficacy of the older rules still holds sway – at least in the narrator's point of view. The conventional notion is advanced to the reader, that 'had she held out till he was crazy he would no doubt have married her; that she had not cared to buy marriage appeared incredible. . . .'[30]

In purely sexual terms, this novel is a Victorian story in 1930s dress, setting forth a conventional tale of tragic passion. Shakespeare's refrain 'Men were deceivers ever' is one of its main themes; or, put more concisely by one of Bowen's contemporary writers, Benedict Kiely, 'Elizabeth Bowen proves that mother was right and all men are snakes.'[31] What he does not add is that which Bowen also implies – that some women are fools to believe them. And she offers a wickedly funny array of contrasting examples of women's choices about matrimony. Gerda Bligh, a discontented young wife, compares her plight with those of other women who complain of their miseries in the local agony columns of the newspaper: 'Gerda went straight to the Woman's Page. It is true, she was more fortunate than Mrs. A. (Mill Hill), Mrs. B. (Sydenham) and "Discouraged." '[32] The implication is that Gerda's social class does a great deal to insulate her from what are no doubt truly appalling situations faced by her less fortunate contemporaries. Bowen satirizes the choices of one segment of a social class at a particular time, as in the vignette where Cecilia goes to meet a group of three women friends for lunch: 'knee-to-knee round the painted table, nibbling salt almonds and twisting the long-stemmed Venetian glasses they confessed they could not understand themselves; each, as she talked, took on an air of childish rarity and importance.' Each defines herself in her role as a woman in relation to an adoring man, with immense egotism:

'one wore frills down her front, she was going to have a baby; one showed a glowing reticence, she had a lover; one, a bride, was called from the *soufflé* to telephone to her husband.'[33]

At the same time, Bowen is serious about portraying the searing pain of unrequited romantic love – and not least, about the inefficacy of anyone else to help or to do anything to alleviate the grief involved. This effort is parodied in the tragi-comic scene at Lady Waters' country house, to which she has swept off a bereft lesbian composer, whose lover has left her:

> So far, Marcelle had been one of her few reverses: Georgina could but regret having carried her off. Alone in her studio scrappy with torn-up letters Marcelle, poor soul, had for days been afloat in whiskey: Georgina had bustled her out of it.

Yet her unsuitability as a house-guest is felt by everyone: 'she drank as much whiskey here and was even more unresponsive: she played the piano at midnight and said next day it was out of tune.'[34] This is intended as an ironic comment on Lady Waters' helpfulness in times of emotional distress; but it also dramatizes a genuine feeling for the sufferer. In a similar way, Emmeline's numbness and grief is made clear in its intensity and its effect on her: 'her hair went darker and dull, her face white: if anyone looked at her in the streets it was to wonder from what she was running away.'[35] Moreover, when Markie rejects her, the travel agency – her great source of delight – begins to fail as she crumples under the strain of grief. The ending of the novel evokes a final disaster, where Cecilia and Julian have belatedly decided to host a small dinner party for Markie and Emmeline, in order to indicate to Markie that they stand behind her. It is when she drives him home that he loses his temper, and she crashes the car – thus irrevocably darkening Cecilia and Julian's approaching marriage, as the two of them wait for Emmeline's return, which will never come.

To the North is a story of expected outcomes, though it is played out with very exceptional and interesting characters. *The House in Paris*, Bowen's next novel, carries all of this one step further towards melodrama, by creating a heroine who is passionate, though she appears to be cool and detached. This also is a novel with specific class associations: 'The Michaelis lived like a family in a pre-war novel in one of the tall, cream houses in Chester Terrace, Regent's Park.'[36] Bowen locates the beginning of passion in adolescence, and, as she did in *Friends and Relations*, she shows a long-term effect of passion which takes shape as a time bomb waiting to explode. *The House in Paris*, however, is interesting in what it says about passion because it is not a formula piece. The central romance lies between a woman who is neither a *femme fatale* nor a calculating bitch, and a man who is self-absorbed, but not a practiced cad. Both Max and Karen are highly romantic and intense, which gives an exalted tone to their passion for each other. As in *To the North*, the main event of *The House in Paris* is that two lovers go to bed together, though in this case the passionate fatefulness of their tryst is underscored by the fact that Karen becomes pregnant (also a stock situation of Victorian melodrama). But this has a special force for her – especially as she has been propelled into the affair by a moment of *memento mori*, when she learns on a visit to Ireland of her aunt's impending surgery, which heralds her relative's death soon afterwards. Karen's reflections during one of the two nights she spends with Max include the thought of a child to come from their union: 'If a child were going to be born, there would still be something that had to be.'[37] The birth of Leopold is only one of the major events which occur after this meeting; Max and Karen's action constitutes the betrayal of Naomi (his fiancée) and Ray (Karen's fiancé), and leads to the ultimate suicide of Max, the related death of Karen's mother, Mme. Fisher's paralytic collapse, and Karen's abandonment of Leopold to adoptive parents. The other main drama of the novel centers around Ray's coming to the house in Paris to collect Leopold and take him to live with Karen and himself in England.

In one sense, this is so conventional a story that it turns on the fact that everything crumbles – from a certain, English point of view – when illicit passion is given full expression. Further, the juxtaposition of the two men constitutes a highly conventional choice for Karen, as a young woman: she can either plunge into sex with Max (the dangerous, exotic, alluring caddish figure) or enter a decorous marriage with Ray (the dull but devoted English husband). It is made clear from the opening of the novel which she has chosen, nor is it any surprise to the reader that this is the outcome. Nor is it surprising that she seems to be punished so cruelly in consequence. (To add to her grief, the two children whom she conceives with Ray, whom she later marries, are both stillborn.) From this point of view, *The House in Paris* is traditional Victorian melodrama: 'Her life had been full of warnings' from her parent figures, which she considers during her night-long vigil when she becomes pregnant with Leopold. She is not sufficiently careful – although, in terms of contraception, the narrator suggests that she has at least thought of this, and has 'done as she knew she must,' on the occasion of her tryst with Max, though ultimately to no avail in preventing pregnancy.[38] The reasons for her rebellion against these social codes are interesting, especially since Bowen is trying to delve to the source of Karen's choices, which are complex. The interlude of her visit to Ireland has impressed upon her the transitoriness of life, in her aunt's plight; and it has also provided a witty way for Bowen to allude to the chemistry involved in any love affair. Meeting another young woman on the crossing to England, of a distinctly different temperament and social class, Karen has the cheerful judgement passed upon her by the privately dubbed 'Yellow Hat' that '*your* poison's not mine.'[39] Poison, in these novels, can be irresistibly sweet.

This novel is fascinating not only for its utterly fantastic melodrama – including the insidiously evil Mme. Fisher and the suicidal Max – but for its scathing comment on Englishness, and on the consummate good manners and chivalry which close around Karen, once she has sinned so blatantly against the social code. Ray – the dull fiancé – gives up a diplomatic career in order to marry Karen, and the two establish themselves as a devoted childless couple, at least in the view of their acquaintances. Bowen raises the question of whether Ray actually loves her more because she is, in strict terms, 'fallen,' and needs to be looked after. In other words, Karen becomes the archetypal example of a 'ruined' heroine, disgraced through sexual excess and the expression of passion. But she attracts a sort of strange compassion that can also be felt as condescension. Bowen's genius lies in showing a bizarre yet important angle on this dynamic. Some long-buried, inescapable tension is always there, between the two decorous married spouses. Leopold, the child, exists, and Karen wants him back. The even more fantastic twist to the story is that Leopold – whereas he might have felt angry and abandoned – also wants Karen, and goes off with Ray willingly at the end of the novel. This is a quintessential female fantasy, where redemption and the forgiveness of a son provide Karen with that which she has not even been courageous enough to seize for herself.

In *The House in Paris*, Bowen has taken her ideas about passion to a stimulating extreme – it would be hard to push them further, unless she verged into the gothic. Also, it is interesting to consider what a riveting story she made from this situation, which is so absolutely rooted in its social context; authors writing later in the twentieth century have infinitely more flexibility in what their heroines are allowed to explore, in sexual terrain. Bowen, however, uses the constrictions which beset her heroine to wring the last bit of tension out of a situation fraught with romantic *angst*.

In *The Death of the Heart*, she creates yet another variation on the damaging effect of passion. Anna Quayne is still riveted by thoughts of her former lover, Robert Pidgeon. He is something of a comic figure, because of his name; but his impact on her feelings is extremely intense. And it is all the more compelling a memory because of her relatively settled position when the novel opens. Anna is married to Thomas Quayne, the owner of a successful advertising agency, and they live in an elegant house in Regent's Terrace. Though bored, she does not have the energy or the desire either to resume her profession again – she has been an interior decorator at one point – or to start an affair, although she has taken up a younger man as her protégé, the mercurial Eddie. Bowen makes Eddie the focus of intense emotion for Anna, yet it is not entirely sexual tension between them so much as it is a power struggle for emotional dominance.

One irony of the novel is the fact that passion is felt by one of the characters for his spouse: Thomas, Anna's husband, finds himself trapped: 'Thomas discovered himself the prey of a passion for her, inside marriage, that nothing in their language could be allowed to express, that nothing could satisfy.'[40]

Eddie's entrance into the Quayne family circle creates an uneasy triangle with Anna, who is older, and who plays the sophisticated woman of the world to his ardent yet embittered troubadour, and with Portia, who at sixteen is still trying to figure out what is happening in the world around her. Neither Anna nor Portia are women with whom Eddie can have a sexual relationship; nonetheless, he has intense relationships with both of them. Eddie fits into Anna's typical pattern, to some extent; her husband, Thomas, views their relationship with resignation born of experience, confident that it will soon falter: 'He had looked on at other declines and falls' in Anna's emotional liaisons. Anna feels justified in this relationship because they are not having physical contact. But the basis of her rejection of Eddie remains the unresolved internal conflict over her former lover: '[Eddie] did not know about Pidgeon, or how badly she had come out of all that – if, in fact, she had ever come out of it.'[41]

Moreover, this view of sexuality (in the head) is directly contrasted with the melodrama of an earlier affair which results in pregnancy and exile. Anna explains the circumstances of Portia's birth to the novelist St. Quentin, in the opening pages of the novel. Mr. Quayne, Thomas's father, has had an affair with Irene, whom Anna describes with malice and loathing: 'She was a scrap of a widow, ever so plucky, just back from China, with damp little hands, a husky voice and defective tear-ducts that gave her eyes always rather a swimmy look.'

This vivid picture of the liaison shows that Anna has been brooding over it with some vindictiveness, as she conjures up an intimate and grotesque view of sexual passion fully consummated. Irene and Mr. Quayne begin an affair which soon leads to her pregnancy with Portia, and Anna offers the following scene: 'I often think of those dawns in Notting Hill Gate, with Irene leaking tears and looking for hairpins, and Mr. Quayne sitting up denouncing himself.'[42] Sexual passion can easily be made to seem ridiculous. While it is more or less tacitly accepted that a young woman such as Karen in *The House in Paris* might fall into bed, in order to '[finish] the past' of her passionate yet unfulfilled adolescence, it is perceived as openly comic that a middle-aged man should do the same.[43] Yet another portrait of the potential silliness of sexual passion is Bowen's parody of adolescent sexual awakening in Portia's school friend, Lillian, who continually complains of feeling 'bilious' with emotion, and who has been taken away from her boarding school after having developed a Grand Passion for the cello mistress, 'which had made her quite unable to eat.'[44]

Part of what Bowen is dramatizing – and what gives her novels such power – is the emotional force that sexual passion has, and can continue to have for years after its original blow. Anna has been deeply impacted by her passionate affair with Pidgeon, although she has not (unlike Karen in Bowen's previous novel) had a child by him. (She has suffered two miscarriages, and responded by withdrawing into irony: the experience has 'turned her back on herself: she did not want children now.'[45]) Pidgeon never appears in person in the novel, having left Anna much earlier. Still, his presence is felt, and she spends a great deal of energy trying to make sense of him and what she felt for him. Late in the novel, she looks through some of his letters, and reflects on her situation in contrast to that of Portia: 'Experience isn't interesting till it begins to repeat itself – in fact, till it does that, it hardly *is* experience.'[46] What Anna intuitively understands is that experience 'repeats' itself, either because one unconsciously recreates it or because some malign fate has designed life to unfold that way.

The Death of the Heart invokes sexuality in conventional terms in relation to Portia, as well: the great question in everyone else's mind is whether or not Eddie is taking sexual liberties with her. He is not, in physical terms; though he does so emotionally. In the middle section of the novel, when Portia is packed off to stay at the seaside with Anna's former governess, Mrs. Heccomb, Eddie does approach another character with frank sexual directness. Daphne, however, the object of his attentions on this occasion, is experienced in such matters, and takes his advances in the spirit in which they are meant: the exchange of covert pleasure. Their hand-holding is intended as much to exult over the feelings of the little group of friends as it is to express a connection between the two of them. The scene occurs in the cinema, where Daphne's brother Dickie extends his cigarette lighter over the row of seated friends, exposing Eddie and Daphne holding hands. They are revealed in an entirely complicit relationship, and one that is portrayed as manifestly ludicrous: 'Eddie's fingers kept up a kneading movement: her thumb alertly twitched at the joint.'[47]

What Bowen understands with deep intuition is the relationship of sex to power, particularly in terms of female rivalry. Portia later asks Daphne to explain the event in the cinema to her, which enrages Daphne almost beyond speech: '"People creeping and spying," said Daphne, utterly tense, "and then talking vulgarly are two things that I simply cannot stick."'[48] To speak of such a thing is to openly acknowledge that Daphne has been trying to hurt Portia by appropriating Eddie (who has been invited to the seaside house, Waikiki, by Portia). In a sense, Daphne's sophistication takes the form of knowing that such a gesture – hand-holding in the cinema – means everything and nothing. As Eddie himself explains, when spurred into speech by Portia, who is still painfully seeking to understand it: 'I have to get off with people. . . . Because I cannot get on with them.'[49] He answers the sexual challenge which Daphne poses to him, but it is merely that. Portia, through loving him with pure affection, actually comes closest to his true feelings – which is what he has both been seeking and what he cannot bear. When she tells him, sorrowfully, 'you stay alone in yourself!' she has given voice to the anguish and loneliness from which he is continually trying to escape. Not surprisingly, this leaves him feeling under attack, and rigid with emotion: 'Eddie, white as a stone, said: "*You must let go of me.*"'[50]

Eddie is not attempting to seduce Portia, as the adult characters suspect. Ironically, their bond is a strong one, because it is of equal intensity between them, but on a different wave-length. In a way, it does have something to do with sexual tension, and yet it transcends that; Portia makes a confidant, even a collaborator, of Eddie, when she asks him to read her diary (something which Anna has been doing throughout the novel, without invitation). The narrator offers a set-piece summary, to describe this union between the two: 'The innocent are so few that two of them seldom meet – when they do meet, their victims lie strewn all round.'[51] Theirs is a more intense connection because it is not conventionally sexual; they are siblings, twins, soul mates.

The novel is fundamentally about two women who are trying to understand sexuality, human desire, and loneliness. Sexuality, in itself, does not necessarily hurt people; lies and deceit and cruelty do this. Portia, as the newly arrived orphan in London, is manifestly trying to make sense of the adult, social world around her. This is expected. What is strange in the situation is that Anna – who sets herself up as a cynical woman of the world – begins to do the same thing, when Portia arrives. In one sense, this happens as pure accident; as she describes it to St. Quentin, Portia's diary lies exposed in her bedroom, and Anna gives in to the temptation to pick it up. Once having done so, she is mesmerized: 'Could I not go on with a book all about ourselves?' she asks, summarizing her reasons for doing so, during a climactic scene at the dinner table, late in the novel, when it is discovered that Portia has run away from home.[52]

The mystery of Portia's whereabouts is soon solved: she has fled to take refuge, as she thinks, with Major Brutt, a safe, solid adult who has attached himself devotedly to the Quayne family. He forms an odd triangle with Anna and Pidgeon, as he is a friend of Anna's former lover – he not only links her with the past, but vividly brings out her own disappointment at Pidgeon's loss. On their first, accidental meeting, in a London cinema, he looks expectantly for the charismatic Pidgeon, who does not appear in Anna's wake. Portia's instincts in fleeing to him are, in one sense, correct: he is kindly, and not only upholds conventionality, but chivalry. From what she understands of the world, it might be possible to strike a bargain: 'Tell Thomas you want to keep me and he could send you my money,' she tells him hopefully, casting this equation in what she understands to be the proper mode by adding, 'Why could you not marry me? I could cheer you up.'[53] The missing ingredient in this equation is sexuality, which is part of the basis of marriage – and it is precisely this that makes their marriage both impossible and ludicrous. Nonetheless, Portia is merely offering a refracted version of what she has been led to believe is the correct way of the world in such situations. Her request comprises the most old-fashioned solution possible for a young, unwanted single woman.

Portia's puzzling out of her situation leads to Anna's attempt to do the same, from her own vantage point. These two strains meet when Anna tries, at the dinner table, to give a cogent account of Portia's view to Thomas and St. Quentin – which reflects on Anna's own way of acting. She describes Portia's probable feelings about their ménage in London with startling clarity, and this crystallizes (perhaps for the first time) what her own feelings are: 'If I were Portia? Contempt for the pack of us, who muddled our own lives, then stopped me from living mine.'[54] What Anna is giving voice to is the dammed-up passion which has been constrained underneath the stilted encounters over the tea table and the flirtatious conversations with Eddie throughout the novel.

Bowen's early novels, from *The Hotel* through *The Death of the Heart*, follow a number of different variations of the expression of intense romantic, sexual passion, within the context of upper-middle-class morality. By the time her next novel, *The Heat of the Day*, appears, World War II has radically changed the tenor of English society, and Bowen's heroine is allowed to pursue a more or less satisfying romance with a man, with no pressing need to marry him. Robert Kelway's proposal to Stella, mid-way through the novel, reflects his panic at being uncovered as an enemy spy; yet also, it expresses the conventional desire (stemming from jealousy) to keep her on a tighter rein. 'You think I run into trouble?' she asks him drily; and in fact, she refuses his offer of marriage. Marriage would not bring them physically closer together, as she points out; she is 'hardly' ever out of Robert's sight.[55]

Bowen's early books, however, set everything within the framework of the world of debutantes and respectable marriage, although they use this to escalate the *angst* of loneliness and sexual passion. What is almost as unbearable to her romantic heroines as being thwarted in love is their inability to feel emotion. Cecilia in *To the North* broods over this numbness, or lack of desire, which in her case stems in part from the grief she still feels over the loss of her husband. The narrator offers a poetic set-piece about this, describing a great house destroyed by fire and replaced by suburbs: 'With [Cecilia], the gay little streets flourished, but, brave when her house fell, she could not regain some entirety of the spirit. Disability seems a hard reward for courage.'[56] This last observation suggests that one cannot will oneself to feel warmth or emotion; many of her heroines are fated – possibly through their own folly, but not always – to lead relatively loveless and disappointed lives. Those who rush off to embrace passion, such as Lady Elfrida in *Friends and Relations* or Emmeline in *To the North*, often fare no better. Bowen's is a dark view; yet it can also be satisfyingly complex.

The other angle brought in by the relation of passion to marriage in the early part of the twentieth century is the attempt that wives can make to substitute satisfaction in their social and family roles for a corresponding lack of purpose. Or, more simply put, these might be the pleasures that one is able to command, either as a spinster or an aging woman, whether married or single. Barbara Pym's heroine, Mildred Lathbury, in *Excellent Women*, listens wistfully to the splendidly competent speakers who broadcast on the 'Woman's Hour,' and keeps cookery books by the bed for late-night reading. When distressed, late in the novel, she decides that a cookery book

> was the best for my mood, and I chose an old one of recipes and miscellaneous household hints. I read about the care of aspidistras and how to wash lace and black woolen stockings, and I learned that a package or envelope sealed with white of egg cannot be steamed open.

The fact that this knowledge is esoteric highlights the absurdity of this endeavour: 'what use that knowledge would ever be to me I could not imagine,' she concludes. Nonetheless, her competence in the kitchen and her being perceived to be a 'sensible person' who keeps an oven cloth 'hanging on a nail by the side of the cooker' is what eventually gains her a husband.[57]

This emphasis on domesticity takes place in a specific cultural context. Anthea Trodd has pointed out that 'the period between the wars saw extensive emphasis on wives' home-making abilities,' especially exemplified in women's magazines.[58] These sought to professionalize the role of the middle-class housewife, who was now experiencing a shortage of daily help (the Servant Problem), and attempting to run the household and raise children single-handedly. For upper-class characters in Bowen's *To the North*, this creates the basis for withering comedy, where a female character such as Gerda Bligh shows off self-importantly with her knowledge: 'Eiderdowns are reduced at this time of year,' Lady Waters explains to Cecilia smugly, about her recent shopping expedition instigated by Gerda. As a competent woman, Cecilia has already mastered this art: '"I know," said Cecilia, indignant. In fact there was little that one could teach her about running or stocking a house. . . .'[59] The crux of the matter is that Gilbert, Gerda's husband, has necessitated the search for new eiderdowns because he has damaged theirs through smoking in bed. This piece of information covertly conveys to the reader one possible source of Gerda's unhappiness in her marriage; whatever goes on in the Bligh bed, it sounds unfulfilling for her.

And this remains a question – possibly, a problem – for wives in these novels. Some authors are inventive in making this domestic scene the source of comedy, as in E.M. Delafield's *Diary of a Provincial Lady*. The narrator's staid husband, Robert, sits in an easy chair reading the newspaper each evening while the heroine's days are spent wrestling with the Servant Problem, trying to mediate between her two lively children and a hysterical governess, planting tulip bulbs, and fending off visits from the local Grand Dame, nicknamed Lady B. She is rueful yet amusing about hosting Lady Boxe to tea, which synthesizes these burdens and anxieties:

> Lady B. stays to tea. (*Mem.*: Bread-and-butter too thick. Speak to Ethel.) We talk some more about bulbs, the Dutch School of Painting, Our Vicar's Wife, sciatica, and *All Quiet on the Western Front.* (Query: Is it possible to cultivate the art of conversation when living in the country all the year round?)[60]

The interweaving of domestic help with one's established, married life is a crucial theme for Dorothy L. Sayers' lovers, Peter Wimsey and Harriet Vane, who marry at the beginning of the novel *Busman's Honeymoon*, and who continue their domestic ménage in *Thrones, Dominations* (which was begun by Sayers, then abandoned in manuscript, and finished several decades later by Jill Paton Walsh). Sayers sets out to grant her characters everything that love and marriage can ideally bring. Passion is a major theme of Lord Peter Wimsey's discourses and his aristocratic bearing – a determined dilettante, neatly escaping matrimonial nets spread by enterprising mothers of debutantes, he unaccountably falls for Harriet Vane at first sight in the novel *Strong Poison*. The poison here can also be understood to mean romantic passion, which in this case appears to be hopeless, as Harriet is charged (on false evidence) with murder and likely to hang; and in any case, refuses his advances flatly. (This very unavailability is naturally one clue as to why he has become so struck with her.)

Wimsey pursues her with ardour through a lengthy courtship of several years, further described in *Have His Carcase*, where the two solve a murder case together, and *Gaudy Night*, where they meet (to Harriet's satisfaction) as 'equals' on symbolically equal territory, in Oxford University. Wimsey's set-piece discussion on his own views of passion are delivered solemnly in this novel, at a point in the plot where he can see the identity of the poltergeist and the solution of the mystery, and she cannot. But it also serves to point the moral of his own views on the subject, as he explains to her later: 'the worst sin – perhaps the only sin – passion can commit, is to be joyless.' As an aristocrat (at least in this cultural context) he does not feel compelled to defend his casual treatment of his sexual partners. This is an accepted part of his social role; when Wimsey's nephew, Gerald, thoughtlessly refers in Harriet's hearing to the most notable of his uncle's courtesans ('spectacular Viennese singers'), she is not surprised. Wimsey nonetheless explains his relationships with paramours to her: 'I have bought it, often – but never by forced sale or at "stupendous sacrifice,"' which implies that he feels he has treated them well and therefore is vindicated.[61]

As for Harriet herself, she distrusts her own emotions, after her grueling public ordeal, when she has been on trial for the murder of her former lover. One aspect of her acknowledgement of her own feelings has to do with the pervasive influence of popularized Freudian theory. In one hilarious scene, Harriet wakes up from a dream in which Wimsey has been embracing her as a lover, an event whose interpretation is obvious enough. Still, she refuses to take it at face value: 'My subconscious has a most treacherous imagination,' she glowers, adding, 'If I really wanted to be passionately embraced by Peter, I should dream of something like dentists or gardening.'[62] What finally breaks down her resistance to her own lack of comprehension about her attraction is an incontrovertible physical phenomenon. The two of them sit alone together in a punt, when Harriet looks at him and flushes deeply: 'she was instantly scarlet, as though she had been dipped in boiling water.' This confronts Harriet with the evidence of her sexual response to Wimsey, which she can either acknowledge or not. 'The only new thing that has happened,' she realizes, 'is that now I have got to admit it to myself.'[63]

Given the conventions of the 1930s, it is understood by the reader that Harriet will muster courage to abandon her falsely donned defenses against male sexuality. As she has cautiously ascertained, marriage to Wimsey would – or could – satisfy her desire for both love and work, and her profession of fiction writing will continue unimpeded. (There is the implication that her novels will gain in depth, through the expression of her own passion, as in her attempts to create more depth in the fictional character of Wilfrid, which Wimsey has advised her to do.) When she accepts his proposal on the final page of *Gaudy Night*, it is reasonable yet also romantic.

The drama of the courtship modulates into the question of how they will convert their passion into a domestic setting. Sayers has created the perfect situation in which to explore this problem, since Wimsey, as the arch aristocrat, has been tended for years by his faithful valet and detective assistant, Bunter. Bunter has been, for all intents and purposes, a wife in the purely domestic sense of the word – cooking his meals, making his travel arrangements and so on. Accordingly, there is a definite sense of Bunter's aid continuing to support his master, although this can only go so far, in the present challenge. On the Wimseys' wedding night, in *Busman's Honeymoon*, Bunter thinks solemnly: 'Though not precisely anxious, he was filled with a kindly concern. He had (with what exertions!) brought his favourite up to the tape and must leave him now to make the running. . . .'[64] In Paton Walsh's completed version of Sayers' *Thrones, Dominations* manuscript – which must be understood to be appealing to an audience in the late twentieth century – she describes an exemplary domestic household in the 1930s. Paton Walsh pays off every arrear of aristocratic dependence on domestic help: in this novel, Bunter himself desires to marry. A brilliant solution is found to the impending disaster of losing such a beloved and valuable companion: he and his new wife will live together in the fully modernized mews apartment behind Peter and Harriet's London house.

Bowen and Sayers portray female sexuality in terms of the socially accepted views of their times on marriage. Writers such as Murdoch and Byatt are able to approach the subject of passion from a very different angle, as their characters are not necessarily doomed to social ostracism, as the result of acting upon their impulses. They also write historical novels which show a different view of sexuality in retrospect, as Byatt does in her novel *Possession*, which I want to discuss in the next chapter. In closing, however, I want to look at one of Iris Murdoch's early novels. In *Bruno's Dream*, Murdoch creates a complicated and interlocking set of relationships in which the pangs of unrequited love anguish many of her characters. This allows the narrator in each novel to theorize about the wild, uncontrollable state of suffering which such obsession brings with it. The plight of the main character in *Bruno's Dream* contrasts with that of the younger people around him. Bruno lies on his death-bed, recalling his past life, and holding illness at bay as best he can. His fantasy is: 'If only he could be loved by somebody new. But it was impossible. Who would love him now when he had become a monster?'[65]

Another kind of suffering is the unwilling passion which Miles, Bruno's son, feels for Lisa, his wife Diana's sister, who comes to live with the couple temporarily. Their passion for each other is mutual: 'there are communications which can be made and certainly made without speech,' says the narrator. 'By the time Friday evening had been reached Miles knew that Lisa knew and he knew that she knew that he knew.' The lure of this emotion is also explained: 'The experience of falling in love, or as it seemed here to Miles, of realizing that one is in love, is itself, however painful, also a preoccupying joy. It increases vitality and sense of self.' The encounter during which the two characters acknowledge this – an embrace – is described as 'a moment of black blissful death. It was also a moment of absolute certainty.' What Miles says is a cliché: 'I feel I've loved you for years only I was blind to it.' This is followed by another ardent yet melodramatic statement, when he informs her, 'I feel I shall die of it.' The stock situation is made still more extreme by Lisa's confession: 'I fell in love with you on your wedding day, the day when we first met.'[66]

Two other variations on this theme occur in the novel. Another character, Danby, also falls in love with Lisa, and succeeds in winning her (to Miles' outraged grief). Nigel, Bruno's paid companion, reveals to Danby that he has been in love with him. He talks also in clichés, writing in a letter: 'Love is a strange thing. There is no doubt at all that it and only it makes the world go round. It is our only significant activity. . . . Yet on the other hand what a trouble-maker it is to be sure.' Part of the point of all of this seeming mismatching of romantic ardour is that characters each have existential choices to make: 'It is a weird thought that anyone is *permitted* to love in any way he pleases,' Nigel goes on. 'Nothing in nature forbids it. A cat may look at a king, the worthless can love the good, the good the worthless, the worthless the worthless, and the good the good.' The novel seems to suggest that instead of being completely fatalistic, love is above all a matter of free choice: 'Love knows no conventions,' Nigel says, 'Anything *can* happen, so that in a way, a terrible terrible way, there are no impossibilities.'[67] In one way, this is simply delusional; and it also ignores the fact that there are conventions in relation to love. But it neatly sets out a view of romance which many of Murdoch's characters seem tacitly to hold, one which combines fatalism and free will.

The two other significant relationships which contrast with this are Lisa's requited passion for Danby, with whom she achieves a blissful union, and Diana's love for Bruno. These comprise different angles on the same reason why love is such a powerful force – even if you possess it, it can easily be taken from you. Miles experiences this, to his rage, first with Parvati (his first wife who died, years earlier, in a plane crash), and later with Lisa. Diana reflects, of her relationship with Bruno: 'I have done the most foolish thing of all, in becoming so attached to someone who is dying. Is this not the most pointless of all loves?'[68] It is also ironic, as Bruno has been wishing for just such an event – the love of someone new, even though he is aged and decaying in body.

As for the romantic union of Danby and Lisa – which occurs at her instigation, as she first says she will go to live in India, but instead returns to find him – it is interesting because it is rational as well as passionate and driven. She tells him, 'Does it seem so strange after all that I should want to make somebody happy and be happy myself?' She describes her coming out of darkness and depression as a deliberate choice; and the usual madness of love (at least, as she herself describes this) is absent: 'I am not mad, Danby,' she insists. 'I have never been more sane, coldly sane, *self-interestedly* sane. I am a woman. I want warmth and love, affection, laughter, happiness, all the things I've done without. I don't want to live upon the rack.'[69]

At the end of the novel, Diana feels that she has lost everything, since Lisa has taken Miles's affection, then she has appropriated Danby; and now Bruno (to whom Diana has become attached) will soon die. She does achieve some serenity and resignation, in the novel's final pages, but what is most clear as a driving force is the compulsive need that all of the characters have to find a partner. Diana thinks: 'We've all paired off really, in the end. Miles has got his muse, Lisa has got Danby. And I've got Bruno. Who would have thought it would work out like that?'[70]

This state of affairs is a given, in Murdoch's novels – the powerful impulse to search out a lover. In one way, the frenetic couplings and regroupings of her tumultuous cast of characters seems surreal; but this is in part because she is not writing in the same vein of realism that authors like Bowen and Byatt (in most of their novels) have chosen. The characters are meant to be puppets, to some extent, in order that we can see the workings of raw emotion hold sway.

Murdoch's blissfully happy couples always have an air of beating tremendous odds against them – or of having overcome great obstacles to their being united. A.S. Byatt is also adept at showing how love can surprise a character – and yet how it can be a logical outcome of that person's life and thoughts. In the case of Daniel Orton, the curate who first appears in *The Virgin in the Garden*, he has thought himself immune to desire, but is overcome by it. 'I was slow,' he tells Stephanie mid-way through the novel, struggling with his passion. 'I should've stopped it all before it properly got going but I was too slow. Such things hadn't happened to me before, as I told you.'[71] He sees in Stephanie Potter a kind of mirror of himself as a helper to humanity; and as such she can be a partner in his work. But his desire for her is both intensely sexual and also a passion for the essential person that she is. 'I just want you,' he tells her, 'I want you, the way you would be, married to me. . . .'[72]

This exchange between the two of them is also amusing because it reveals the essential qualities in Stephanie which have drawn him to her: 'People always do,' she tells him, 'Want to marry me. It's frightening. Men at Cambridge. People I've only met twice, even only once. . . . I think I must – it isn't sex appeal, it's always marriage – I think I must just look comfortable.' From her own perspective, however, it seems humiliating: 'They don't say, let's go dancing, let's have a holiday, let's go to bed, or anything but I want to marry you, with a sort of awful reverence.'[73]

In a reverse of the usual stereotype of the age, Stephanie is sexually experienced (from her years as an undergraduate at Cambridge) while Daniel is not. When they first sleep together, in his lodging at the vicarage, she is the practical partner: 'We shall need a towel,' she informs him.[74] This is comical, yet also sweet; and it is not the masculine, sexual finesse which he displays which wins her, but the love and affection which he displays. His enthusiasm is for her, rather than for the excitement or relief which she can offer (in contrast to the importunate undergraduates of her earlier experience). When Stephanie tells her sister Frederica that she has agreed to marry Daniel, she refers to their encounter in this way: '"It was a revelation," said Stephanie with dignity.'[75] While this statement as made to Frederica has a great deal to do with jealousy and sibling rivalry, it is also true that Stephanie is in love with Daniel, and both of them are happy together.

Frederica, by contrast, has determined to take a practical approach to sexual matters, though she also suffers for love; as a schoolgirl, in *The Virgin in the Garden*, she has a hopeless crush on Alexander Wedderburn, a master at the school in which her father also teaches. In *Still Life*, she repeats this pattern by falling in love with Cambridge don Raphael Faber. But she is not hampered by lack of choice in sexual partners, once she has left home; her career as an undergraduate at Cambridge is marked by wide experimentation with a number of eager young men. Byatt also offers us a briefly romantic moment, in her suggestion that one man only would have suited this particular heroine. An aside tells us: 'It was by chance that Frederica did not meet Ralph Tempest at Jeremy Laud's formal gathering, at Harvey's debate, at Mike, Tony and Jolyon's smoky talk with pasted mottoes on the walls.' As the ideal mate for her, 'He would have made her happy and left her free, Frederica.'[76]

For each of these novelists, Bowen, Murdoch, Sayers, and Byatt, the intensity of passion which their heroines feel is also accompanied by some desire to understand it – even if they would prefer to shut out thought. Frederica Potter, in Byatt's *Still Life*, is cast as one of 'the intelligent, the watchers, the judicious,' who crave in love to 'be let off, to *feel* incontrovertibly.' Yet she remains 'doomed to be intelligent, a watcher, judicious,' rather than to be swept along on a tide of pure feeling.[77] The melodramatic events of women's lives remain the same, in these novels: pregnancy, quarrels, passion, the terror of death. Yet while these characters apply a judicious use of reason and analysis to universal problems, it is often intended to heighten the passion with which they greet them, and to emphasize their bravery. To think and also to feel is the highest value in these novels, producing prickly heroines such as Harriet Vane and Frederica Potter. Still, they are sometimes allowed happy endings, thus proving that Victorian sentimentality still exerts its own irresistible pull.

5
Betrayal

In descriptions of exalted romantic passion, betrayal is almost a mandatory part of the emotional landscape for writers such as Elizabeth Bowen and Molly Keane. It increases the tension of the drama, and also makes it more wide-ranging in its effects, since it involves other people as well. Betrayal of their two fiancés proves that Karen and Max's love in *The House in Paris*, for instance, is fateful and overmastering. It also renders their tryst deliciously secret, as Karen meditates – while in bed with Max – on the fact that her affair will never be known to have occurred by her family. This same sense of secret power is felt by Mary, in Molly Keane's *Taking Chances*, whose magnetic attraction to a dashing Irishman causes her to sleep with him, though he is her best friend's fiancé, and it is the night before the wedding. As she observes to herself, 'Love is pagan, and knows not compassion.'[1] Betrayal is appealing as a plot device, first of all because passion can be seen to overwhelm conscious thought (or at least, to obliterate any sense of possible consequences), and second, because once a deception has been perpetrated, the characters must continue to think furiously in order to sustain the web of lies they have built. In both *The House in Paris* and *Taking Chances*, Karen and Mary have become pregnant, which forces the issue, and makes their deceptions all the more dramatic when they are unveiled.

At the same time that betrayal can generate great tension in a novel, it is somewhat risky for novelists to employ it, because it can make their characters appear foolish. Those who have been deceived by their husbands, lovers or friends seem naïve. Those who have given in to passion and deceived others can appear wicked or cowardly when they are unmasked. Georgette Heyer scarcely uses it as a theme in her novels, since her forte is to rehabilitate her selfish characters (at least, the elegant and eligible rakes who wear many-layered riding capes and own large country houses). These aristocrats on the point of being reformed are always carefully painted as not having willfully deceived any of their many sexual partners, since this would place them almost beyond the pale, even if they were to seem to repent. (And, it goes without saying, they are invariably male and never female.) Thus, the amours of the Duke of Alverstoke, in *Frederica*, are described as having been numerous simply because he is 'rapidly bored' – not because he is consciously cruel, nor because he is lacking in sexual desire. His two censorious sisters cannot 'suppose, reviewing the numerous dazzling barques of frailty who had lived under his protection, that he was impervious to feminine charms. . . .'[2] More to the point, his current lover (when the novel opens) is painted as being worthless: 'A nice bit of game,' Alverstoke informs his secretary, 'but as birdwitted as she's avaricious.' The implication is that his many lovers have used him, rather than the reverse:

> Fanny, he decided, was becoming an intolerable bore. A dazzling creature, but, like so many prime articles, she was never satisfied. She now wanted a pair of cream-coloured horses to draw her barouche; last week it had been a diamond necklace. He had given her that, and it would serve for a farewell gift.[3]

Having paid off his emotional debts, he cannot be perceived as having betrayed his paramours. His fastidiousness (in terms of the social system which Heyer has constructed) in only forming liaisons with women whose hearts are incapable of being broken qualifies him for marriage to the spunky heroine, Frederica, to whom he is supposed to have developed a deep attachment by the novel's end. Moreover, the earlier amours both set her off to advantage (she does not bore him) and they are justified because they have driven him to pessimism (which is now resolved): 'he wished to spend the rest of his life with her, because she was the perfect woman he had never expected to encounter.'[4]

Those virtuous characters in Heyer's novels who feel driven to deceive others are seen to be fully conscious of the terrible evil they are perpetrating, and if they are truly good, are even rescued from the act of betrayal in the nick of time. Frederica's younger sister, Charis, in the same novel, elopes with her suitor, Endymion, leaving behind an explanatory note to her sister which bears evidence of tears having been shed over it, and which 'consists entirely of pleas for forgiveness, mingled with assurances that only desperation could have driven the writer to take so dreadful a step.' Still, Frederica remains furious at her sister's defection. 'At first glance, Charis appeared to have subscribed herself *wicked Charis*; but closer scrutiny revealed that the word was not *wicked*, but *wretched*. Frederica thought bitterly that *wicked* more exactly described her sister.'[5] Since Heyer does not allow her characters to lose face, however, the guilty lovers are apprehended during the middle of the ceremony, and persuaded to desist from their hasty action. The Duke's secretary, Charles, reports having seen the pair enter St. George's, and recounts to the Duke and Frederica his masterful diversion of the proceedings, which have led to Charis being taken to her fiancé's mother's house (a course which is in every way proper). The older characters are able to contrive a respectable marriage for the young pair.

Good women do not deceive others. This is the basic rule. Likewise, they are not, themselves, betrayed, without considerable cost to self-esteem (and, thus, to the reader's admiration for them). Olivia Manning, for instance, takes especial care to never allow a hint of Guy Pringle being sexually unfaithful to his wife, Harriet, in her two World War II trilogies. Harriet feels personally betrayed by her husband again and again, suffering from his carelessness in appropriating her possessions and ignoring her in preference to his large and convivial group of friends. He teaches late nights at the university, mounts Shakespearean dramatic productions that keep him out until all hours, and reads continually instead of spending any time with her when they go away on holiday together. Every example of his relative indifference to her is given – except that of a particular interest in another woman. Manning goes so far as to underscore this, in her depiction of the *femme fatale* character, Edwina, with whom the Pringles share a flat in Cairo, in the final novels of the series. The annoying presence of the wildly popular (and single) Edwina comprises the epitome of female rivalry for Harriet. In one crucial scene, Guy takes a heart-shaped brooch from Harriet's bedside, as she lies suffering in hospital, and pockets it (over her outraged objections) in order to give it to Edwina, as it will complete her costume for a play which he is producing.

The fact that this action is not supposed to signal a romantic attraction to Edwina, however, is emphasized in two ways, in Manning's final novel, *The Sum of Things*. Guy remembers the taking of the brooch and regrets it later, when he believes that Harriet has died. And during this period of grieving for her, Edwina tries to seduce or at least to attract him – something which she has succeeded in doing with a number of male characters. But he pays her no attention. This absorption in ideas and genial camaraderie is, perhaps, intended to be indicated by such behavior on Guy's part. However, it would also have been humiliating in a particular way for Harriet to have been deceived, and Manning seems careful to avoid this.

In this chapter, I want to look at various examples of novels in which betrayal plays a large role. It is an important theme in many of these books, and is often an integral part of the fabric of these plots because it provides a possible intersection for violent, obsessive emotion with reason and thought. For novels in which melodrama is habitually tempered by irony, it is an excellent way of focusing the question of self-justification for the heroines. Desire generates rivalry between women who – ideally – ought to be respectful to each other, rather than competing in vicious ways. Their desperate passion offers the only excuse for such behavior.

I want to start with the betrayal that the older generation makes, in relation to younger people in the novels: this is an abnegation of their social role, and a moral defection from what they ought to be doing. Many of the older characters are destructive parents, through carelessness or downright greed and exploitation, and some of the novels follow the progress of decay through a couple of generations. In Molly Keane's *Treasure Hunt*, for example, the older generation has eaten up all of the capital which sustains the family estate. Elizabeth Bowen's older characters range from being simply selfish and thoughtless (Elfrida in *Friends and Relations*) to silly (the buffoonish Lady Waters in *To the North*) to intensely wicked (Mme. Fisher in *The House in Paris*). The most poignant of these failures is that of Anna in *The Death of the Heart*, who refuses to be a surrogate mother to her orphaned half-sister, Portia, and who ends by betraying her utterly.

I then want to go on to look at straightforward sexual rivalry, in Molly Keane's *Taking Chances*, where the 'gallant' yet rapacious *femme fatale* steals her best friend's husband. This novel is written in a tradition of realism, and thus it makes a contrast to the more stylized fictions of Iris Murdoch, who makes betrayal a central theme in her novels *A Severed Head* and *The Sacred and Profane Love Machine*. Psychologists play major roles in both of these novels, thus drawing a direct connection between the ways in which the characters think about their actions of betrayal. Next I consider Salley Vickers' novel *Miss Garnet's Angel*, which achieves a resolution of the wound which a betrayal inflicts. This plot is a double twist of betrayal, as the heroine is tricked into betraying another character; but forgiveness is found to be possible. I finish by looking at Barbara Pym's *Jane and Prudence*, which turns betrayal to positive effect.

The older generation in Molly Keane's *Treasure Hunt* has betrayed its younger family members through thoughtless selfishness stemming from hedonism; it is not intended as a malicious act, yet it has this effect. When the novel opens, Sir Roderick, the owner of Ballyroden, a large Anglo-Irish country house (who has spent all of the available capital on himself and his dependents in the mansion) has just died, and the bankruptcy is shortly to be discovered. One of the family members calls for champagne to drink a tribute to his memory. But the departed squire has drunk all of them out of house and home, as is soon made apparent by the insistence of the lawyer who reads the will. It is left to the young hero, Phillip, who has come back from grim experience fighting in the Great War, to organize everything, and to institute economies which his mother and uncle find horrifying and unthinkable.

Part of the comedy is the incomprehension of the older generation, who cannot believe that what either the lawyer or the young squire tells them is true. Phillip attempts to explain: 'Darlings, we're pretty well sunk and broke. Dear old Dad just spent it all – his own and yours, too, I'm afraid.' His mother and uncle object to this strenuously: 'Consuelo said hotly: "He spent it on us as much as on himself."' This is immediately seconded: '"Yes," Hercules clamoured, "he gave us a royal time always."'[6] Such gratitude and good-heartedness earns these characters eventual redemption – the sheer ebullience of spirit of Consuelo and Hercules cannot be damped, even when they are allowed only a single glass of sherry per day, and when they must put up with the infuriating imposition of Paying Guests who come to share Ballyroden from London.

Since this is a comedy, the Paying Guests eventually prove to be the salvation of the entire situation. The ultimate result of the original betrayal (or, at least, mismanagement) of the older generation is a happy ending – though it must occur through a *deus ex machina*, when the long-lost treasure hoarded by the charmingly mad Aunt Anna Rose is discovered. A large part of the comic drama, however, is that the parent figures, Consuelo and Hercules, are like children; they cannot be reformed, and it is impossible to discipline or control them. Phillip forbids his widowed mother and his uncle to spend any money; but they sneak out to the races, and lose huge sums. The irony inherent in this situation is that the younger generation are the sensible ones; in the eyes of Eustace, one of the Paying Guests, Phillip and Veronica 'seemed to him like the Victorian age succeeding the age of Elegance.' Yet it is also their humility and lack of rancour that makes them deserve their eventual good fortune – which Eustace helps to bring about. He tries to rouse them to a sense of urgency about claiming their inheritance (in the form of the long-lost rubies):

> Their outlook, he sometimes thought with a certain sadness, was not unlike that of two plumber's mates looking backwards without much interest or rancor to an illegitimate ducal grandfather. The present struggle to live and continue to live blinded them to the color and glamour of their family's yesterdays and days before yesterday.[7]

The 'treasure hunt' takes the form of breaking through Aunt Anna Rose's self-protective madness, which masks a long-ago trauma on her wedding night, a task of discovery which Eustace sets himself as a quest to perform. Her deliberate escape into fantasies of continual world travel is both consciously willed and involuntary, as a psychological response. He is fascinated by her, yet also angry at her unfair advantages in assuming an escape from life which seems to affect others adversely:

> She was in no sense a shadow of that desperate child-bride she fled. She was alluring, preposterous, amusing, teasing, adorable, what lady you would have her be. And she was carried, upborne, isolated on the air and breath of beauty. It glorified unfairly every little action, amplifying and enhancing all she did. Exaggerating all she was.[8]

This novel offers a picture of a complex family dynamic which is successfully resolved, by the agency of a kindly outsider. Still, it is made clear that the abnegation of responsibility by Sir Roderick and others of his generation has heavy consequences for later generations.

A similar situation is portrayed in Caroline Blackwood's *Great Granny Webster*, which describes the figure of Lady Dunmartin, the narrator's grandmother, who goes progressively mad in her huge, Anglo-Irish mansion, while her husband either will not or cannot see the extent of her insanity. His determination to believe that she is at least nominally the head of the household makes him insist that the footman consult her daily with the household dinner menus, which she counters with various responses:

> Some mornings she asked him to come in. She would take the menus from him and, while he waited uneasily, glance down them with the unseeing eyes of someone in a dream, and finally place a few impatient random ticks next to some of the names of the French dishes which had been suggested to her.

On other occasions, his appearance 'had the effect of inflaming her most paranoid and irrational terrors'; or she might throw a hysterical scene and '[scream] obscenities.' This behavior is, in a way, consistent for her with her view of the task which the footman has been made to perform: 'she saw his whole mission with the menus as totally insane.' Yet, poignantly, this daily power struggle stems from a desire for proper order from the head of the household, who wants to show his wife honor and respect: this 'unnerving situation [was] created by Grandfather Dunmartin, who still refused to abandon the idea that it was important for his wife's self-esteem and her emotional well-being that she be allowed to choose the food that was to be served that day in her household.'[9] This constitutes an oblique betrayal on the part of the grandfather, for allowing her to retain her position of authority.

Her husband eventually takes her to London, in hopes of a cure for her mental derangement, but nothing can be done. The most dramatic scene occurs at the occasion of her grandson's christening, which the narrator has heard by report from other members of the family, many years later. The grandmother has been brought back from London to Ireland to attend the celebration, and makes an attack upon the baby, attempting to kill him. This is directly allied to her own sense of her dementia: '"He has bad blood!" my grandmother started screaming. "Can't you see that I'm doing it for *him*? Can't you see it's better for the poor little creature if I smash out his tiny brains against a stone!"'[10]

This is a novel about total dissociation from one's family, particularly in the dominating figure of the dour, Scottish elderly woman, the narrator's Great Granny Webster, of whom she observes:

> Her own heart was all she cared about. She had produced three generations of descendants and lived to know that none of them could have the slightest importance to her, any more than all the leaves that have flown yearly from its branches can have much importance to an aged oak.[11]

While this novel is not exactly bitter in tone, it has a haunting sense of sadness for an older generation which has so closed itself off from life. The young woman who narrates the story keeps herself deliberately in the background, revealing almost nothing of herself – which suggests that the telling of these tales is undertaken in order that she might understand her background, but is not prepared to speak of their ultimate effects on her life. This makes the novel much less of a story of direct, personal betrayal – merely one of malicious egotism and withdrawal.

Elizabeth Bowen's fiction, being much more concerned with social situations and interconnecting social circles, offers an extraordinary range in characters of the older, fiendishly dominating type. Mrs. Kerr, in *The Hotel*, is infinitely remote and malicious; Lady Elfrida in *Friends and Relations* is a dangerous but comic buffoon, as is Lady Waters in *To the North*; Mme. Fisher in *The House in Paris* is both desperate and rivetingly evil, representing the extreme of this type of older women who deliberately meddle in younger characters' lives.

Elfrida in *Friends and Relations* affects the younger generation largely by her outrageous behavior as a mother – this is a very conventional kind of failure, and carries with it a suitably Victorian ring of reproach. She describes her resulting situation of being a social outcast to Janet, years later, when she recounts an episode where she has met her cook on the street, wearing one of Elfrida's own dresses: 'Of course I am always ruined: one can't be more.'[12] What is amusing in Bowen's portrayal, however, is that Elfrida has ebulliently survived. Janet tells Edward wearily, when he objects to his mother's apparently light-hearted behavior, that everyone in their circle is secretly jealous of her: 'she seems to have such a lovely time.'[13] Still, the root of the dysfunction in the novel stems from her desertion (as even Elfrida sees it) of Edward during his early childhood. Though Janet reproves him for his resentment, saying, 'Nothing ever happened to *you*,' the pain of the situation remains.[14]

Lady Waters, in Bowen's *To the North*, is a comic figure as well, and she is a contrast to Elfrida in Bowen's previous novel because most of her effect on others is deliberate meddling (not the thoughtless by-product of passionate behavior), and it is usually done to adults, rather than to hapless children. Her reputation for interference is notorious, and in the specific context of an amateur who wishes to behave like a professional consultant. When she makes her entrance at a party in Gerda's flat, mid-way through the novel, she has garnered a reputation as a formidable antagonist: 'she sat down and gazed round the room with impartial interest. The psychologist, who had met her, hastily looked away.'[15]

Lady Waters is dangerous because she stirs up emotion in others: 'she enlarged her own life into ripples of apprehension on everybody's behalf . . . she entered one's house on a current that set the furniture bobbing; at Rutland Gate destiny shadowed her tea-table.'[16] The response of the two heroines to her is a key indication of their different temperaments, and her effect on their lives – yet this also shows why she exercises so magnetic an attraction on Cecilia. She feels drawn to her aunt, fascinated by the chance to pour out her heart in a confessional setting. Emmeline avoids her altogether: 'While Emmeline simply said, gently and not very often, that she wished Georgina'd been dead for a hundred years, Cecilia daily declared her to be a scourge and a menace.'[17] This is what she proves to be, though by no means intending it. While Lady Waters is not responsible for Emmeline – who, although orphaned, is fully grown – she does fail to be of material use in Emmeline's *débâcle* with Markie. Lady Waters' betrayals are those of omission, yet they remain a huge and adverse influence on her circle.

As for Mme. Fisher in *The House in Paris*, she is the archetype of a fiendish, controlling older woman. As a young man just arrived from the provinces, Max becomes her protégé, describing Mme. Fisher's formidable powers to his lover Karen, years later: 'I was given a letter to her when I first came to Paris. Twelve years. Till this year, I have not tried to separate what she made me from what I am.' This attempt at self-definition sends danger signals about Mme. Fisher's continued hold over him; her influence remains all-pervasive: 'From the first,' Max explains, 'she acted on me like acid on a plate. . . . What her wit ate out is certainly gone.'[18] Her taunt about his affair with Karen leads directly to Max's suicide, and her resulting state of paralysis can be seen to be a melodramatically poetic justice. She is contrasted in this novel with Karen's mother, Mrs. Michaelis, who does try to exert a proper yet respectful and solicitous control of her daughter's passionate impulses, but whom Karen despises for her distance and discretion.

Bowen's older women characters are aggressively unmaternal. The one who seems most to *want* to become a mother-figure – the dreaded Lady Waters in *To the North* – does a great deal of harm, by encouraging her protégés to pity themselves. Anna, in *The Death of the Heart*, is placed in a painful dilemma as a mother-figure, as she does not choose this role; it is thrust upon her. It is assumed that she will act as a mother to Portia, whose mother has just died. But Anna has lost two children of her own, through miscarriages, and in a way, Irene's mothering of Portia is a silent reproach. (The Quaynes' house-keeper, Matchett, tells Portia, '*She* never filled [the nursery] for all she is so clever.') In more than one way, Anna must fight with the ghost of Irene, whom she despises. Matchett is the one who takes over the role of comforting Portia, telling her that Anna had had the right 'to be where I am this minute,' at her bedside; but Anna has clearly rejected this.[19] This domestic background is crucial to the profound betrayal which Anna perpetrates, by reading Portia's diary. This revelation is the catalyst which sends Portia hurtling out of the house, to seek refuge with Major Brutt. It is a fundamental betrayal, because it symbolizes looking at someone's private thoughts without compassion.

Part of Anna's lack of maternal caring comes from the fact that she too has lost her mother at an early age; the parallels with Jane Austen's *Emma* are clear, in the fact that she has had a governess, Mrs. Heccomb. She is inadequate, and in the modern age she cannot prevent Anna from taking up with a cad such as Robert Pidgeon. This is still a sore point between Thomas and Anna, as he asks in disdain, late in the novel, 'was she ever much of a chaperone?'[20] But the dissociation between Anna and Portia runs deeper than this. Anna observes, in the final conversation over dinner, 'Though she and I may wish to make a new start, we hardly shall, I'm afraid. I shall always insult her; she will always persecute me. . . .'[21]

The betrayal of the younger generation by its elders is a theme which is handled in various ways in these novels; it can be reclaimed and reversed, as in Keane's *Treasure Hunt*, or rendered a curiosity with only distant effects, as in Blackwood's *Great Granny Webster*. In Bowen's novels, it becomes a force with many and varied influences.

In more direct confrontation between characters, female rivalry occurs when one woman takes away another's lover. In Molly Keane's world, this happens because love is so overwhelming a passion. The *femme fatale*, Mary, in *Taking Chances*, wonders, 'Just why is it so appallingly difficult to get what one really wants from life?' and is not restrained from seizing her desire by consideration for others' feelings.[22] Her betrayal of another does not stem from a desire to hurt or punish, but has been caused by a sudden flaring of unexpected, intoxicating passion. Visiting a country house in Ireland in order to be a bridesmaid in her friend Maeve's wedding, she falls into bed with Rowley, the bridegroom, on the night before the wedding. She soon discovers herself to be pregnant from this encounter, and to try to cover this situation, she quickly marries Maeve's brother, Roguey (who also adores her). Her despair – when she and her lover next meet in company – leads her to try to commit suicide, or at least to abort her pregnancy. In the end, however, Rowley determines to elope with her – by which action she is not only 'taking chances,' but taking her best friend's husband away from her. The kind of temperament which both lovers share is that of sublime ruthlessness: an older character, Edyth, pronounces that 'Those two are past ordinary pales, because they're not afraid of anything. And when you fear nothing for yourself you've no pity for other people.' In Mary's own experience, 'love is pagan and knows not compassion,' and the thrill of it compels her: 'a hell of a rake she was, and chanced things gallantly.'[23]

This is one kind of heroine – the frankly sensuous *femme fatale*, who is contrasted with the virginal, sweet, docile Maeve, who, on her wedding day,

> was woven through with the bright, intense glamour that endues only the actions of those single-hearted and respectable virgins who have journeyed circumspectly down the happy canal of uneventful maidenhood to the lock whose first name is wed.[24]

Although this is a labored construction, it expresses what several of the characters in Keane's novel have been thinking or fearing. They wonder if Maeve, in her modesty and sedateness, will be able to satisfy the notably adventurous Rowley once they are married. The answer, resoundingly, is no – from the very start of their marriage. And it is based on predictable character types.

This is one way of presenting a drama centered on female rivalry: defining women in terms of two opposing types, either innocent and virtuous or daring and dangerous. Also, however, this serves as a useful plot device because it sparks extreme tension over the question of what her characters will decide to do. When Mary and Rowley meet up again, later in the novel, it is a purely melodramatic situation. Rowley does not know that Mary still loves him, and that moreover, she is carrying his child (rather than that of her husband). The two lovers eventually decide to go off together, even though this means living in exile (since they cannot stay in Ireland). The betrayal is made complete, when Maeve's hapless brother, Jer, tells Maeve after their departure that Mary's unborn child does not belong to her (recently deceased) brother – thus completely destroying even her illusion of happiness. Keane's novel is manifestly melodramatic, punishing its virtuous characters and rewarding the *femme fatale* and her lover – or at least, sending them off-stage together. Yet in this instance, their betrayal of Maeve acts as an affirmation of their compelling passion for each other, in the height of romantic union.

Iris Murdoch is much more stylized in her portrayal of sexual betrayal; the characters in her fiction move with a jerky, predictable instability. But her use of it stems from the same source as Keane's does. Her narrator Martin Lynch-Gibbon in *A Severed Head* tells us, at one point, 'Extreme love has a voracious appetite.'[25] Betrayal is an extension of the intensity of passion, and it overrides any objection to it by means of its fantastic power. Three of Murdoch's novels show different angles on this.

The hero of her early novel *The Nice and the Good*, John Ducane, is caught in relationships with two women who feel themselves to be rivals for his affections. A civil servant in his forties, he begins an affair with a younger woman, Jessica Bird, and is appalled at the frantic grief she shows when he wants to end their relationship, finding himself unable to break with her. In part out of apathy, in part out of hapless good-heartedness (her sobbing makes him feel 'like a murderer'), he continues to see her, since she has threatened suicide in the extremity of her pain at abandonment.[26] At the same time, he begins a flirtation with Kate, the wife of Octavian, who is Ducane's boss in the Civil Service. The married couple have created their own stylized formula for adultery, in which Kate reports her conquests and *affaires du coeur* to her husband. Kate tells Octavian of her impending conquest of John's heart – with the understanding that theirs will be a platonic affair only. She gravely discusses the arrangement with John, who agrees with its essential rightness: '"Yes," he said gravely. "Yes. I have thought about it a lot and I do think it is all right."' She replies, 'Octavian – well, you know what Octavian feels. You understand everything.' This scene is comic because of the arrogant self-assurance of the two characters, and the solemn contract which they make – and which will obviously fail: 'Dear Kate,' John tells her, 'I'm a lonely person. And you're a generous woman. And we're both very rational. All's well here.'[27]

Still, Murdoch suggests that betrayal of any kind, even of this seemingly frank and above-board nature, is fraught with potential danger. Octavian, for his part, engages in some activities which he does not report to his wife, such as trysts after hours with secretaries at the Civil Service offices. Both Kate and Octavian, who are described as being 'ebulliently married,' nonetheless use their position as minor royalty (they are 'well off and enjoyed the deep superiority of the socially secure') to manipulate others for their own pleasure.[28] Their endless discussions of Kate's conquests are intended to excite themselves sexually in their marriage. Kate is duly punished for this acquisitiveness, however, when she learns of John Ducane's previous relationship with Jessica. Ironically, she is deeply hurt, feeling that she has been deceived; but this anguish reinforces the basic point of betrayal. Everyone expects to be the one and only lover in a beloved's life. John Ducane appals both Kate – although it is understood that he has taken her as a flirtatious, platonic lover – and Jessica, his former lover whom he now wishes to abandon, by the fact of their simultaneous presence in his life. Both women are indignant at learning that he has talked to both of them at the same time, and regard themselves as having been basely deceived by him. He confesses to Kate (after she has received a letter from Jessica): 'You'll just have to digest it, Kate, if you can. I've acted wrongly and I have in a way deceived you. I mean, I implied I had no entanglements and this certainly looks like one. I'm sorry.'[29]

A darker triangle of betrayal is also set up in the novel between two married characters who have parted from each other when Paula, the wife, has taken a lover. Richard, the husband, has discovered the two together, and has struck Eric; in a tragi-comic scenario, a bookcase falls on the hapless Eric and he eventually loses his foot in consequence of this injury. Although Richard and Paula have long been separated, they are clearly still in love and are suited to each other. Part of John Ducane's penance, as he reformulates his erroneous view of himself as an essentially good character, is to help to reunite these two. (The existence of the nine-year-old twins, children of Paula and Richard, also serves to point a moral of the inherently gripping irrationality of sexual passion; the older characters think to themselves that when the children grow into their sexuality, their characters will change.) This novel gains part of its force from the redemption of previous betrayals; even the deeply melancholy Willy, who earlier in his life has suffered in concentration camps (and who finally confesses that he has betrayed others in this situation) is granted a lover in the form of Jessica.

Murdoch makes betrayal the key situation in her novel *The Sacred and Profane Love Machine*, whose elaborate title refers to the human mind, and its predictable, mechanistic responses to sexual stimuli – and also, its opposing yet complementary passions for sacred and profane elements. This is one of the most elaborate of Murdoch's stories of sexual betrayal, as it describes an affair which has been going on for some nine years, as yet undetected. Blaise Edward has had a mistress in London for many years, while living in the country with his wife, Harriet, and their adolescent son, David. He is a psychologist, and has developed an ingenious means of getting away once each week in order to see Emily, his mistress, and their son, Luca. He creates the fiction of a patient, Magnus Bowles, whom he must counsel in an overnight session. Blaise is – figuratively – of two minds about these domestic arrangements, compartmentalizing his life so that he can move back and forth between the two ménages. Harriet has been seemingly won over to his weekly sojourns in town: 'She was now entirely used to Blaise's regular absences with his nocturnal patient,' the narrator says. But the impact of this on her subconscious is apparent: 'Only, as it seemed to Blaise, Harriet's curious and more frequent night fears attested some unconscious feeling in his wife that all was not well.'[30]

The appearance of Luca at Blaise's house in the country, at the opening of the novel, signals the impending revelation of his long-standing betrayal of his wife. The novel depicts the raging and contradictory responses of each of the major characters to this fraught situation. Part of the comedy of this is Harriet's attempt (as a wife) to patronize Emily (the mistress), when the two first meet. Harriet tells her: 'Naturally you know it isn't my fault – but I can imagine how you feel. I'm sorry you've had such a bad time. Blaise has behaved badly to you, I know, he has told me everything.' Emily has the last word, here, as she snaps in response, 'I doubt if he has told you *everything*,' going on to patronize Harriet in return: 'And I haven't had a bad time, though I'm sure you'd like to think so. I've had the fun. You're the one who's been swindled. Poor old you.'[31] This is another fantastically melodramatic novel, in which, among other exotic events, Harriet eventually abducts Luca and is shot by terrorists in an airport lounge. Part of its power stems from this inventiveness on Murdoch's part; she is never afraid to make dramatic events occur in her novels, to astonish her reader. But part of its interest lies in the internal psychological battle and the female rivalry which underlies the plot. These characters struggle to be rational, and to control their thoughts and actions – not least, so that they can manipulate their antagonists into acceding to their own desires. They realize that they are driven by the passions of their minds, which exist tantalizingly outside of their own control, as with Harriet's dreams and 'night fears.' The pack of stray dogs which Harriet has gathered around her, at her house in the country, acts as a tangible expression of her internal rage, and almost succeeds in killing Blaise, late in the novel.

The resolution of the romantic triangle is predictable in its simplicity: Harriet dies, and Emily is left with a clear field of entitlement to Blaise. She entirely supplants her rival, replacing the symbolic kitchen table with a modern, modish Scandinavian one, devoid of sentimentality. The two marry and create a new household together: '[Blaise] and Emily worked silently, surreptitiously, feverishly, like people trying to conceal a crime, to erase all traces of Harriet's existence from Hood House.'[32] The novel is, finally, as much about the continuation of deception, or of the fantastical self-deceptiveness of the human mind, which pursues Blaise. Though he realizes that his predicament has been settled in a bizarre way, he soon adapts to what appears to be good fortune: 'Secretly, cautiously, he felt that he had come through the fire and had probably emerged unscathed. He had *survived*.' What Murdoch emphasizes is the readiness of the mind to adapt to good fortune, even to appropriate it as deserved. Blaise mourns his wife, yet marvels at his sheer good luck in having painlessly been relieved of her existence:

> That Harriet should simply have been killed, meaninglessly slaughtered by people who knew nothing of *his* predicament, that his problem could have been so absolutely solved in this extraordinary way, struck Blaise first as being unendurably accidental, and later as being fated.[33]

This irony bracingly counteracts the melodrama of the plot.

Murdoch's *A Severed Head* also portrays adultery and deception, in a fiendishly complex tangle of interlocking betrayals. The narrator, Martin Lynch-Gibbon, begins to tell the story while having a tryst with his mistress, Georgie Hands, and goes home to discover his wife, Antonia, in bed with Palmer Anderson, her psychoanalyst. While he urges calm discussion of what is to happen next, Martin must cope with his shock; and this is merely the first of successive revelations of betrayal, which continue to unfold. The immediate irony is that the betrayer, Martin, has been betrayed. But when the full intensity and range of his wife's deception are subsequently revealed, he becomes completely disoriented. When he learns that Antonia has been having a long-standing affair with Alexander, his brother, he must revise his whole view of the past. The most wounding betrayals are incestuous; and they strike at deep articles of faith. 'No marriage is ever quite right,' he observes, late in the novel, 'But I believed in ours.'[34]

Part of the outrage in Martin is spurred by the fact that, between them, Palmer Anderson and Alexander take away each of the women whom Martin has loved. This results in grieving and outrage on his part. At the same time, he is given a prime opportunity to blackmail Anderson in turn, which is satisfying to the reader as well. And he ends the novel by having obtained the one thing he has most passionately desired, a fulfillment of his visceral attraction to Honor Klein, who is Palmer's half-sister, a passion which is magnetic. They both view this as being beyond any ordinary emotion or desire: as Honor asserts, it has 'nothing to do with happiness, nothing whatever.'[35] In a way, this novel offers such a dizzying succession of changing partners that it can be difficult to take the characters' feelings seriously. They move in a well-choreographed constellation of betrayals and counter-betrayals; yet it is the seeming fatefulness of the plot's resolution that is so satisfying. Each of the characters is alternately punished and rewarded, in fairly equal measure. Part of Murdoch's genius is to show the almost independent actions of the brain in times of extreme emotional duress, and sexual betrayal provides an excellent stage for this drama.

Salley Vickers' *Miss Garnet's Angel* combines a story of sexual betrayal with a Cinderella plot, which is a fascinating twist because the woman who is translated into a delightful situation is found to be naïve – a handicap which then transforms her elevation into grand company into an experience of suffering. The heroine, Julia Garnet, is a retired schoolmistress who has gone to Venice to live for six months upon retiring from her job. She shows herself to be brave in setting out alone to go abroad, yet this act also acknowledges the generosity of a recently deceased friend, Harriet, who has willed her modest fortune to Julia. Upon her arrival in Italy, Julia tentatively begins to make friends, one of whom is Carlo, a cultured older man who takes her to musical events and to meals in expensive restaurants. Although she puzzles over why such an elegant man should want to spend time with her, she convinces herself that she must, contrary to her belief, be a worthy companion. The shock of betrayal, when it comes, is severe: she realizes that he has courted her as a way of trying to ingratiate himself with Nicco, the young Italian boy to whom Julia is teaching English. This is a double shock, because she has unwittingly betrayed a third person, without even knowing that she was doing so.

Vickers shows very accurately the precise way in which the heroine's mind works, when she discovers the betrayal which Carlo has perpetrated. Her first clue is that Nicco begins to avoid her. (Part of the dynamic of this book is that the reader realizes long before the heroine does what has happened.) But when she finally discovers the truth – that Carlo has been using her to get closer to Nicco – her mind suddenly flashes back to the exact moment when she appeared in the framing shop with him:

> Out of her memory, clear and unprocessed, came the recollection of the day she had gone with Nicco to the glass-cutters. A man. A man had come out as she had been worrying about paying for the picture, fussing with the Italian currency. The man and Nicco had collided. . . .

Her brain suddenly connects the identity of the man with the man whom she knows:

> The man, tall and silver-haired, she suddenly perceived was Carlo, and in a moment of painful understanding she saw, watching his

> hungry, yearning look after the retreating Nicco, that she had been the unwitting dupe of his wish to find the boy who had accompanied her that day.

This is a fundamental betrayal of her hard-won sense of self-worth: 'It was not her whom Carlo had wanted to befriend – it was Nicco.'[36]

As the novel unfolds, she becomes reconciled to Carlo – even though he has done her the further disservice of destroying her relationship with Nicco, who no longer trusts her. Still, the betrayal has a significant mitigating aspect to it: Miss Garnet is a fool, and not a knave. Her betrayal was unwitting, and not intended to cause harm. This makes recovery possible, and she is rewarded with other friends and passions, including a fierce aesthetic attachment to the 'angel' – painted on a rare panel – of the title.

One final example of the dark side of passion that I would like to discuss briefly is Byatt's novel *Possession: A Romance*. The subtitle announces the book's main preoccupation, and almost verges on defensiveness, in insisting that this is the focus in what is otherwise a satirical novel about academic research. The plot turns on the revelation of a sexual betrayal, in the passionate, month-long tryst in Yorkshire of two Victorian writers, Randolph Henry Ash and Christabel LaMotte. This constitutes a double betrayal: Ash of his wife, Ellen, and Christabel of her lesbian lover, Blanche. It gives the twentieth-century academic scholars something significant to discover, a century later, and the lurking secret gives the plot some of the impetus of detective fiction. But part of the result of uncovering this long-hidden mystery is the revelation of all of the subsequent destruction and estrangement that has occurred in consequence of it. The events which occurred in this Victorian (and tacitly oppressive) context are chilling – both in conventional yet melodramatic terms. Unbridled passion, in the shape of a month spent together as lovers in Yorkshire, results in the birth of a child to Christabel (although the daughter fares well with her adoptive parents), but also the alienation and humiliation of Ash's wife and the suicide of Christabel's life-long companion.

This is a novel written for a late-twentieth-century audience, and appeals to the values which have been encouraged by the sexual revolution of the 1960s; therefore, it is deliberately anachronistic. But this also means that it is interesting to consider what the novel does with the change in cultural views about sexual fidelity. In contemporary terms, it seems reasonable – even deserved, in relation to Ellen Ash – to suffer her husband to spend one month in Yorkshire with a passionate female poet.

Ellen has been frigid since the beginning of her marriage, which means that Ash has never been given the chance to have sexual relations in the approved, Victorian manner. Still, she is deeply wounded, punishing him even on his death-bed with the withholding of Christabel's final letter to him. Blanche is similar, in that she takes Christabel's defection grievously to heart, going so far as to purloin Ash's letters before they have come to Christabel's hand. Her jealousy burns from the first, when she sees that her lover is receiving letters from Randolph Henry Ash, and as Christabel describes it, somewhat acidly, their ménage has become one of mutual resentment: 'This house – so happy once – is full of weeping and wailing and Black Headache like a Painful Pall. . . .'[37]

What Byatt shows so skillfully in this novel is the embarrassment of having a jealous partner. Christabel might insist that she is not betraying Blanche, but she knows that this is not strictly true, in terms of the unspoken agreement which they have made. Their choice has been to live apart from the world, as women together. Ash rends this willed enclosure.

But this makes the drama all the more intense, and our *Schadenfreude* at these characters' actions all the greater. Since part of this novel is set in the Victorian period, it is expected that its nineteenth-century characters will value loyalty and integrity. This makes their defection all the more passionate and significant; no casual decision has been made, when Ash and LaMotte travel north to Yorkshire together. Furthermore, it is intended to be a doubly romantic tryst, since the two also write poetry about their feelings for each other, and are presumed to be inspired by their mutual passion. All of these elements combine to make their affair a betrayal of particular people (Ellen and Blanche) and also of a code of values (sexual fidelity and a wider conception of loyalty to a spouse or friend).

The theme of betrayal in these novels, whether it is the abnegation of responsibility of parent figures to their protégés, or the ruthless snatching of a friend's lover, has its roots in selfishness. Often it is desperation to survive that causes these fictional characters to act in a malicious way; or, as in the case of Mary in Molly Keane's *Taking Chances*, betrayal is perceived as an expression of gallantry and adventure, which will have no adverse consequences. It is almost invariably allied to dark passion, lending portentous weight to these decisions.

Still, it can be made the source of comedy, where characters do not have their feelings engaged too deeply. Barbara Pym's *Jane and Prudence* offers a bizarre yet cheerful version of this story. It is a novel in which the less sympathetic woman triumphs over her competitor, and carries off the man in question. Yet although the heroine is indeed beaten out by a female rival, she turns it into an acceptable occurrence, lightly rushing through her grieving, and setting out on fresh adventures. The undercurrent of real emotion can be felt, or these books would not be so compelling as they are; still, Pym hits off a certain resonance of emotional detachment that is both shrewd and poignant.

In *Jane and Prudence,* two women compete for the same man, the elegant yet superficial widower, Fabian Driver. One is Jessie Morrow, the paid companion of the elderly and authoritative Miss Doggett: Jessie is a manifestly neo-Victorian figure, in terms of her dependent position to the older woman. The other is a very modern young woman, Prudence Bates, who holds a degree from Oxford, and works as a research assistant for a scholar in London. Jessie is more cunning, and moreover, lives next door to Fabian, and so has more opportunity to plan a seductive strategy. She is also more cynical, as she has witnessed his chronic infidelities to his former wife. As she tells the newly-arrived vicar's wife in the village, Jane Cleveland, 'Her death came as a great shock to him – he had almost forgotten her existence.'[38] This line takes its place in a tradition of British comedy, and might have come from a Noel Coward play; we understand the ridiculousness of such a man, yet also the fact that this is one way in which such feelings are allowed to be expressed. Fabian may be a habitual deceiver of women, but Jessie wants him as a husband nonetheless.

The most direct expression of antagonism between the two rivals for Fabian's attention occurs during tea-time in the village, where Fabian and both women are present, in addition to several other characters. Jessie deliberately spills a cup of tea over Prudence's lilac cotton dress, necessitating her withdrawal from the fray. This is masterful in that it focuses all the attention on the dress itself, thus diminishing Prudence as a person and also annoying the men, who have been dominating the scene: 'Prudence felt foolish and irritated at being the centre of so much fuss. Edward and Fabian were perhaps a little annoyed at having attention diverted from their weariness, and it seemed inevitable now that the party should break up. . . .' The older women are relentlessly practical, talking over Prudence's head: '"I am worried about Miss Bates's dress," said Miss Doggett to Jane. "If you don't put it to soak in cold water at once that tea will stain."' But its real effect is to disrupt the parting between Fabian and Prudence, as she must now be led away for ministrations to her clothes: '"Well, Prudence," said Fabian, rather at a loss, "I expect I shall be seeing you soon in Town."' As Jane notes, this is 'Not a very satisfactory leave-taking. . . .'[39]

Part of the comedy of this chasing after Fabian is the uncertainty on everyone else's part as to precisely what extent feminine wiles have been employed in pursuit of him. Has Jessie slept with Fabian? Miss Doggett shudders when she considers this possibility, though she is never to know. As for Prudence, her friend Jane tries to ascertain the same thing, when she visits her overnight at her flat in London: was she or was she not Fabian's mistress? Prudence's reply is wonderfully evasive: '"Well, I mean to say – one just doesn't ask," Prudence went on. "Surely either one is or one isn't and there's no need to ask coy questions about it. Now, Jane, what about a hot-water bottle?"'[40]

Yet it is not a light question. After Fabian's engagement to Jessie is discovered, Jane concludes that Prudence 'had not been Fabian's mistress, after all,' more for her own sense of defining the situation than because she actually knows it to be true; and she comforts herself with this reflection:

> it did seem as if the worst – which was what Jane called it in her own mind – had not happened. This should certainly make the situation easier. Prudence's feelings would be less deeply involved and there could be no chance that she might be going to have a baby.[41]

This places the novel firmly in the twentieth century, yet with lingering Victorian values still present.

The humor of this situation stems from the fact that Fabian has now been caught out, by Jessie; he must relinquish Prudence. He makes a theatrical show of 'wretchedness' over this loss, to Jane, when promising to write a farewell letter to Prudence. Jane's further thoughts on the matter combine pity with satire:

> Presumably attractive men and probably women too must always be suffering in this way; they must so often have to reject and cast aside love, and perhaps even practice did not always make them ruthless and cold-blooded enough to do it without feeling any qualms.

The question for both characters in this affair is how much they actually have felt, and thus might be likely to suffer now that the relationship has ended. Jane, as an outsider, wonders how deeply Fabian has been touched, and also concludes that Prudence cannot have been in love with him – yet this also represents 'an effort to relieve her own misery and her feeling of guilt for the part she had played in bringing them together.'[42]

Pym writes sympathetically yet humorously of Prudence's rituals of mourning, once she learns of Fabian's defection to Jessie. She spends the weekend doing as Jane has earnestly suggested, when she urges: 'on the morning when you get this letter you will be alone, darling Prue, so be sure and give yourself a *good breakfast*, if you possibly can. . . .'[43] Prudence enjoys the drama of playing her role of rejected lover, going out to lunch alone during the following week and considering the tragic figure she must seem to other viewers: somebody might ask, 'Who is that interesting-looking young woman, with the traces of tears on her cheeks, eating smoked salmon?'[44]

She also succeeds in immediately turning her rejection by Fabian into a means of alluring another, younger man: Geoffrey Manifold, who works in her office, gruffly takes on the role of confidant, and soon becomes her next romantic interest. The drama all along for Prudence has been one of enjoying a succession of adoring lovers, beginning with her memories of suitors while she was still at Oxford, who came 'up the drive, in a great body, it seemed . . .' in her recollection of undergraduate days.[45] Part of the underside to this romantic scene is that Prudence's days as a *femme fatale* are numbered. Her practical friend Elinor, who is also single, looks on at Prudence's romantic adventures and considers that they cannot last forever. 'One had to settle down sooner or later into the comfortable spinster or the contented or bored wife,' in her view.[46] Still, Prudence has taken on love affairs as an absorbing occupation, or vocation; and part of the pleasure of this is to compare herself favorably with spinsters such as Elinor, whom she takes to dinner after the demise of her affair with Fabian, and to whom she '[hints] at tragedy.' While her friend sympathizes, she also acknowledges that it is what Prudence has chosen: 'Still, you were just the same at Oxford, I remember. Whoever was it then – Peter or Philip or Henry or somebody?' This shows the other benefit which Prudence derives from her numerous relationships, as she retains an air of mystery: 'Prudence smiled. It had been Peter and Philip and Henry at one time or another. Not to mention Laurence and Giles.'[47]

The price which Prudence pays for her continued romantic adventures is the occasional betrayal. Still, it is made clear that she accepts this, and would (to some extent) prefer it to any other alternative. This is an addictive and in many ways an alarming or sad pattern. But it is something that she wants. As for Fabian, he is suitably punished for his light-hearted abandonment of Prudence; pondering marriage with Jessie, he realizes that it will not be 'like life with Constance all over again, with little romantic episodes here and there.' He is hemmed in by her sharpness and vigilance: 'It was as if a net had closed round him.'[48]

While it is impossible to feel that either of these characters is tragic, the destructive effects of betrayal – and the frantic efforts to hold realization of it at bay – are at the heart of this novel. Each of these writers – Bowen, Keane, Murdoch, Byatt, and Pym – portrays characters who struggle with grief and abandonment by warding it off, trying to diminish it, or travestying its effects by consciously dining well. It remains a powerful theme because reason does not affect it; one cannot think one's way out of emotional pain of this kind, although a great deal of thinking is applied to these situations.

In the preceding chapters, I have discussed interconnections between novels which take passionate, romantic themes and dramatic situations and present them hedged with irony. These writers love ideas, and are fascinated by the power of the mind. This makes the drama of ineffectual reasoning all the greater – and suffering in the mind all the more intense. But there is also an obverse side to this, where the use of rationality does begin to affect the characters' lives for the good. Especially in genres which celebrate this quality, such as academic and detective novels, reason can be seen to prevail against fatalism. This will be the subject of the final section.

Part III
Wit and Reason

When contrasted to the sweep of grand passion, the cool light of reason can seem ridiculous or – at best – a compromise with the highest claims of the heart. And yet, it is intriguing and compelling in its own right: in the deliberately rational world of a detective or academic novel, it is possible to reason one's way out of a dilemma. Villains can be apprehended, crimes thwarted, and theoretical or scholarly ideas can be examined with a critical eye, as in Byatt's *Possession*.

Still more amusing is the use of cheerful humor in domestic novels in which a skillful and diplomatic heroine becomes a catalyst for the transformation of an entire family circle, as in Gibbons' *Cold Comfort Farm* or Georgette Heyer's *The Grand Sophy*. Intended as a sly corrective to brooding Lawrentian passion, Gibbons' Flora Poste advocates the adoption of 'the Higher Common Sense.'

6
Academic and Detective Novels

In the midst of a furor caused by the dreaded 'poltergeist' in Dorothy L. Sayers' Oxford novel, *Gaudy Night*, Lord Peter Wimsey tells his fellow investigator, Harriet Vane, that the problem can be solved by the application of 'a little straight and unprejudiced reasoning.' This is the *sine qua non* of a detective novel: everything – including the source of a malign passion – can be discovered and corrected by means of rational thinking. Sayers underscores this point by making it a primary conflict for her heroine, who desperately wants to believe in the efficacy of the intellect, but is beginning to doubt its power, since one of the college fellows appears to be mad. The usefulness of rationality is an important article of faith for her: 'the reason why I want to – to get clear of people and feelings and go back to the intellectual side is that is the only side of life I haven't betrayed and made a mess of,' she tells Wimsey. He understands her dilemma: 'it's upsetting to think that it may betray you in its turn.' His contribution to her understanding of it is to challenge this assumption: 'But why should you think that?'[1] The novel is satisfyingly complex because she wants to trust in 'head' rather than 'heart,' thinks furiously (though to no avail), and ends by having both: reason and passion, work and love. *Gaudy Night* is a novel where reason triumphs, since the mystery is solved; yet emotion is shown to be equally formidable, since Harriet herself fails as a detective, unable to reason cogently because of her emotional panic.

Twentieth-century detective novels, and their distant counterpart, academic fiction, gain their dramatic power from this juxtaposition: characters who pride themselves on having superior intellect are found, nonetheless, to be affected by passion. The growing emotional attachment between Byatt's two twentieth-century scholars in *Possession* is meant to provide sexual tension in this story, as is the prickly relationship between Harriet Vane and Peter Wimsey in several of Sayers' detective novels. The irony of this approach serves both of these authors well. They use the expected and conventional emphasis on reason in these genres to contrast with the highly irrational effects of obsession, jealousy, self-protectiveness, and fierce power struggles among university members. Academics, they suggest, may think of themselves as being level-headed, but nothing could be further from the case.

The question about the possible ravaging effects of emotion is crucial, since it directly impacts the cause of feminism – without which women would not have been admitted to the university. This stereotype of hysteria haunts them. Women are assumed to be more emotional than men (to the detriment of their work), and in novels about academe, the female characters must fight to show that they can also be cool and objective in their scholarly roles. One result of this effort to claim their places in the academic world is that women in these novels who pursue and who have gained Oxbridge degrees seem to have tacitly agreed to ignore their initial difficulties in getting into the university. To make an indignant stand now, when the point has been gained, would be to draw attention to something they would wish to forget: their admission was so recent, and so resentfully contested.

And because this remains a sore point, Sayers and Byatt continually raise the subject of women and learning in order to test the relative merits of intellect and emotion. Women are traditionally supposed to be unfit for learning, at least in the context of Sayers' 1930s Oxford college and Byatt's 1950s Cambridge. Frederica Potter, as an undergraduate in *Still Life*, poses this to herself as a significant issue, especially when trying to gain respect from academic men. 'There is something both gratifying and humiliating in watching a man who has taken you for a routinely silly woman begin to take you seriously,' she thinks after her first serious conversation with the elegant don, Raphael Faber. She goes on to make a generalization from this: 'It was always happening to her; her social life was a battle to establish the idea that she was intelligent, was capable of intelligent talk, in the minds of others.'[2] But she is irritated by the effort, because it implies that she exists only insofar as she is perceived as a certifiably intelligent person: 'Surely, surely it was possible, she said to herself in a kind of panic, to make something of one's life *and* be a woman. Surely.'[3]

This wish has as much to do with ambition and a passionate desire to live, as it does with academic prowess. As the half-disapproving, half-admiring Raphael Faber tells her, mid-way through the novel, 'You only want everything. You're a formidable girl, Frederica.'[4]

This is by no means a whimsical observation. The hard-won privilege of gaining an Oxbridge degree intensifies the importance of what these women do with their adult lives beyond their undergraduate days. In *Gaudy Night*, Sayers makes this a constant theme; the Gaudy Night itself gathers together college graduates, who meet to celebrate their companionship in scholarly matters, and to covertly compare how far each of them has succeeded in life. It remains a matter of deep honor and pride that women who have gained university degrees use them intelligently. The professionally successful graduates who are gathered together at the Gaudy make fun of the current enthusiasms of over-emotional 'old girls'; Phoebe Tucker delights in informing Harriet of these absurdities, listing: 'Trimmer's mental healing, and Henderson going nudist. . . .' Another guest at the dinner is Broadribb, who is reported to have gone 'absolutely potty on some new kind of religion and joined an extraordinary sect somewhere or other where they go about in loin-cloths and have agapemones of nuts and grape-fruit.'[5] These emotional excesses seem to have negated the women's Oxford education into rationality. The more sophisticated graduates comfort themselves in the face of this spectacle by finding a reason for it all: Phoebe diagnoses Broadribb's defection as stemming from 'Reaction, I expect. Repressed emotional instincts and all that. She was frightfully sentimental inside, you know.'[6] This is the great danger, as the 1930s women characters feel.

It also returns the reader to an earlier theme, of the uneasy relationship between thinking and feeling. What the detective heroine has half feared is, to some small degree, proved to be true: it is possible to be learned and smart, and yet also to be unstable and irrational, psychologically speaking.

The novel is very much a set-piece of its era, and can appear quaint in its insistence upon old-fashioned ideas (or old-fashioned ways of saying them) about the importance of hard work, and the generally good and acceptable thing that the British class system can be (if it produces such a paragon as Lord Peter, who is moreover willing to flout aristocratic prejudices and marry a country doctor's daughter). At the same time, the novel deals astutely with some highly complex issues. And it typifies a particularly British way of doing so: while tentatively invoking psychological terminology (all the while pretending that it is really rather foolish), it tries to fathom the way in which people's minds work. The irony of this is that characters can seem utterly transparent in their rage and jealousy, even though – or, especially because – these feelings are being expressed in Freudian terminology. When the history don, Miss Hillyard, loses her temper about the extra allowances which are made to married women in college employment, she casts it in this language:

> The fact is, though you will never admit it, that everybody in this place has an inferiority complex about married women and children. For all your talk about careers and independence, you all believe in your hearts that we ought to abase ourselves before any woman who has fulfilled her animal functions.[7]

The resulting argument among the assembled dons is heated; they deny that such partiality is wrong or destructive, although the particular subject under discussion is a crucial one. The woman who is being exalted above the other employees is given her own room in the servants' lodgings, which allows her to carry out her depredations on the college. Miss Hillyard's objections are thus prescient, as it is the poltergeist whom they are favoring. The don's remarks also give an opening for the other fellows to label her as having an 'inferiority complex' in return.

The novel turns repeatedly on the relative merits and power of emotion (allied with courtesy and compassion, as in the treatment of college servants) and of intellect (which is connected to rewards for hard work). The actions of the poltergeist are particularly effective at upsetting the college's equilibrium, because they disrupt a rational system which is designed to keep excessive emotion at bay. The college fellows are taxed, emotionally, by the persistent attacks of the poltergeist, and begin to quarrel spitefully with each other. Their sense of professionalism restrains them from allowing this to damage the cause of women at Oxford, however, and Wimsey congratulates them on this, when the mystery is solved. Their collective belief in rationality allows them even to erase past grievances: 'They were all normal again,' the narrator informs the reader at the close of the novel. 'They had never been anything else.'[8] The conclusion of the detective plot allows the college dons to display yet again their faith in reason and justice: when the criminal is exposed, she is allowed to defend herself against the charges against her. As a consummate representative of warped thinking, she uses this opportunity instead to make an attack on Harriet, the college, Miss de Vine (the don whom she held to be indirectly responsible for her husband's suicide), and scholarly women in general. Their response is to take her away, to be handed over to a psychologist: 'the problem,' Wimsey tells Harriet at the end of the novel, 'is being medically dealt with.'[9] This denouement satisfies all requirements, defending the rights of women to be and to remain in such an exalted place as Oxford. It was never one of them in the first place, who caused such disruption. Still, Sayers does skillfully bring out the particular problems which academics (who are also emotional, as well as intellectual beings) can experience.

Although Byatt is not writing directly about women's entry into Oxbridge, in the way that Sayers is in *Gaudy Night*, she does consider many of the same questions about women and scholarship that Sayers does. As a student at Newnham in 1954, Frederica's first encounter with the world of Cambridge is unsatisfactory because it is expected that she define herself as a woman student: '[the college] was a setting for cocoa, toasted crumpets, tea parties. Frederica wanted wine, argument, sex.'[10] In the 1950s world of *Still Life*, Frederica Potter possesses the kind of sexual freedom which Sayers' undergraduate women in *Gaudy Night* could only dream of; while they climb stealthily over college walls in order to circumvent curfew, Frederica self-consciously continues her quest for sexual experimentation. Part of the humor of this novel lies in the mutual distrust which both male and women undergraduates show towards each other in this endeavor. One of Frederica's first lovers at Cambridge is a man who is somewhat experienced with women, though he also is learning: 'She had the sense that she was one of a number of girls he was observing and practicing on: she didn't mind this, since she was observing and practicing on him.'[11]

True to her academic heritage, Frederica attempts to bring an intellectual, analytical mode to bear on sexual adventures: 'She judged and categorized men,' the narrator says, adding that this has its roots in an attempt to hold emotion at bay. 'If men wanted "only" one thing, so could, and would, and did, Frederica Potter.'[12]

The issues for women have altered slightly, in Byatt's novel, to the more fundamental desire for inclusion in an Inner Ring – and the question here is whether exclusion from it happens because of gender or because of other, intangible qualities. Frederica complains to one of her male undergraduate friends, 'Oh, Alan. I want to be part of things. You get shut out, as a woman.' He objects immediately to this characterization of her place in the university: 'You're at the centre. In a way most men can't be.'[13] Part of what Byatt suggests in this novel is that both things are true. Later in her life, Frederica looks back on her undergraduate experience, and concludes that she possesses 'the sexual self-confidence, over-confidence perhaps, of her curious historical position, brief and anomalous, a Cambridge woman when there were eleven men for every woman.'[14]

Another implication of her 'historical position' as a highly intelligent and educated woman is that she takes her career choices after university extremely seriously. Nearing the end of her undergraduate days in *Still Life*, she considers various alternatives: 'There were two hypothetical future Fredericas – one closed in the University Library writing something elegant and subtle on the use of metaphor in seventeenth-century religious narrative, and one in London, more nebulous, writing quite different things, witty critical journalism, maybe even a new urban novel like those of Iris Murdoch.'[15] These are not simply two alternate career choices, but two essentially different individuals – two 'hypothetical future Fredericas.' Part of the interest of her character as an intellectual woman is that she pursues more or less the latter course, eventually living in London, teaching, writing, and becoming involved in television broadcasting. Yet in *A Whistling Woman*, she is seen to have retained her connection with the University of North Yorkshire, and continues to wonder if she would not prefer to return to writing scholarly treatises.

The main issue for Frederica is not so much what particular work she undertakes, as the fact that there must be intellectual effort involved in it. Stephanie's sudden and accidental death prevents any choice at all for Frederica at a crucial moment, and she is stunned into marrying Nigel Reiver in her grief, just after leaving the university. But when this crisis abates, and Frederica finds herself stranded in the country, she cannot help protesting. Early in *Babel Tower*, she begins to realize her incipient panic: 'She does not blame Nigel yet for her unhappiness, although she is constantly angry at his long absences, and at his failure to see what she needs, by which she means *work*, not too well defined, but *work*.'[16] Later in the novel, when she has escaped from her domestic enclosure with Nigel, she verbalizes this more clearly to her friends in London: '"I must *work*," says Frederica. "It kills you, unused energy, it turns against you."'[17]

The counterpart to Frederica's passion for work is that of her sister, Stephanie, whose absorption into domesticity through her marriage to Daniel Orton has separated her from literature, teaching, and reading. Attending to her young children, Will and Mary, she realizes her loss. 'I've been thinking,' she tells Daniel late in *Still Life*, 'I suffer from having to use a limited vocabulary. All the time.'[18] Yet she also does something immediate to try to remedy this, taking up scholarly work again. When she first goes to the library, intending to start a dissertation on Wordsworth's poetry, she experiences momentary panic: 'She had with some pain cleared this small space and time to think in and now thought seemed impossible.' Still, she recognizes this as part of the process of writing or reading:

> One had to peel one's mind from its run of preoccupations.... There had to be a time before thought, a wool-gathering time when nothing happened, a time of yawning, of wandering eyes and feet, of reluctance to do what would finally become delightful and energetic.

The most interesting part of this venture is its very formlessness, in terms of the academic framework in which she has been trained. When she first lays out her books, she realizes that: 'Never before had she attempted to work without the outside sanction of an essay to write, an exam to pass, a class to prepare.'[19] This requires considerable concentration and bravery, and Byatt honors this attempt in her heroines.

Byatt's tour de force about academe, *Possession*, weaves together many of her ideas about academe, creativity, and romance – particularly as this relates to women scholars in the late twentieth century. The novel combines an academic setting with a detective and a romance framework, and also interpolates a kind of historical novel in its text (all the while mocking tenets of literary criticism which are contemporarily in vogue, such as deconstruction and feminism). Since genre is defined by its accepted patterns, there are a number of expectations that this intertwining creates. In its character as a detective novel (in its most specialized sense, a 'research' novel), we feel convinced that the answers which the scholars seek about historical events will be forthcoming. Appropriate documents or clues will be discovered, and links will rapidly be established. As an academic book, it is expected to satirize ridiculous stereotypes – the lesbian American feminist, the rapacious manuscript-hunting American male professor, the sexual predator deconstructionist critic, and so on. And in its genre as romance, it offers a ritual transformation of the beleaguered female – in this case, a minor character, Val – by a worldly man, Euan MacIntyre, who transfigures her, by the skillful application of proper lipstick, high fashion and sensual pleasures. When Roland (her former lover) sees her again after their separation, he is astonished: 'Roland stared at sleek Val, who had the shine of really expensive and well-made clothes, and more important and unmistakable, the glistening self-pleasure of sexual happiness.' Part of this newly acquired beauty is aesthetic: 'She was all muted violets and shot-silk dove-colors, all balanced and pretty, stockings, high shoes, padded shoulders, painted mouth.' But as Roland recognizes, her true regeneration has come from within: 'He said, instinctively, "You look *happy*, Val."' Her reply is concise: 'I decided I could be,' she tells him, almost as a reproof.[20] The implication (which is amusing in this context) is that academics have more difficulty in discovering this possibility than those who are not scholarly and encumbered with excessive intellectual scruples, like Val and Euan.

Still, the main characters are also granted their desires. The frozen maiden (the heroine, Maud Bailey) becomes transformed by the relatively mousy hero (Roland Michell), and the desperately romantic Victorian poets, Randolph Henry Ash and Christabel LaMotte, are granted a month's idyll together in Yorkshire. Theirs is the most supremely romantic tryst, as they part irrevocably, at the end of this period.

At the same time, Byatt recognizes – as Sayers does – that gender questions are also linked to class-consciousness. Roland worries that he would not be acceptable as a potential romantic partner to Maud Bailey, since she is 'County, and he [is] urban lower-middle-class.' Academe is supposed to be, in the abstract, a democratizing leveler, where great minds meet, unhampered by class prejudice. But another irony is that this inherent competitiveness is refined and removed to another sphere. Old-fashioned insecurities prevail, in Roland's self-doubts: 'Maud was a beautiful woman such as he had no claim to possess,' he warns himself, going on to contrast their relative positions in the academic class system: 'She had a secure job and an international reputation.'[21] Byatt makes the competitive and acquisitive nature of academics central to her novel. Sayers' female dons in *Gaudy Night* seem positively quaint, in comparison, exalting pure learning for learning's sake, and earnestly approving of 'getting on with one's work.' Byatt's characters are infinitely more worldly; they want jobs with definite income, and provenance of literary papers which they can dispose of to their favored archival research center. (Yet another irony of Byatt's characters' insistence on the ownership of manuscripts is their relative unimportance, in contemporary literary criticism.)

If these late-twentieth-century characters want love as well as work, they are much cagier about admitting it (if they are English, that is – for American feminists, it is different). Romance works backwards for Roland and Maud, by virtually 'deconstructing' their notions about sexuality: they confess to each other that they dream of solitude, and a 'white bed,' which provides a respite for them both, before their physical union at the end of the novel.

Byatt's satirization of feminist critics conjures up the stereotype of over-emotional women which Sayers has used earlier in the century, in

Gaudy Night. By making Leonora Stern, the feminist critic, evangelistically lesbian, aggressive and over-emotional, she reinforces by contrast the traditional values of heterosexual romance. (Leonora's nineteenth-century counterpart, the quasi-lesbian Blanche Glover, is possessive to the point of becoming hysterical and self-destructive. She ultimately proves disastrous to Christabel LaMotte.) Men in the novel do not fare any better; Byatt's equally rapacious male character, Fergus Wolff, counterbalances the odious Leonora – both are poison for the delicate (and indecisive) Maud Bailey.

In several variations, the romantic entanglements in *Possession* carry out a staple idea in academic fiction: the irony of intellectual characters leading irrational, driven emotional lives. This is shown in specifically academic terms by applying some sort of rationality to it: in Sayers' *Gaudy Night*, the paradigm is quasi-Freudian. The academic characters are willing to acknowledge the power of the unconscious mind, although they parody this elaborately (and continue to practice denial about their emotions) by assuming that nothing is what it seems. In Byatt's fictional world, several decades later, Freud's ideas have been further refined by literary critics, who dislike the implications which they draw from his paradigms, but who nonetheless embrace many of Freud's views: 'We live in the truth of what Freud discovered,' Maud Bailey tells Roland, mid-way through the novel. 'Whether or not we like it. However we've modified it. We aren't really free to suppose – to imagine – he could possibly have been wrong about human nature.'[22] This interchange between two of the main academic characters suggests that they have allowed themselves to become defined by their chosen research specialties. Roland wonders at Maud's devotion to a Freudian paradigm, yet accepts it as her viewpoint: 'Roland wanted to ask: Do you like that? He thought he had to suppose she did: her work was psychoanalytic, after all, this work on liminality and marginal beings.'[23]

Part of what Byatt is dramatizing through the insistence on various academic paradigms is that scholars are bound to find whatever they are already looking for. Feminist critics such as Leonora Stern and Maud Bailey have assumed that Christabel LaMotte, the Victorian poet who is the subject of their own writings, lived in a harmonious lesbian relationship with another woman, Blanche Glover. (The fact of Glover's suicide does not seem to have altered their views about the happiness of this ménage.) The benefit of doing historical scholarship, based on actual original materials, is the chance to work from the other direction: to begin to see from the nineteenth-century characters' perspective, rather than to impose a later paradigm on their work. As Roland tells Maud, when they are together in Yorkshire following their earlier counterparts: 'It makes an interesting effort of imagination to think how they saw the world. What Ash saw when he stood on perhaps this ledge.'[24] This attempt to 'imagine' transforms both the scholars and their view of the past: at the end of the novel, the appearance of new evidence causes them to redraft their understanding of relationships between various characters, and to establish a new relationship themselves.

But the heart of the novel lies in the relationship of the text (or texts) to the reader. Whereas the twentieth-century scholars search diligently for revelatory manuscripts, they can never directly know the experiences of their nineteenth-century counterparts. The narrator offers to the reader of the novel a glimpse of the past – the 'truth' about the Victorian characters – which the scholars within its pages can never have in such a direct way. This can provide a highly gratifying reading experience.

In *Possession*, Byatt works from the latter end of the equation: her characters, for the most part, possess their chosen work. What they still seek is love – especially, perhaps, when they vigorously reject the assumption that they are looking for it. Maud Bailey's dream of autonomy and solitude is a deliberate construction of defenses against the encroaching fellow scholars who would breach her integrity. Similarly, Sayers' Harriet Vane stresses her commitment to her writing, in *Gaudy Night*. (Part of Wimsey's attraction becomes evident when he helps her with a novel in progress, thus suggesting that he is a fit husband for her.) This puts both heroines in a laudable position: they are not cast as single-minded romantic heroines, but rather, as independent women who can hold their own in the world. At the same time, the almost inevitable clinch between hero and heroine at the end of each novel merely spins out this pleasurable tension a bit longer – the reader is always certain of the outcome.

The ultimate female fantasy novel is for the heroine to end the novel with everything she desires. An academic setting enables her to have an impressive self-identity (she is theoretically equal to a man, as a fellow scholar), and a detective framework gives the two romantic lovers something else to concentrate on while they spar wittily with each other. They can 'work' together – which is held up tacitly as the ideal, thus exalting the chosen work of both sexes.

In these novels in particular, Byatt and Sayers shrewdly incorporate two things at once: their heroines are not feminist – in any particular sense of the word – yet they possess the spirit of independence which feminists would promote. In the most conventional decision possible, Harriet agrees to marry the ardent (and impossibly devoted) Lord Peter Wimsey. In Byatt's novel, Maud Bailey and Roland embrace a suitably open-ended, 'modern' relationship – but their sexual coupling, after so much earnest discussion of separateness, marks a romantic merging. Furthermore, Byatt seems to be deliberately forestalling a feminist reading of her fictional text by writing in as realistic a manner as possible – rather, she constructs the novel as a straightforward narrative (with flashbacks, in an echo of detective novel conventions), and satirizes scholarly attempts to analyze texts.

Academic and detective novels are similar (and can mesh so well together, as genres) because they share the same indeterminate ground regarding the definition of a 'professional' as opposed to an 'amateur.' Both kinds of work call for cogent reasoning, and this invites another question – can the amateur rival the professional in this endeavor? It becomes important to many of the characters in these novels to define their status, relative to the academy; in Byatt's *Possession*, the feudal spirit of the university is continually stressed. Roland Michell is Prof. Blackadder's research assistant, and therefore lower in the ranks than someone like Fergus Wolff; and this is never forgotten by any of the group of academics. There is a great emphasis on competitiveness, among the various scholars, which makes a cynical comment on academia in the late twentieth century. In this novel, the question is not so much whether an amateur can do as well as a professional, as whether a person lower on the scale can do so. The related question is: whether Roland sets out on his quest to discover the truth about Randolph Henry Ash's possible love affair because he is an amateur (in the sense of loving his work and having a passion for research) or because he wants to seize all the glory of possible scholarly discovery for himself, and triumph over his more successful rivals.

Byatt extends this concept of amateur scholarship to heartfelt romantic love, in suggesting that academe has professionalized the characters in relation to their own emotions. Commenting wryly on the exquisitely self-conscious twentieth-century characters, the narrator observes: 'They were children of a time and culture that mistrusted love, "in love," romantic love, romance *in toto*, and which nevertheless in revenge proliferated sexual language, linguistic sexuality, analysis, dissection, deconstruction, exposure.' The same over-analytical approach characterizes Roland's view of himself: 'Roland had learned to see himself, theoretically, as a crossing-place for a number of systems, all loosely connected. He had been trained to see his idea of his "self" as an illusion, to be replaced by a discontinuous machinery and electrical message-network of various desires, ideological beliefs and responses, language-forms and hormones and pheromones.' The advantage of this intellectualized view of life in holding emotion at bay is obvious, as the narrator points out, adding in explanation: 'Mostly he liked this.' Yet Roland and Maud can both be seen to be overlooking the obvious; they are physically attracted to each other, in chaste yet obvious ways, late in the novel. 'They took to silence. They touched each other without comment and without progression.' When Roland wonders 'what their mute pleasure in each other might lead to,' he is phrasing a lover's question, though without admitting this to himself.[25]

The profound distrust of emotion which an academic setting evokes for readers can provide endless grounds for ironic comment, especially in relation to women, who continually resist being labeled as hysterical or as being ruled by passion. Byatt shows a great deal of rivalry among women characters in the scholarly and teaching profession – even to the extent of aggressive personal challenges being made. Maud Bailey confesses to Roland that she has cut off her hair, at one point, to prove her solidarity with fellow feminists – a gesture which is intended to prove an ideological point, but is manifestly a childish gesture expressing hurt and grief. To some extent, the women academics in *Possession* are much more defensive about their place in the profession than the dons in Sayers' *Gaudy Night*, even though they are much more well-established within the university system.

At the same time, both Sayers and Byatt are fully aware that one advantage of an Oxbridge degree – as garnered by their heroines Harriet Vane and Frederica Potter – is that one does not need to be part of the university, in the sense of having a title or a job, in order to be a writer. This makes it a profession that is particularly suited to women, who can sometimes work outside of the existing structure with great success. When Harriet Vane first appears, in the novel *Strong Poison*, the judge sums up her achievements, which are formidable for a young woman in her late twenties, as follows:

> she was left, at the age of twenty-three, to make her own way in the world. Since that time – and she is now twenty-nine years old – she has worked industriously to keep herself, and it is very much to her credit that she has, by her own exertions, made herself independent in a legitimate way, owing nothing to anybody and accepting help from no one.[26]

It is made a heavily significant point, later in the novel, that she earned four times as much money as did the man with whom she lived for some time (and whom she is now accused, falsely, of having murdered). Her genre is detective stories, and she has been both hard-working and successful. By the time she comes back to stay at Oxford, some years later, in the novel *Gaudy Night*, she returns to considering scholarship, particularly undertaking a biography. But the real reason that she has been invited to come and stay at Shrewsbury College is that she is being consulted as a detective (which is a kind of off-shoot of her actual profession, as a writer of detective stories). Still, she is an amateur, as she protests to the Senior Common Room, when they invite her to solve the problem. This, however, is the basic point: they feel much happier with an amateur, since she is an old member of the college, and is part of their clan.

Lord Peter Wimsey is the archetype of an amateur sleuth, since he is a wealthy aristocrat who does not need to take up any profession (except, perhaps, out of a sense of *noblesse oblige*). Some of the Oxford dons look askance at his activities, judging him to be a dilettante, while Harriet defends him: 'Catching murderers isn't a soft job, or a sheltered job. It takes a lot of time and energy, and you may very easily get injured or killed.' He himself continually jokes about his pretensions to be like the master detective figure, Sherlock Holmes, who represents the pinnacle of being both amateur and highly professional at the same time. No one is more obsessively devoted to the study of his craft than Holmes, who makes detailed studies of cigar ash, types of dirt, bloodstains, and so on. Yet, while he does accept private clients who come to him for help, he markedly leaves the public triumphs of detection to members of the official London police force. Wimsey conceives of himself as a sleuth who derives his identity from this kind of heritage, making humorous reference to it. Near the end of *Five Red Herrings*, he confronts the other investigators: '"This," said Lord Peter Wimsey, "is the proudest moment of my life. At last I really feel like Sherlock Holmes."' His situation is akin to Holmes, in that as an outsider, he is able to illuminate the true state of affairs for those who are supposed to be the professional detectives: 'A Chief Constable, a Police Inspector, a Police Sergeant and two constables have appealed to me to decide between their theories, and with my chest puffed like a pouter-pigeon, I can lean back in my chair and say, "Gentlemen, you are all wrong."'[27]

Sayers' creation of Wimsey's character evolves in complexity throughout several novels, although she never alters his essential qualities. This is a great achievement, since he begins the detective series as so stock

KING ALFRED'S COLLEGE
LIBRARY

a type as to verge on P.G. Wodehouse's Bertie Wooster; yet she turns this to his advantage. His Man of the World persona enables him to be able to talk to many different kinds of characters, and he also possesses the ability to disguise himself on occasion. One obvious irony is that he can appear to be a foolish wastrel; when Harriet sees him among a sea of billowing hats at Ascot, she thinks instinctively of his utterly Mayfair persona, inferring that he has adopted it in order to be efficiently 'detecting' something. Sayers plays this to the hilt, in the novel *Have His Carcase*, in which Harriet discovers a corpse while on a solitary walking holiday. The great joke here is that Wimsey, who comes to join her, continually despises such 'watering places!'[28]

But his class superiority does serve to protect Harriet in *Have His Carcase* (much as she disdains this, and believes that she requires no help), and his manner is judged to be so extreme that he cannot even be taken seriously for what he is, an aristocrat. At one point in the novel, a theatrical producer is struck with admiration of Wimsey's air, and becomes entranced with the possibility of casting him in a drama entitled *The Worm that Turned*. Another character asks, dubiously, 'but can he act?' to which the producer's response is: '"Act?" exploded Mr. Sullivan. "He don't have to act. He's only got to walk on. Look at it! Ain't that the perfect Worm? Here, you, thingummy, speak up, can't you?"' Wimsey plays along with this fantasy, placing his monocle more firmly into his eye. 'Really, old fellow, you make me feel all of a doodah, what?' When offered the role on the spot, he refuses with a flourish: '"I have played lead," he announced, "before all the crowned heads of Europe. Off with the mask! The Worm has Turned! I am Lord Peter Wimsey, the Piccadilly Sleuth, hot on the trail of Murder."' This combines several fantasies in one – being a good performer (an admiring spectator pronounces his final line to be 'good curtain'), and an amateur who could have become a professional (actor, in this case), and finally, exactly what he is at the moment.[29] Taking to himself the fanciful title of Piccadilly Sleuth, he is, in fact, searching for the murderer.

While the stratification of English society is such that he is bound to be recognized as a particular type wherever goes, Sayers nonetheless emphasizes that he is able to achieve some measure of disguise. This confirms both the amateur and professional sides of his work – he is able to pretend to be what he is not, and yet to be an excellent detective because of this. In the novel *Murder Must Advertise*, he takes on a brief spell as copy-writer for a London advertising agency, in order to investigate a death. In addition to conscientiously appearing each day at the office and producing copy with the other writers, he appears disguised as a Harlequin figure at a party, where he displays a dazzling athletic prowess in the garden fountain: 'He was climbing the statue-group in the centre of the pool – an elaborate affair of twined mermaids and dolphins. . . . Up and up went the slim chequered figure, dripping and glittering like a fantastic water-creature.' One onlooker concludes that 'the fellow's a tight-rope walker,' while another dares him to dive into the shallow pool, which of course he does with consummate ease.[30]

It is crucial for the validation of his detective abilities that Wimsey be seen as being neither effete nor cowardly. While he hides, on occasion, behind the mask of assumed aristocratic silliness, he makes it clear that he is able to recognize antagonism when it confronts him and to counter it with all the accustomed frostiness of his class. In *Have His Carcase*, the murderer (as yet unrevealed in the plot) insults him, in an attempt to prevent him from investigating the case at hand:

> 'I see your game all right. You're nuts on this kind of thing and it's all a darn good advertisement, and it gives you a jolly good excuse for barging round with the girl. That's quite all right. But it's not quite the game to go playing my mother up, if you see what I mean. So I thought I'd just give you a hint. You won't take offence?'

Wimsey's answer is intended to show that nothing can intimidate him: '"I am quite ready," said Lord Peter, "to take anything I am offered."' He is, furthermore, willing to give an exact account of his background, when these are required as credentials of a combative and unyielding spirit. In this case, he unhesitatingly flies the banner of class privilege. When the murderer queries Wimsey's nerve and athletic prowess, he replies, 'I hunted pretty regularly with the Quorn and Pytchley at one time, and I shoot and fish a bit.'[31]

The point in many similar exchanges with men who show contempt for Wimsey, throughout these novels, is that he is a fully masculine being in the accepted way – his athleticism, stemming from years of brilliant cricket-playing, is continually recalled. And he effortlessly fits into the social scene in a number of places, such as the quintessential gentleman's club in London, where the dead body of an elderly member is discovered in *Unpleasantness at the Bellona Club*. Most important, Wimsey is able to relate to these increasingly anachronistic characters because he himself has been on the front lines in the Great War, and knows first-hand the sufferings that such men have endured. His personal heroism and the bonding that this gives him with other male characters is stressed in encounters such as that which he has with

Padgett, the porter at Harriet's college in Oxford in *Gaudy Night*, who greets him enthusiastically and hero-worships him still.

Yet another advantage that Wimsey possesses derives from his instinctively shrewd sensitivity to women. His aristocratic bearing gains him access to many different kinds of women, and his elaborate courtesy makes him an excellent confidant (as does the hope of securing him for a husband). In the novel *The Unpleasantness at the Bellona Club*, he visits a bohemian sculptress, Marjorie Phelps, in quest of information about a suspect in a murder case. Marjorie dismisses the woman in question, Ann Dorland, as unattractive and defensive (and, moreover, inartistic). Nothing points up the competitive line between professional and amateur in these novels so much as the subject of art. Marjorie explains that Ann has been living with a rich relation, who has just died. Wimsey characterizes her as 'A well-off amateur with a studio,' which hits off this resonance exactly. Marjorie agrees with this label – although at the same time, she acknowledges Ann's other abilities: 'Ann ought to have been something in the city. She has brains, you know. She'd run anything awfully well. But she isn't creative.' Furthermore, she isn't temperamentally suited to be a bohemian, since she is not sufficiently attractive – although passionate, and desperately in search of a lover. Marjorie blithely characterizes Ann as having 'a complex of some kind,' and goes on to explain the way in which she is a misfit in the bohemian crowd: 'Ann has a sort of fixed idea that she couldn't ever possibly attract any one, and so she's either sentimental and tiresome, or rude and snubbing, and our crowd does hate sentimentality and simply can't bear to be snubbed.'[32]

This thumbnail sketch – and instant analysis – provides the key to Wimsey's handling of Ann Dorland, when he meets her later in the novel. (She is suspected of murder, and in some danger of being implicated through her lover, but is entirely cleared of any involvement in it.) Wimsey is able not only to interpret Ann's misplaced and awkward passion correctly, thus discerning that she is not guilty of murder, but he also takes a hand in rehabilitating her, and setting her on the right path. He acts as father-confessor to the humiliation she has suffered at the hands of a former lover: 'he said I had a mania about sex. I suppose you would call it Freudian, really,' she tells him, mortified. Wimsey neatly defuses this, declining to be shocked: '"Is that all?" said Wimsey. "I know plenty of people who would take that as a compliment."' He also fortifies her self-respect, drawing a comparison between her character and a 'harsh' yet spirited red wine which he has ordered at dinner, as a moral lesson: 'Look! That wine I've sent away – it's no good for the champagne-and-lobster sort of person, nor for very young people – it's too big and rough. But it's got the essential guts. So have you.'[33] This effects a brilliant recasting of her passionate nature into an acceptable form. Wimsey is portrayed in this novel as a man who possesses keen insight into women's weaknesses, but who is willing to use his analytical powers for good. He is portrayed as a man with a kind heart, as well as a keen mind.

The final piece of heroic trappings with which the character of Wimsey is overlaid is his devotion to scholarly pursuits. 'I collect first editions and incunabulae,' he tells Harriet, the first time he speaks to her, while she is held in prison on suspicion of murder in *Strong Poison*.[34] By the time *Gaudy Night* opens, and she begins to think of him in terms of his intellectual interests, Harriet learns that he apparently continues some (mostly unspecified) form of amateur scholarship, connected with his collecting. A point is made by the female Oxford dons of Wimsey's ability, when they note that he could have been a professional scholar.

Wimsey succeeds in winning the reader's admiration (or the reverse) on the grounds of many and varied aspects of his character, most of which are related to this fine line between amateur and professional which – in the period in England when Sayers was writing these books – is a quintessential English approach to the question of *noblesse oblige*. While he will readily give account of himself, he is not defensive about his position in society, nor does he appear to attempt to impress others with his sleuthing successes. On the contrary, the sensitivity of his nature is shown by the fact that he hates bringing murderers to justice. It is reported that he usually suffers some kind of reaction or breakdown, upon completion of a case. Yet another aspect of his heroism is seen in the fact that Wimsey's efforts on behalf of society are unselfish, in not courting personal glory, and disinterested, in that they extend beyond working out potentially interesting intellectual problems. In *Strong Poison*, he has hired an inquiring spinster, Miss Climpson, to supervise a crew of women who work together to expose mail fraud. His mother, the Duchess of Denver, refers obliquely to the work of this group – although she does so in a way which also makes a comedy of this effort, rather than exalting it:

> 'Yes – such a good thing too, answering all those shady advertisements and then getting the people shown up and so courageous too, some of them the horridest oily people and murderers I shouldn't wonder with automatic thingummies and life-preservers in every pocket, and very likely a gas-oven full of bones. . . .'[35]

Sayers does a remarkable job of developing the character of Wimsey throughout her series of detective novels. He first steps onstage as the personification of rationality, under a self-protective mask of aristocratic vapidity. The appearance of Harriet Vane in *Strong Poison* makes him passionate about something. As the novels progress, he retains his intellectual character as a detective who likes solving problems, yet who also has compassion for other people's feelings. He is depicted as being entirely manly – both in his athletic prowess and in his sexual abilities (at least he explains to Harriet on their initial acquaintance that he can produce 'quite good testimonials' attesting to his ability as a lover).[36] But his intuition and his courtesy towards women endows him with qualities that are also (in this cultural context) feminine. And Sayers neatly retains an amateur status for her detective hero, while showing his fanatical devotion to a self-appointed task, which is not frivolous.

But Wimsey cannot reason his way out of one particular dilemma: his passion for Harriet Vane. In this situation, Sayers reformulates the problem which afflicts her academic women characters. A man who lives by rationality is gripped by unreasoning passion. The paradox comes full circle when he is able to gain her love through the exercise of his reasoning faculties, and solve the college mystery in *Gaudy Night*.

Both Dorothy L. Sayers and A.S. Byatt use this contrast between passion and intellect to dramatic effect. Academic and detective novels emphasize the latter skill – thinking one's way out or through a difficult problem. The Duchess of Denver, Wimsey's mother, observes the value of this when he becomes engaged to Harriet Vane, and she must adapt to his way of life. Writing in her diary, she observes of Harriet: 'Evinces dogged determination to do thing properly while she is about it . . . and resolutely applies intelligence to task. Something apparently to be said for education – teaches grasp of facts.'[37] But the challenge of sexual attraction always sparks an irritated reaction in the academic characters. One of the most amusing contrasts which Byatt makes is between university scholars and the work of D.H. Lawrence, whom highly intellectual Europeans like Raphael Faber disdain (possibly because they are afraid). He tells Frederica Potter in *Still Life*: 'I can't read Lawrence. I dislike his hectoring tone. And I find his characters incredible.'[38] Frederica herself has expressed a similar revulsion to the exaltation of Lawrence's novels, though on different grounds; her father's adulation of Lawrence causes her as an adolescent to reject him utterly. Later on, she expresses ambivalence towards the author, in a conversation with Alexander Wedderburn: 'I love Lawrence and I hate him, I believe him and I reject him totally, all at the same time. It's wearing.'[39]

These novels thrive on this contradiction. Byatt makes one more connection with this novelistic style which I would like to consider here. Improbable as it may seem, her character Frederica Potter shows a predilection as an adolescent for the Regency romance novels of Georgette Heyer. This is directly opposed to her father's passion for Lawrence's work, certainly in terms of class-consciousness: Heyer's main characters are relentlessly aristocratic. But it is nonetheless entirely fitting that – at least at an early period of her life – Frederica should be drawn to these novels, as they dramatize the same dilemma (in a different context) that she will face at Cambridge and in her adult life: the unexpected impact of passion upon a reasoned and controlled emotional life. Her father mistakenly disdains them as romances – which they are – yet their primary characteristic is the exaltation of reason. In his zealous quest for 'mystical palpable otherness' he is thus right to despise Heyer's works, though not for the reason – sentimentality – which he assumes they possess.

Many of Heyer's heroes and heroines think of themselves as being entirely rational and level-headed, only to be seized unexpectedly by romantic passion. This provides a satisfying contrast with their former, self-possessed state of emotional independence. Whereas Sayers and Byatt create the same kinds of tensions in an academic context, Heyer does so in the enclosed social world of early nineteenth-century England. Her heroines concentrate on their chosen work – as they have defined it – and gaily and resolutely renounce all pretensions to romance for themselves. In the context of the aristocratic circles in which they move, social reputation is all – and marriage contracts are the primary business of young women and their guardians. Although Heyer is infinitely more conventional in portraying the role of women, there is a corollary here with academic novels, since the traditional preoccupation of women has been with caring for children. The twentieth-century academics seem far less concerned with their students than with pursuing their own research. This is seen as a respectable way of being selfish, though; writing and scholarship in particular are given privileged status in novels about academe (which seldom touch on student–tutor relationships). In Heyer's novels, concern with the younger generation – particularly by aunts or guardians – is viewed as being highly commendable in its unselfishness.

Still, these novels turn on the same axis as academic fiction: reason and rationality. In Heyer's Regency world, as she reconstructs it for twentieth-century readers, a strict code of behavior prevails, and one false step can sink an aspiring female's reputation irrevocably. Therefore, the wits and resourcefulness of many of her adult heroines are engaged in preventing younger, headstrong adolescent characters from flouting social conventions (thereby ruining their chances for an eligible match). The game consists of a straightforward set of rules, which either must not be transgressed, or must be hidden from view. The older heroines try to manage younger ones within this framework. This externalizes what is an internal drama within twentieth-century academic characters such as Harriet Vane, Frederica Potter, and Maud Bailey.

Their focus on the welfare of others makes Georgette Heyer's heroines attractive because they are not, themselves, trying to catch a man (therefore, they escape being perceived as rapacious – and the hero himself becomes free to find them delightful on his own). Thus, a heroine like Frederica, in the novel of that title, is entirely consumed with launching her younger sister, Charis, into society and acting *in loco parentis* to her two highly strung younger brothers. Abigail Wendover, in *The Black Sheep*, watches anxiously over her ward, Fanny, and Anthea Darracott in *The Unknown Ajax* worries about her younger brother, Richmond. Venetia in the novel of that title, cares solicitously for a difficult younger brother. (Suffice it to say, this is a usual plot device.) In all of these cases, the heroines regard themselves as being unfit for any romantic nonsense, and they decide that they themselves will be free of suitors – nor is this an unrealistic assumption in this social context. This paves the way for a double reversal: they wear the superficial trappings of feminist, independent heroines – whereas in fact, they embody the most intense maternal feelings possible, for their charges, and must be persuaded to share this burden with the admiring hero. He in turn proves his own worth by recognizing the heroine's true value, and by undertaking the role of fellow guardian of the unruly younger crew.

Reason and family obligation are stunningly shattered by romantic love. Yet Heyer transfigures this formula. The heroes in these novels are transformed into protective fathers, as well as into lovers. The latter role may seem to be the one that they assume, but it is the sincere attention which they pay to the well-being of younger characters which seems to bring about their transformation into manly ardor. This gives the hero and heroine absorbing work to undertake together, thus uniting them in a common purpose.

The genre of the historical novel serves the author well: by transplanting the twentieth-century reader into a much earlier time period, Heyer has appropriated the best of all worlds. She can create a closed society (which she based on extensive research of the period – but which obviously is overlaid with her own preoccupations), and she can exalt the value of rationality, echoing Jane Austen's fiction. Her self-consciously sensible heroines are contrasted with the silly, flighty over-emotional ones (whom only the dim-witted males in the novels seem to prefer). A reasonable end is the one that is desired – therefore the passionate and unrestrained heroines are brought to heel, while the merry but self-deprecating heroines are coaxed into romance with the (fully reformed) heroes. These are admittedly stock situations, but Byatt has argued persuasively for their appeal, observing that 'by deflecting attention from the passions to the daily life of her romantic characters, she manages to create an escape world of super-sanity in her fantasy.' Moreover, as Byatt points out, there is true camaraderie in these books: 'men and women really *talk* to each other.'[40]

Still, it is easy to dismiss them. One of the funniest episodes in Byatt's *The Virgin in the Garden* is Frederica Potter's fury, when her father self-righteously burns her hidden cache of *Girls' Crystals* and Georgette Heyer novels (which are moreover 'borrowed from that almost-friend I once had, and . . . weren't even *mine*'). At the bonfire which Bill Potter makes of these volumes, Frederica 'danced round him on the grass, tossing her arms and screaming with highly articulate fury.' She defends these books on the most straightforward of grounds: 'They were harmless. I liked them,' going on to counter his objections with the belief that: 'A little fantasy never hurt anyone.'[41]

Part of their importance in Frederica Potter's 1940s Yorkshire adolescence is these novels' depiction of a heavily gendered society, where men are emphatically men (except if one tarts himself up as a dandy, thus looking to censorious eyes like 'a miserable man-milliner') and women must be under the protection of a respectable parentage as ward.[42] Heyer capitalizes, of course, on the relaxed social standards of the mid-twentieth century, during which she is evoking – with this mind-set – the ideals of an earlier age (as much as these can be determined and recreated in her fiction for a later time period). But it is part of the convention of a historical novel to seem – in some sense – fairly silly or antiquated, in contrast to contemporary sensibilities. And in relation to the group of twentieth-century women writers whom I am gathering together loosely under a 'not especially feminist' label, historical fiction plays a particular role: it allies the reader with the seemingly sensible or rational characters (who are closer to modern view-points, and thus seemingly more clever and admirable). The same is true of detective and of academic fiction. In the broadest sense, these novels suggest that women can be just as rational as men are, and that reason itself extends beyond gender to be a useful ideal. The continual corrective to this is issued in the form of unexpected eruption of passion; yet reason remains an important value, and none of the sensible characters are made to suffer long for love. Byatt's Frederica Potter, who wants – emphatically – 'everything' is more or less granted this wish.

In the on-going attempt to avoid being seen as sentimental, twentieth-century writers such as Sayers, Byatt, and Heyer employ various tactics to defend themselves against this possible charge. Their heroines are ambitious yet self-mocking; alternately, as in Heyer's novels, they can be self-sacrificing, yet they possess a solid sense of their own self-worth. Still more interesting, however, are the rare instances when reason triumphs in a novel by means of persuasion, rather than by passion, fury, or force. This is the subject of the final chapter.

7
'The Higher Common Sense'

Reflecting on the contemporary English novel in 1947, Elizabeth Bowen concluded that 'we live in an age of ideas and passions, in which individual destinies count for less. . . .'[1] Since two world wars have rent the fabric of British society, there are ample grounds for offering this as a realistic picture of the modern age. Writers such as Bowen and Olivia Manning, who take World War II as their subject matter, convincingly evoke the darkness inherent in such a time. Those authors in the twentieth century who show characters determinedly attempting to combat despair tentatively suggest in their fiction that one might think one's way out of a problem. Yet they reserve an attitude of suspicion towards the power of individual ingenuity to accomplish this feat: the human mind itself may be deceived – in madness, in romantic love, or in unimaginable betrayal. It becomes difficult for characters to make their own choices, or to have 'individual destinies' that seem meaningful.

The problem with pronounced fatalism in a fictional context is that it tends to make the novels less interesting.[2] Unless characters are seen to possess some latitude of choice, there cannot be a plot, which works by means of cause and effect, and which assumes that individual choices carry definite consequences. And plot is a crucial part of the nineteenth-century novel form, which the twentieth-century authors whom I have been discussing drew on as a pattern for their own work.

One way of dodging this difficulty is to recast the question in a quintessentially modern way, which seeks to locate the source of free will at some overruling, mysterious level of consciousness. In her critical study of Iris Murdoch's novels, A.S. Byatt describes them as combining a sense of both forces being at work. She characterizes Murdoch's novels as suggesting that

> life has finally no pattern, no meaning, that we are ruled by necessity and chance, yet one of the strengths of both her plotting and her symbolism is that it explores fully the sense in which we feel that our lives *are* gripped by formative forces which function below our conscious knowledge or choice.[3]

This argument is particularly clever, as it suggests that characters and readers alike might be choosing the course of their lives after all, but without knowing it. This is part of the appeal of Freudian paradigms in the twentieth century: they explain reasons for human motivation, which gives the illusion of being able to obtain more control over one's life, and so theoretically to prevent disaster. At the same time, they suggest that the individual cannot access these hidden sources (this is the special role of the analyst), which negates their effectiveness as powers for choosing good.

In relation to the novel form, there is also a large degree of fatalism inherent in the construction of a given book as an artistic entity. Elizabeth Bowen explains her own view of her craft as being integrally linked to this idea: 'Plot might seem to be a matter of choice. It is not. The particular plot for the particular novel is something the novelist is driven to.' This sense of inevitability is connected with Bowen's concept of character: 'By the end of the novel, the character has, like the silk worm at work on the cocoon, spun itself out.'[4] Its potentialities are seen to have been expended, in a logical extension of choices made throughout the course of the book. And this makes possible a kind of retrospective revelation of what has been occurring all along; the ending of a novel impacts the reader's understanding of the characters' motivations.

As for the kinds of fictional endings offered to readers in both the nineteenth and twentieth centuries, these are strongly influenced by contemporary literary styles. With the innovations of the modernists in the early part of the twentieth century, open-ended possibilities became the more expected resolution for fiction. Byatt's narrator in *Still Life* observes:

> Once novels ended with marriages: now we know better, we lumber on inconclusively into the sands and swamps of married life, ending in a query, an uncertainty, a bifurcation of possibilities that allows the reader to continue the story with his own preferred, desired projection.[5]

This distinction is particularly important for women writers, who in the twentieth century are seizing the greater freedom of opportunity which their heroines have potentially been granted. If we compare these plots to the nineteenth-century conventions, a contrast is immediately apparent. The nineteenth-century writers fully embraced the idea of closure in their fictions, since female experience was so limited that we as readers wanted to know how their stories would end, for any characters we came to care about. The social constrictions of the time meant that great weight was placed on one particular choice, which would determine an entire life of either fulfillment or despair. The terrible fate against which their heroines fought was the bleak prospect of being boxed into a hateful domestic role, which would sentence them to self-negation forever. Because of this stark necessity of choice, the authors were able to give their novels closure in a way that could be seen to be a manifestly happy ending. Since the absolutely crucial denouement was a suitable marriage, it simplified things: if this could be achieved for the heroine, everyone (including the reader) felt the goodness of that resolution. This might take the form of the ending of *Pride and Prejudice,* where the vexatious results of the first, blighted season of courtship might be seen to be hastening to their same dreadful conclusion, but are averted. Elizabeth marries Mr. Darcy, and Jane marries Mr. Bingley. A satisfying romantic conclusion is also achieved in the union of Anne and Captain Wentworth in *Persuasion,* which has a longer and more bittersweet period preceding it, but which does at least end well for the characters. Many critics have been skeptical of the relative merits as husbands of such characters as Mr. Rochester (for Jane Eyre) and Will Ladislaw (for Dorothea Brooke), and rightly so. Still, within the conventions of the time, these can be seen as happy endings, and are preferable to the alternatives. The heroines are each undoubtedly in love with their spouses, when they marry. And the narrator in *Middlemarch* tells us that her heroine's union has prospered; indeed, that Dorothea's marriage to Will has been fulfilling:

> They were bound to each other by a love stronger than any impulses which could have marred it. No life would have been possible to Dorothea which was not filled with emotion, and she had now a life filled also with a beneficent activity . . . .

Moreover, in terms of ambition – which the onlookers grumble about, implying that she ought to have done something grander – this objection is countered by the narrator. Her life is seen to have been a great success, once the paradigms for judging this have been properly adjusted:

> Her full nature, like that river of which Cyrus broke the strength, spent itself in channels which had no great name on the earth. But the effect of her being on those around her was incalculably diffusive, for the growing good of the world is partly dependent on unhistoric acts. . . .[6]

The twentieth century offered women novelists a chance to write more openly of sexuality, and to offer their characters resolutions that could be considered happy endings, but were not necessarily dependent upon the heroines being married to the 'right' men. There was more freedom to give passion wider scope into other alternatives, or else to follow the darker side of romanticism still further into despair, as Elizabeth Bowen did in her fiction. The limited number of resolutions for Victorian heroines, as has often been pointed out, consisted of either marriage (as in *Middlemarch*) or death (as in *The Mill on the Floss*). In the twentieth century, there were more options; this was an advantage for heroines, because if one became a fallen woman (a distinction which in any case began to disappear), one could still carry on with life, and was not sentenced by the author to drown.

In terms of what their heroines were allowed to do in the world, the novelists seized on the sense of possibility which became available when new vistas were opened. At the same time, the plots of their novels – in contrast to what Byatt has suggested as their modernist characteristics of 'bifurcation' and 'possibilities' – were often decisively conclusive. Bowen, for instance, consciously strove to make her fictional endings seem inevitable, and Byatt admired her for the 'simple brilliance' of the plot of *The House in Paris*, which Byatt considered to be 'of considerable primitive force.'[7] Iris Murdoch's novels almost inevitably resolve the dilemmas of her characters – or, at the least, they make clear to the reader whether the main characters have been granted the object of their desires (nearly always the fulfillment of a romantic passion) or not. To take only one example, Martin Lynch-Gibbon ends *A Severed Head* by returning to his flat in London, after the departure of the other main characters (as he thinks) from the airport:

> I sat thus for a long time surrendered to grief and to the physical pain which is the mark of a true emotion. Then suddenly I heard, as if inside my head, a strange sound. I looked up sharply. The second time the sound came I recognized the front door bell.

This heralds the appearance of Honor Klein, for whom he has felt violent passion, and who has come to seek him out. The dizzying romance of this scene is heightened by his blissful query: 'I wonder if I shall survive it.'[8] Yet this self-doubt is immaterial to the satisfying nature of such a closure to the book. Survival in any case is irrelevant to romantic love – even the antithesis to it – and the geometric pattern of the book has been brilliantly fulfilled.

In a more direct echo of Victorian novel forms, A.S. Byatt ends her tetralogy with an extravagant array of closures. *A Whistling Woman* satisfies the reader's curiosity about the fates of various characters who have been suffering and striving for the decades which have been described in the novels. And those contemporary readers who have read the novels as they appeared might well feel something akin to the experience of those Victorian readers of serial novels; this protracted reading experience makes genuine closure all the more satisfying. The particular resolution of this final novel for one of the main characters, Frederica Potter, is as much a beginning as an ending: she is pregnant, which marks the beginning of the 'long biological process' she has spoken of in such cavalier terms on her television program discussion of women's lives in the 1960s. But this satisfies both requirements: the novel is both open-ended and firmly resolved.

Twentieth-century novelists who are distinctly writing in a tradition of social comedy are more or less bound to offer happy endings, as in Georgette Heyer's romances and Dorothy L. Sayers' detective fiction. But these genres offer great latitude in the tone of the comedy, which can be condescending or wittily ironic. Georgette Heyer invariably rewards her sensible heroines, thus implying that it is beneficial to the individual to remain level-headed, and therefore as an author pointing an expected moral. The more interesting fictional conclusions grapple with the problem of excess emotion in women who find insufficient outlet for their passion. In at least one instance, in addition to her rehabilitation of Harriet Vane in *Gaudy Night*, Sayers champions the cause of those women characters who are seen to possess too much passion, but are merely undirected, thus making a happy ending at once reasonable and surprising. The unfortunate Ann Dorland, in *The Unpleasantness at the Bellona Club*, is lectured at the close of the novel by Peter Wimsey as to her intrinsic worth and her potential value to a future husband: 'Not an artist, not a bohemian, and not a professional man; a man of the world. . . . That is the kind of man who is going to like you very much,' he tells her. The reasons he gives for this optimism are more or less convincing: 'you'll find that yours will be the leading brain of the two. He will take great pride in the fact. And you will find the man reliable and kind, and it will turn out quite well.' Her good fortune is particularized immediately, when Robert Fentiman, another character in the novel, becomes her admiring suitor. Lest this seem too facile a resolution, however, we can recall that she is justified in having an admiring husband; Ann is possessed of a bad complexion and 'rather sticky-out teeth,' in Marjorie's earlier description of her, and therefore qualifies as a plain woman who nonetheless ought to be loved for herself.[9] And she has suffered extremely, from rejection by a former fiancé, and so is all the more deserving of happiness. By making her heroine slightly ridiculous, Sayers minimizes the sentimentality which might attach to her fortuitous union. But she also points the moral that women must first learn to value themselves, before they can be supported in their worth by the approval of men.

At the same time that many twentieth-century novels offer the reader closures which echo Victorian happy endings, there is a definite pattern of heavily ironic conclusions in these novels as well. While a given ending might be joyous for the main characters in its immediate effects, it can be heavily qualified. This stems from the authors' lurking fear that happy endings might be regarded as simple-minded or as too predictable. I would like to consider some of the examples of markedly ironic endings, as they reflect a tacitly fatalistic view of human nature in its capacity to change or mature. In an age which has been heavily influenced by a popularization of Freudian psychoanalysis, it has become more usual to doubt the possibility of true emotional growth for characters. An important test case for this idea is the work of Susan Howatch, who takes psychological crises as her subject. She details an entire process of breakdown and rehabilitation for several individuals. In each case, the main character is delusional to some degree or other – or, is simply refusing to see that he or she is on a destructive path through addictions adopted in order to minimize pain by avoidance. The first part of each book leads the main character deeper into trouble, until an explosive crisis propels him or her unwillingly to seek help from a spiritual mentor. The process of resolving the psychological tangle often involves facing up to repressed pain from the past, or an uncovering of lies which have affected a character's self-image. A character like Charles Ashworth in *Glittering Images* might be forced to learn that he had a profligate father (whose identity and existence has been hidden from him), and to extend forgiveness to – and obtain it from – his stepfather.

Howatch does offer a genuine resolution to all of these emotional traumas, often with a moral imperative to send the character on his way with a more disciplined path ahead, in order to ward off future disasters of the same kind. Jonathan Darrow in *Ultimate Prizes*, for instance, counsels the wayward clergyman Neville Aysgarth, first telling him that 'As with all distressed people . . . one has to locate the source of the distress in order to heal the wound in the psyche.' After exploring the background causes of Aysgarth's anguish, however, he also looks to the future, giving him an imperative to devote himself to his second wife (who has been a significant part of the unfolding drama). While Darrow is certain of the direction he points for his protégé, he also disclaims clairvoyance on his behalf:

> 'Aysgarth, there's no board outside this office which says: "Fortune-telling by Appointment." All I can tell you as a priest is that you've sinned, you've repented and now by the grace of God you'll be redeemed – although the manner of the redemption is still to be revealed.'[10]

This is sensible advice, and constitutes proper penance for Aysgarth's having severely mistreated his first wife, who has died early in the novel, in part through his neglect.

The psychological cure is only partial, however. Howatch does not denigrate it as merely a quick fix; the characters are considerably better off than they were in the throes of their main crises. Still, they are fully capable of sinning again, and in the same way. Aysgarth notes at the conclusion to *Ultimate Prizes* that he 'was an old hand at taking scandalous risks' and had always 'liked to live dangerously.'[11] He appears again in the novel *Scandalous Risks*, seducing a young woman, and refusing to recognize his actions as being either wrong or selfish. Another psychologically reformed character, Charles Ashworth, lives a relatively productive life until he reappears in the later novel, *Absolute Truths*, and his wife Lyle (who has been a mainstay for him) dies, catapulting him into a dramatic reenactment of rivalry with his old enemy, Jardine. In one sense, this is the best kind of ending for this sort of psychological novel, as it does not ask too much credibility from the reader. It seems much easier to believe that he will fall again than it would be to believe that he lived a pious and sober life thereafter. In another sense, though, it is rather uncomfortably ironic. This is almost as much of a cliché as the reverse would be. Since we have seen, first-hand, the extreme agony which the narrator has gone through in the course of the novel, it would be reasonable to think that he would do anything rather than repeat it.

Elizabeth Bowen's later novels become increasingly ironic, verging on surrealism, which sits uneasily in the paradigm of largely realistic fiction. In *A World of Love*, for instance, the final scene of the novel sends the heroine to meet another character for the first time, offering the Shakespearean resolution: 'They no sooner looked but they loved.' Bowen's most melodramatic novel ending occurs in her final work, *Eva Trout*, in which the hero and heroine are being seen off on their honeymoon by well-wishers from Victoria station. The farewell speech, given by her former guardian, Constantine, meditates on the fickleness of fortune: 'On behalf of all, I wish you a pleasant future. The future, as we know, will resemble the past in being the result, largely, of a concatenation of circumstances. Many of our best moments, as well as our worst, are fortuitous.'[12] This sense of existential flux is immediately reinforced, however, by the fact that Jeremy, Eva's adopted child, rushes up to the bride and shoots her dead with a revolver. This can seem gratuitous fatalism.

Even those writers who seem determined to work a fortuitous resolution for their characters, such as Barbara Pym, cannot help seeming rather desperate to bring this about. Again, the answer to this problem for the novelist can be the use of irony – and, in particular, ironic reference to the nineteenth-century novel, which seems to demand a happy ending for the main characters. *No Fond Return of Love*, for instance, closes with the improbable scene where Aylwin Forbes directs a taxi to the house of the heroine, Dulcie Mainwaring, intending to propose to her:

> As for his apparent change of heart, he had suddenly remembered the end of *Mansfield Park*, and how Edmund fell out of love with Mary Crawford and came to care for Fanny. Dulcie must surely know the novel well, and would understand how such things can happen.

Lest this seem too whimsical a solution, the hero's egotism is seen to be motivating his actions after all:

> For what might seem to the rest of the world an eminently 'suitable' marriage to a woman no longer very young, who could help him with his work, now seemed to him the most unsuitable that could be imagined, simply because it had never occurred to him that he could love such a person.

This satisfies Aylwin's vanity, as he concludes: 'It was all delightfully incongruous. Just the sort of thing Aylwin Forbes would do.'[13] Twentieth-century writers who bring together the heroine and the object of her affection almost cannot help quoting Jane Austen – either in outright irony, or in playful tribute to the mistress of this art.

To return again to the quintessential nineteenth-century happy ending for deserving heroines – marriage – I would like to give one final example here of an excessively ironic modern reworking of this same theme. It is also important as a recasting of the basic problem with which twentieth-century women writers often wrestle in more or less open terms: what is to be done with excessively passionate women characters? Stella Gibbons alludes to the uneasiness which her female characters feel with expressing or acknowledging emotion – and which some of her readers in the 1930s might be expected to share. She caricatures her professional young female character Edna Valentine Lassiter, in *Miss Linsey and Pa,* as a 'dedicated artist, patiently recording her sensitive reactions to the enormous multiplicity of phenomena which we have agreed to call life,' yet who understands nothing of it all (including the violent passion of her lesbian flat-mate), and ends by marrying a cheerful, solid professional man. 'She who had thought of herself as the artist set apart from normal experiences strayed too near to life and was quietly swallowed, joining the huge company and sharing the joys and griefs of the happy obscure.' This reassures the reader that an oversensitive, artistic woman would be more fulfilled as an ordinary housewife. Not only is artistic work seen in itself to be overrated – E.V. does not publish fiction again – but the possible effects of feminism are painted as being suspicious and even dire. The Bohemian scene which E.V. Lassiter inhabits in London is characterized as follows:

> She had lived for nearly ten years in a set which assumed men and women to be intellectual, financial, spiritual and sexual equals, thereby creating a desert in which Meyestein, Colbrooke, Roger and Swettin [various male suitors] told you about their sorrows, subsequently putting their heads on your chest and going to sleep.[14]

This kind of writing reinforces traditional gender values (and judgemental superiority as well). Its tone of rather ponderous satire reveals the fear of feminist equality which might be seen to emasculate men and transform them into unsuitable husbands, which would cause the chance for a happy outcome to vanish. In this context, women – like men – are seen to want only 'one thing,' though these differing desires can seem to be mutually exclusive.

But this essential gender difference is part of the fun of many of these novels, which depict the intricate interplay of sexual politics. While social conventions can be seen to have changed in the twentieth century, women still wrestle with many of the same problems. And feminism, as Gibbons suggests, can occasionally alienate men and women from each other, though needlessly so. Sometimes the best way in which to combat this competitiveness is by laughing at it. In regard to the vexed question of female passion, Gibbons suggests that it makes intellectuals, in particular, nervous. She ridicules male vanity in the figure of her comic character Mr. Meyerburg (nicknamed Mr. Mybug) in *Cold Comfort Farm*, who is clearly running scared. A self-styled intellectual, he explains to the heroine, Flora Poste, that he is at work on a 'psychological study' of Branwell Brontë, whom he claims has written the novels of his three sisters, who were 'passing his manuscripts off as their own.' His argument is based on the intensity of passion in *Wuthering Heights*: 'You see, it's obvious that it's his book and not Emily's. No woman could have written that. It's male stuff. . . .'[15] The intention of this claim is to seduce the heroine – or any other woman who may cross his path – by talking frankly about sex. This fails notably with the sensible Flora, and the author's response as a novelist is to grant Mr. Mybug a wife at the end of the novel.

The irony of these endings stems mostly from the fact that authors seem reluctant to suggest that their characters can change. In most of these fictional worlds, the characters can alter neither their circumstances, nor their basic temperaments. Thinking does not work; and feeling is not allowed. There is little faith expressed in the intrinsic goodness of emotion – except on rare occasions – or in the passion portrayed by D.H. Lawrence, which makes female authors especially nervous because if they echo it, they might seem (since they are judged severely as women) to be hysterical. An obvious defense against this fear of emotion is humor; but the adoption of this sort of tone alarms the authors into thinking that they might not be taken seriously. If a 'mannered, edgy style [which is] a humorist's tool' is employed by a writer such as Elizabeth Bowen, it is done in order to 'express a severe judgment on a diminished society,' as Hermione Lee has remarked.[16]

This creates a profound distrust of Victorian happy endings, along with the increasing doubt about characters being able forthrightly to choose their own destinies. Influenced by the novel form itself – which seems to demand a resolution – the authors often provide closure in these novels, though not usually in the sense of the characters having worked something through emotionally. In the twentieth century, it may well be assumed that it is only possible to do this with humor, which deprecates the attempt at the same time that it brings it about. But this is not necessarily a drawback, and works that offer this kind of plot need not be dismissed as superficial. I would like to end this study with a couple of examples of happily resolved novels which achieve an integrity in plot. They set out to solve complex problems through the agency of an objective outsider, yet they accomplish this in a fairly convincing manner that works with, rather than against, the unhappy characters' desires and temperaments, rather than imposing a false resolution on them.

The best example of this is Stella Gibbons' *Cold Comfort Farm*, a satire with realist trappings. It is a fascinating contrast to the work of novelists such as A.S. Byatt, because Gibbons also is reacting against the power of Lawrentian passion, though by the use of humor to show up its potential weaknesses. Her heroine, Flora Poste, goes to stay with relations in the country, who embrace fatalistic melancholy in a parody of the rural novel. Flora Poste embodies the concept of reason; her intention is to help her benighted family members by showing them reasonable alternatives to their fatalistic and masochistic acceptance of domination by the family matriarch. When she departs for Cold Comfort Farm, she does so in a spirit of adventure, telling her friend in London, Mary Smiling, that 'there is sure to be a lot of material I can collect for my novel; and perhaps one or two of the relations will have messes or miseries in their domestic circle which I can clear up.' Mary labels Flora immediately as a masochistic Victorian figure, observing, 'You have the most revolting Florence Nightingale complex.' But Flora derives her sense of self-identity from Jane Austen, with whom she feels she has much in common: 'She liked everything to be tidy and pleasant and comfortable about her, and so do I.'[17] Rather than being officious, however, Flora improves the 'untidy lives' which she finds at the farm in a way which evokes each of the characters' innate desires, and therefore fulfills rather than punishes or ridicules each of them. This dramatizes a way of thinking which effects good results, yet is not condescending.

Two novels by Georgette Heyer, *The Unknown Ajax* and *The Grand Sophy*, achieve a similar resonance – not by means of dramatic or overly subtle deductive reasoning, but by the application of common sense. Both of the main characters in these books rescue an entrenched, unhappy family, but they do so in a way which does not seek to alter the deepest desires of the other characters.

In *The Unknown Ajax*, a distant relation unexpectedly succeeds to the family title and inheritance of an estate in Kent when the heir dies in a sailing accident. The family instantly patronize him, when he arrives to meet them – but it is they who are blinded to their own danger, as the youngest son has assumed leadership of a band of smugglers on the coast. Discovery of this would be a grave blow to aristocratic respectability, but they realize that the true disaster is to the future career of Richmond Darracott, the young man. Hugo Darracott, the capable, newly arrived member of the family, orchestrates a beautifully theatrical display, intended to deceive the Prevention Officer who comes to the house to arrest Richmond at the end of the novel. Richmond has been shot in the shoulder by an excise man on his way home from a smuggling escapade, but the family pretends that another character, Claude, has been wounded while returning from a midnight tryst with the local blacksmith's daughter, and that Richmond (who necessarily appears to be somewhat wobbly) has been drinking and playing cards all evening. This ensemble acting piece unites the family together in loyalty. It also procures a second chance for the morally chastened and repentant Richmond, who exits the novel with intentions to enlist in the army, which has been his true desire all along.

Heyer's *The Grand Sophy* also depicts a sensible yet dashing outsider who appears in the midst of an unhappy family scene and sets all to rights. Sophy's first entrance into the house of her London relations convinces her that Charles Rivenhall, the hero, is about to marry an entirely unsuitable (though aristocratic) woman, who is making his family miserable while she is merely his fiancée. The prospect of her ascendency over them when the two are married appals Sophy. When she confides her indignation to a friend, he pronounces it to be a 'Very bad business. . . . Nothing to be done, though.' The heroine declines to take this view: '"That," said Sophy severely, "is what people always say when they are too lazy, or perhaps too timorous, to make a push to be helpful! I have a great many faults, but I am not lazy, and I am not timorous. . . ."'[18] This is an especially successful novel because the heroine is spirited and yet also compassionate. She helps each of the characters to solve his or her individual problems in inventive ways, though always with full respect for the integrity of the individual. She does not force confession from the younger son, Hubert, her cousin, whom she sees to be in distress. (Sophy does, however, confront the evil money-lender who has fleeced Hubert, visiting him in his lair and threatening him with a pistol – all of which is evidence of her flair and self-possession.) She dissuades Cecilia, the eldest daughter in the family, from an unsuitable engagement, by pretending to supplant her in the affections of the eminently suitable duke whom Cecilia has rashly refused, rekindling her passion through female rivalry and jealousy. The novel ends with another set-piece of dramatic action, as in *The Unknown Ajax*, where all crises are resolved, potentially disastrous marriages are averted through engagements being broken, and all of the characters are linked with the romantic partners of their choice. Although Georgette Heyer is not always successful at resolving her novels in a way that seems to illustrate a trajectory from the plot which precedes them, in these particular novels she shows herself to be brilliant at constructing fictional endings that honor the thoughtful choices which her characters have made. Where they have been wrong, such as Richmond Darracott, they have repented; and where they have been afraid to reach for their desires, they have summoned the courage to do so.

Moreover, in *The Grand Sophy*, the heroine – whose passion and verve have never been doubted – is claimed by the young man in the novel who has the most ardent spirit amongst her various suitors. Heyer offers readers the quintessential romance novel ending, where the heroine is seen to be crushed against the male tweeds:

> 'Charles!' uttered Sophy, shocked. 'You cannot love me.' Mr. Rivenhall pulled the door to behind them, and in a very rough fashion jerked her into his arms, and kissed her. 'I don't: I dislike you excessively!' he said savagely. Entranced by these lover-like words, Miss Stanton-Lacy returned his embrace with fervour, and meekly allowed herself to be led off to the stables.[19]

It will be self-evident that all of these books are intended as comedies – which strongly suggests that this offers the best format for such positive and cheerful thinking. Moreover, the novels are further distanced from their contemporary audiences by being set in different time periods – in Heyer's case, early nineteenth-century England, and in Gibbons' *Cold Comfort Farm*, in a future period of time. Whether these are too simplified as plot structures will be judged differently by different readers. But it is worth appraising these novelists' application of reason to human sufferings, in an attempt to lighten them through concerted effort. This cannot provide anything other than temporary relief, as all solutions are necessarily short-term. At the same time, Heyer and Gibbons dramatize ways in which characters not only come to a better situation in life through making wiser choices; but they also behave with honor (a great point in their favor, as these are, above all, moral tales). They do so with great wit, though also with astutely rational decisions being made by the leading characters. These twentieth-century writers are trying to depict larger-than-life psychological struggles in their characters; but they are also interested in applying reason and rational solutions to those problems. It may be that such an effort is in vain; in cases of madness and fixed irrationality, it is difficult to apply a corrective. But the reason that Heyer and Gibbons succeed so brilliantly is that they bring viable emotion into their books, as well as reason.

Stella Gibbons' *Cold Comfort Farm* achieves part of its effect from the comic contrast of its modern heroine to the dark, melodramatic passion which infuses the rural characters. When Flora Poste arrives at the farm, she does so with the intention of making things 'tidy.' Her first suggestion, upon discerning the pall that covers the Sussex farm, is that the family sell it and move elsewhere. But the second phase of her improvements strike to the root of the problem: Aunt Ada Doom holds everyone in the family in thrall, and it is she who must be tackled, in order to loose her paralytic hold on the Starkadder family. The process of transformation takes two forms: Flora aids each member of the family in achieving or reaching out for his or her secret desire, and she also confronts Aunt Ada with her selfishness. The latter's resentfulness towards everyone else is a wonderful parody of psychological blackmail. As a child, she has seen 'something nasty in the woodshed,' which gives her the conviction that she has the right to demand abject loyalty from the rest of the family, who must never be allowed to abandon her. Flora ponders the astuteness of making such a claim:

> It struck her that Aunt Ada Doom's madness had taken the most convenient form possible. If everybody who went mad could arrange in what way it was to take them, she felt pretty sure they would all choose to be mad like Aunt Ada.[20]

She breaks the hold of an oppressive parent figure, by showing that it is possible to stand up to her, and she also gives a positive direction to everyone's pent-up energies. Her basis for these efforts towards rationality are the teachings of the Abbé Fausse-Maigre, as expressed in a book entitled *The Higher Common Sense*, which is what she opposes to the irrational, fatalistic passions of the Starkadder family.[21]

Part of what is so humorous about the novel is that each of the characters lusts after something different, and Flora employs immense creativity to help them towards their desires. The young woman, Elfine Starkadder, is in love with the local squire, Richard Hawk-Monitor. Flora persuades her to come to London, effecting a Cinderella transformation which prepares her to go to his twenty-first birthday party where she hopes to capture his heart (and accordingly to overcome the social differences between them, allowing him to propose to her). This means that she must be able to present herself to him and to his family as someone who is able to enter his social class and to hold her own. Flora instructs Elfine in proper clothing and proper upper-class sentiments, yet she does not seek to alter Elfine's essential character, or to make her into another kind of woman. Flora says: 'I tell you of these things in order that you may have some standards, within yourself, with which secretly to compare the many new facts and people you will meet if you enter a new life.' Nor is the proposed transformation intended to be only superficial; Flora determines that she must 'be transformed indeed; her artiness must be rooted out. Her mind must match the properly groomed head in which it was housed.'[22]

The comedy here lies in the fact that Elfine has a passionately romantic (and also naïve) nature, which causes Flora to 'coldly [raise] her eyebrows,' when she hears the thought expressed that: 'I thought poetry was so beautiful that if you met someone you loved, and you told them you wrote poetry, that would be enough to make them love you, too.' She objects entirely: '"On the contrary," said Flora firmly, "most young men are alarmed on hearing that a young woman writes poetry. Combined with an ill-groomed head of hair and an eccentric style of dress, such an admission is almost fatal."'[23] Elfine's compromise, which unites both artistry and propriety, is to decide to write poetry 'secretly' and publish a volume when she turns fifty.

As for the other characters, various resolutions are offered. Flora helps Amos Starkadder to find the courage to set out on a preaching tour – this is his passionate calling in life, as evidenced by his delight in denouncing those members of the Church of the Quivering Brethren who gather to hear his sermons. His departure frees Amos' eldest son, Reuben, to take over the running of the farm, which affords him the deepest possible satisfaction; the morning following his father's dramatic departure, 'He now thought of himself as master of the farm, and a slow tide of satisfied earth-lust indolently ebbed and flowed in his veins as he began his daily task of counting the chickens' feathers.'[24] The playboy younger son, Seth, is helped to a realization of his Grand Passion, which is to become a Hollywood film star. Even the officious and insecure Mr. Mybug is married off to Rennet, one of the minor characters.

The most crucial transformation is that which Flora works for Aunt Ada, who has been barricaded in her room for decades, with rare exceptions. One possible resolution of the novel would have been for Aunt Ada to be properly punished for having dominated the rest of the family so ruthlessly. Instead, she appears at the wedding of Elfine and Richard Hawk-Monitor at the end of the book, to everyone's surprise, announcing, 'we must hurry up and begin the wedding breakfast. I leave for Paris by air in less than an hour.'[25] This gives a truly comic resolution to the novel. The villain of the piece is forgiven, which makes everyone freer to pursue his or her individual bent without lingering resentment; moreover, there is a supreme excellence in the plan, since she literally leaves the farm.

The most melancholy of the Starkadders is Aunt Ada's daughter, Judith, to whom Flora presents a Freudian analytical solution. She introduces Judith to Dr. Müdel, who convinces her to stay at his clinic in London for treatment. (Gibbons gleefully satirizes this kind of psychological therapy: 'It was one of his disagreeable duties as a State psychoanalyst to remove the affections of his patients from the embarrassing objects upon which they were concentrated, and focus them, instead, upon himself.') Still, it is an acceptable resolution for her, and the analyst decides immediately that he will eventually redirect her energies towards the study of 'olt churches,' which will give her an occupation.[26] *Cold Comfort Farm* is manifestly a comic tale, but it uses humor to be kind as well as scathing to its characters. Gibbons uses rationality, or common sense, to show that her characters can better their lives by exercising careful thought and by having the courage to reach out for their desires.

The major nineteenth-century novelists influenced these twentieth-century women writers in incalculable ways. When Barbara Pym's heroine in *Excellent Women* wished to explain her own character, she contrasted herself with its antithesis: 'Let me hasten to add that I am not at all like Jane Eyre, who must have given hope to so many women who tell their stories in the first person, nor have I ever thought of myself as being like her.' When Stella Gibbons wanted to announce her counter-attack to sentimentality, she borrowed from *Mansfield Park*, putting as epigraph to *Cold Comfort Farm* the phrase, 'Let other pens dwell on guilt and misery.' A.S. Byatt's tetralogy is very like Eliot's *Middlemarch*, with its impressive historical sweep, its detailed scientific interests, and its continual theorizing by the narrator. Elizabeth Bowen must have longed to capture in her own work some of the 'fire and ice' which she admired in Emily Brontë's *Wuthering Heights*.[27] Living in a different cultural context, yet drawing consciously on a literary heritage, these authors reshaped the novel to reflect their own times. Taking into fiction their academic backgrounds, they brought into their novels an intellectual zeal and (as they hoped) a new basis for relationships with men. Their passion for ideas, for the inexorable fatefulness of plot, and for the power of the mind to overcome obstacles infuses their works. These authors wrote as women, but also as novelists who strove to transcend the defining limits of gender – not as a political statement, but because a writer most wishes to explore in the realm of the imagination, and to find what she does not yet know.

Notes

Introduction

1. A.S. Byatt, *Passions of the Mind: Selected Writings* (New York: Random House, 1992), p. 11.
2. A.S. Byatt, *Babel Tower* (London: Chatto & Windus, 1996), p. 159.
3. A.S. Byatt, quoted in Olga Kenyon, *Women Novelists Today: A Survey of English Writing in the Seventies and Eighties* (New York: St. Martin's Press, 1988), p. 53.
4. John Carey, *Pure Pleasure: A Guide to the Twentieth Century's Most Enjoyable Books* (London: Faber & Faber, 2000), p. 87.
5. Ruth Robbins, *Literary Feminisms* (London: Macmillan, 2000), pp. 6–7.
6. Gillian Hanscombe and Virginia L. Smyers, *Writing for their Lives: The Modernist Woman 1910–40* (London: The Women's Press Ltd, 1987).
7. Nicola Humble, *The Feminine Middlebrow Novel, 1920s to 1950s: Class, Domesticity and Bohemianism* (Oxford: Oxford University Press, 2001), p. 5. Humble's admirable and far-ranging study seeks to 'rehabilitate' the term 'middle-brow' and its generic application to certain novels. Her personal statement about having discovered and enjoyed these novels defines their essential components: 'The generic "girly book" combined an enjoyable feminine "trivia" of clothes, food, family, manners, romance, and so on, with an element of wry self-consciousness that allowed the reader to drift between ironic and complicit readings.' As she goes on to observe, there is a seriousness of purpose which underlies this fiction as well, and I have followed her example in including an eclectic range of types of literature.
8. It will be argued that Virginia Woolf says the same thing; but I think that Byatt and Murdoch mean it in a different, less consciously feminist sense. Woolf's ardently feminist agenda as expressed in her work caused her to use 'androgyny' to promote a particular view about women, rather than to 'escape' from its perceived limitations, as Byatt has suggested.
9. Kenyon, *Women Novelists Today*, p. 53.
10. A.S. Byatt, quoted *ibid.*, p. 55.
11. Byatt, *Passions of the Mind*, p. 239.

Chapter 1 The world gone mad in wartime

1. Olivia Manning, *The Great Fortune* (1960; published in *The Balkan Trilogy*, London: Penguin, 1981), p. 267.
2. I am doing a disservice to Manning's wartime novels, by over-simplifying here. Part of her strength as a writer is that she does a very creditable job of creating a panoramic view of the war, particularly in her rendering of the characters Prince Yakimov and the young British soldier, Simon Boulderstone. As Jenny Hartley points out in her excellent study *Millions Like Us*, Manning has been praised for her astonishingly realistic portrayal of battle scenes.

Jenny Hartley, *Millions Like Us: British Women's Fiction of the Second World War* (London: Virago Press, 1997).
3. Elizabeth Bowen, *The Heat of the Day* (1948; New York: Knopf, 1949), p. 99.
4. *Ibid.*, p. 147.
5. That this has to do with class issues is self-evident.
6. Baroness Orczy, *The Scarlet Pimpernel* (1905; New York: Nelson Doubleday, Inc., 1935), p. 42.
7. Bowen, *The Heat of the Day*, p. 102.
8. Elizabeth Bowen, *The Last September* (1929; New York: Knopf, 1964), p. 49.
9. *Ibid.*, p. 64.
10. *Ibid.*, pp. 143, 146.
11. *Ibid.*, p. 298.
12. *Ibid.*, p. 301.
13. *Ibid.* This is absurdly stylized, in the context of the novel; a 'few pieces of skin' cannot but be acutely painful. But Marda wishes to minimize the drama of the event immediately – which brings out the even more shocking passion of Hugo Montmorency (which is adulterous, and therefore forbidden), and casts it in these terms.
14. Bowen, *The Heat of the Day*, p. 103.
15. *Ibid.*, p. 26.
16. *Ibid.*, pp. 30, 26.
17. *Ibid.*, pp. 29, 33, 30.
18. *Ibid.*, pp. 33, 30. In Harold Pinter's screenplay version of Bowen's novel, this scene acquires very vivid force and power, even without the perspective of Bowen's narrator, who dominates so much of the book.
19. *Ibid.*, pp. 211, 214.
20. *Ibid.*, p. 214.
21. *Ibid.*, pp. 213–14.
22. *Ibid.*, pp. 152, 263, 269.
23. *Ibid.*
24. *Ibid.*
25. John Coates, *Social Discontinuity in the Novels of Elizabeth Bowen: The Conservative Quest* (Lewiston, NY: Edwin Mellen Press, 1998), p. 162.
26. Manning, *The Great Fortune*, p. 67.
27. *Ibid.*, pp. 268–9.
28. *Ibid.*, p. 270.
29. Olivia Manning, *The Spoilt City* (1962; published in *The Balkan Trilogy*, London: Penguin, 1981), p. 317.
30. Lest Harriet appear too much of a whiner, Manning also gives us Guy's view of their marriage – one which is suspiciously admiring of his wife, whom he genuinely pities in her discontentedness, and whom he approves for having '[come] from the narrowest, most prejudiced class, she had nevertheless declassed herself.' He sees his own mission as one of giving her life meaning (though she has rejected his efforts at her 'political education'): 'Harriet, he felt, must be protected from the distrust that had grown out of an unloved childhood. He would say to himself: "Oh, stand between her and her fighting soul," touched by the small, thin body that contained her spirit. And he saw her unfortunate because life, which he took easily, was to her so unnecessarily difficult' (*The Spoilt City*, p. 343).

31. *Ibid.*, p. 316.
32. Olivia Manning, *The Danger Tree* (London: Weidenfeld & Nicolson, 1977), p. 94.
33. Olivia Manning, *Friends and Heroes* (1965; published in *The Balkan Trilogy*, London: Penguin, 1981), pp. 671–2.
34. Olivia Manning, *The Sum of Things* (London: Weidenfeld & Nicolson, 1980), pp. 145–6.
35. Manning, *The Danger Tree*, p. 158.
36. Manning, *The Sum of Things*, pp. 148, 150.
37. *Ibid.*, pp. 145–6
38. Manning, *The Sum of Things*, pp. 9–10.
39. *Ibid.*, p. 149.
40. Manning, *The Danger Tree*, p. 158.
41. *Ibid.*, p. 55.
42. Anthea Trodd, *Women's Writing in English: Britain 1900–1945* (London: Routledge, 1989), p. 125.
43. Orczy, *The Scarlet Pimpernel*, pp. 41–2.
44. *Ibid.*, p. 58.
45. *Ibid.*, p. 43.
46. *Ibid.*, pp. 146, 148.
47. *Ibid.*, pp. 161–2.
48. *Ibid.*, pp. 196–7.
49. *Ibid.*, pp. 199–200.

Chapter 2 Gothic and fabulist tales

1. John Sutherland, *Is Heathcliff a Murderer?: Great Puzzles in Nineteenth-Century Literature* (Oxford: Oxford University Press, 1996), pp. 59–65.
2. Dorothy L. Sayers, *Gaudy Night* (1936; New York: Avon, 1968), p. 66.
3. *Ibid.*, pp. 61, 68.
4. *Ibid.*, p. 47.
5. Elizabeth Bowen, 'The Cat Jumps,' *The Collected Stories of Elizabeth Bowen* (London: Jonathan Cape, 1980), p. 362.
6. *Ibid.*, p. 363.
7. *Ibid.*, pp. 368–9.
8. *Ibid.*, p. 366.
9. Elizabeth Bowen, 'The Demon Lover,' *The Collected Stories of Elizabeth Bowen*, pp. 661–2.
10. *Ibid.*, pp. 663–4, 666.
11. *Ibid.*, p. 663.
12. A.S. Byatt, 'The July Ghost,' *Sugar and Other Stories* (New York: Penguin, 1988), p. 40.
13. *Ibid.*, p. 46.
14. *Ibid.*, pp. 50, 56.
15. *Ibid.*, p. 54.
16. A.S. Byatt, 'The Next Room,' *Sugar and Other Stories*, pp. 58, 67.
17. *Ibid.*, pp. 66, 70.
18. *Ibid.*, pp. 74–5.

19. *Ibid.*, pp. 80–1.
20. Iris Murdoch, *Nuns and Soldiers* (1980; New York: Penguin, 1988), p. 296.
21. *Ibid.*, pp. 291, 294.
22. Byatt, 'The Next Room,' p. 81.
23. Susan Howatch, *Mystical Paths* (New York: Fawcett Crest, 1992), p. 3.
24. *Ibid.*, p. 48.
25. *Ibid.*, p. 49.
26. *Ibid.*
27. *Ibid.*, p. 97.
28. Susan Howatch, *Scandalous Risks* (New York: Fawcett Crest, 1991), pp. 361–2.
29. Howatch, *Mystical Paths*, p. 451.
30. *Ibid.*, pp. 431, 435.
31. *Ibid.*, pp. 435, 476–7.
32. *Ibid.*, pp. 431, 448.
33. A.S. Byatt, 'The Djinn in the Nightingale's Eye,' *The Djinn in the Nightingale's Eye: Five Fairy Stories* (London: Chatto & Windus, 1994), pp. 95–6.
34. *Ibid.*, pp. 201, 203.
35. *Ibid.*, p. 193.
36. *Ibid.*, p. 206.
37. Mary Stewart, *Touch Not the Cat* (Greenwich, CT: Fawcett Publications, Inc., 1976), p. 12.
38. *Ibid.*, pp. 12, 234, 238.
39. *Ibid.*, p. 236.

Chapter 3 Grieving and madness

1. William Shakespeare, *Hamlet*, IV.v.174.
2. Iris Murdoch, *Nuns and Soldiers* (1980; New York: Penguin, 1988), p. 466.
3. *Ibid.*, pp. 101, 144, 101, 467.
4. *Ibid.*, p. 143.
5. *Ibid.*, pp. 465, 481.
6. Iris Murdoch, *The Bell* (1958; New York: Penguin, 1986), pp. 99, 107, 103.
7. *Ibid.*, pp. 106, 104, 107.
8. *Ibid.*, p. 158.
9. *Ibid.*, pp. 104, 105.
10. *Ibid.*, p. 280.
11. *Ibid.*, pp. 288, 296.
12. *Hamlet*, V.ii.244–8.
13. Elizabeth Bowen, *To the North* (1932; New York: Avon, 1979), pp. 257–8.
14. Elizabeth Bowen, *The House in Paris* (1935; New York: Avon, 1979), p. 181.
15. Caroline Blackwood, *Great Granny Webster* (1977; New York: New York Review of Books, 2002), p. 34.
16. Iris Murdoch, *The Book and the Brotherhood* (1987; New York: Viking, 1988), p. 116.
17. *Ibid.*, p. 385.
18. A.S. Byatt, *The Virgin in the Garden* (1978; New York: Penguin, 1981), p. 57.
19. *Ibid.*, pp. 62–3.
20. *Ibid.*, p. 60.

21. In Byatt's final novel of the tetralogy, Marcus is shown as being happily settled in Cambridge in a gay relationship.
22. Byatt, *The Virgin in the Garden*, p. 383.
23. A.S. Byatt, *A Whistling Woman* (London: Chatto & Windus, 2002), p. 309.
24. *Ibid.*, p. 200.
25. *Ibid.*, p. 18.
26. *Ibid.*, pp. 23–5.
27. *Ibid.*, pp. 123, 125.
28. *Ibid.*, pp. 235–6.
29. A.S. Byatt, *Possession: A Romance* (New York: Random House, 1990), p. 496.
30. A.S. Byatt, *Sugar and Other Stories* (New York: Penguin, 1988), pp. 130, 145.
31. *Ibid.*, p. 145.
32. *Ibid.*, p. 134.
33. Iris Murdoch, *The Good Apprentice* (1985; New York: Viking, 1986), pp. 424–5.
34. Iris Murdoch, *The Sacred and Profane Love Machine* (1974; New York: Penguin, 1983), pp. 340–1.
35. Molly Keane, *Treasure Hunt* (1952; London: Virago, 1991), pp. 34–5.
36. *Ibid.*, p. 75.

Chapter 4 Romance

1. Elizabeth Bowen, *The Hotel* (1927; New York, Penguin, 1987), p. 102.
2. Hermione Lee has pointed out that Bowen seems to have learned a great deal from Henry James, to whose work hers has often been compared. See Hermione Lee, *Elizabeth Bowen: An Estimation* (London: Vision Press, 1981).
3. Elizabeth Bowen, *The House in Paris* (1935; New York: Avon, 1979), p. 106.
4. Bowen, *The Hotel*, p. 11.
5. *Ibid.*, pp. 11, 102.
6. Olivia Manning, *The Wind Changes* (1937; London: Virago Press, 1988), p. 319.
7. A.S. Byatt, *A Whistling Woman* (London: Chatto & Windus, 2002), p. 24.
8. *Ibid.*, p. 12.
9. *Ibid.*, pp. 142, 415.
10. A.S. Byatt, *Babel Tower* (London: Chatto & Windus, 1996), p. 155.
11. Byatt, *A Whistling Woman*, pp. 258, 149.
12. *Ibid.*, p. 11.
13. Agatha Mond has also written what turns out to be a best-selling book, in the course of reading her fiction aloud to Frederica, hers and Frederica's children, and other friends.
14. The ending of Byatt's tetralogy gives a sense of almost Dickensian closure, which again reflects the novels' echoing of nineteenth-century form and twentieth-century content.
15. Bowen, *The Hotel*, p. 53.
16. *Ibid.*, p. 56.
17. *Ibid.*, p. 114.
18. *Ibid.*, pp. 136–7.
19. *Ibid.*, p. 102.

20. Elizabeth Bowen, *The Last September* (1929; New York: Knopf, 1964), pp. 98, 187.
21. Elizabeth Bowen, *Friends and Relations* (1931; New York: Penguin, 1986), p. 25.
22. *Ibid.*, p. 104.
23. *Ibid.*, p. 105.
24. *Ibid.*, p. 106.
25. *Ibid.*, p. 99.
26. Elizabeth Bowen, *To the North* (1932; New York: Avon, 1979), p. 19.
27. *Ibid.*, p. 129.
28. *Ibid.*, p. 187.
29. *Ibid.*, p. 232.
30. *Ibid.*, p. 194.
31. Benedict Kiely, *Modern Irish Fiction: A Critique* (Dublin: Golden Eagle Books, 1950), p. 157.
32. Bowen, *To the North*, p. 5.
33. *Ibid.*, pp. 28–9.
34. *Ibid.*, pp. 164–5.
35. *Ibid.*, p. 236.
36. Bowen, *The House in Paris*, p. 66.
37. *Ibid.*, p. 152.
38. *Ibid.*, pp. 153, 152.
39. *Ibid.*, p. 90.
40. Elizabeth Bowen, *The Death of the Heart* (1938; New York: Avon, 1979), p. 33.
41. *Ibid.*, pp. 58–9.
42. *Ibid.*, p. 13.
43. Bowen, *The House in Paris*, p. 159.
44. Bowen, *The Death of the Heart*, p. 44.
45. *Ibid.*, p. 33.
46. *Ibid.*, p. 7.
47. *Ibid.*, p. 189.
48. *Ibid.*, p. 198.
49. *Ibid.*, p. 191.
50. *Ibid.*, p. 208.
51. *Ibid.*, p. 97.
52. *Ibid.*, p. 298.
53. *Ibid.*, p. 289.
54. *Ibid.*, p. 305.
55. Elizabeth Bowen, *The Heat of the Day* (1948; New York: Knopf, 1949), p. 220.
56. Elizabeth Bowen, *To the North*, p. 102.
57. Barbara Pym, *Excellent Women* (1952; New York: Harper & Row, 1978), pp. 171, 189.
58. Anthea Trodd, *Women's Writing in English*, p. 15.
59. Bowen, *To the North*, p. 85.
60. E.M. Delafield, *Diary of a Provincial Lady* (1930; London: Virago Press, 1985), p. 3.
61. Dorothy L. Sayers, *Gaudy Night* (1936; New York: Avon, 1968), pp. 145, 379.
62. *Ibid.*, pp. 91–2.

63. *Ibid.*, p. 247.
64. Dorothy L. Sayers, *Busman's Honeymoon* (1937; New York: Avon, 1968), p. 57.
65. Iris Murdoch, *Bruno's Dream* (1969; New York: Penguin, 1986), p. 17.
66. *Ibid.*, pp. 168, 170.
67. *Ibid.*, p. 268.
68. *Ibid.*, p. 309.
69. *Ibid.*, p. 269.
70. *Ibid.*, p. 308.
71. A.S. Byatt, *The Virgin in the Garden* (1978; New York: Penguin, 1981), p. 159.
72. *Ibid.*, p. 115.
73. *Ibid.*
74. *Ibid.*, p. 185.
75. *Ibid.*, p. 188.
76. A.S. Byatt, *Still Life* (1985; New York: Penguin, 1988), p. 298.
77. *Ibid.*, p. 205.

Chapter 5 Betrayal

1. Molly Keane, *Taking Chances* (1929; London: Virago, 1987), p. 121.
2. Georgette Heyer, *Frederica* (1965; New York: Harlequin, 2000), p. 15. One is tempted to wonder whether Byatt's notable character with this name is an ironic connection with Heyer's novels.
3. *Ibid.*, pp. 26–7.
4. *Ibid.*, p. 330.
5. *Ibid.*, pp. 372–3.
6. Molly Keane, *Treasure Hunt* (1952; London: Virago, 1991), p. 41.
7. *Ibid.*, pp. 154–5.
8. *Ibid.*, p. 201.
9. Caroline Blackwood, *Great Granny Webster* (1977; New York: New York Review of Books, 2002), pp. 72–4.
10. *Ibid.*, p. 20.
11. *Ibid.*, p. 23.
12. Elizabeth Bowen, *Friends and Relations* (1931; New York: Penguin, 1986), p. 104.
13. *Ibid.*, p. 94.
14. *Ibid.*
15. Bowen, *To the North*, p. 133.
16. *Ibid.*, p. 8.
17. *Ibid.*, p. 27.
18. Elizabeth Bowen, *The House in Paris* (1935; New York: Avon, 1979), p. 138.
19. Elizabeth Bowen, *The Death of the Heart* (1938; New York: Avon, 1979), p. 74.
20. *Ibid.*, p. 300.
21. *Ibid.*, p. 306.
22. Keane, *Taking Chances*, p. 190.
23. *Ibid.*, pp. 124, 121.
24. *Ibid.*, p. 128.

25. Iris Murdoch, *A Severed Head* (1961; London: Chatto & Windus, 1972), p. 199.
26. Iris Murdoch, *The Nice and the Good* (1968; London: Triad/Panther Books, 1977), p. 30.
27. *Ibid.*, pp. 49–50.
28. *Ibid.*, p. 19.
29. *Ibid.*, p. 266.
30. Iris Murdoch, *The Sacred and Profane Love Machine* (1974; New York: Penguin, 1983), p. 77.
31. *Ibid.*, p. 157.
32. *Ibid.*, p. 339.
33. *Ibid.*, p. 337.
34. Murdoch, *A Severed Head*, p. 191.
35. *Ibid.*, p. 207.
36. Salley Vickers, *Miss Garnet's Angel* (London: HarperCollins, 2000), pp. 77–8.
37. A.S. Byatt, *Possession: A Romance* (New York: Random House, 1990), p. 207.
38. Barbara Pym, *Jane and Prudence* (1953; New York: E.P. Dutton, 1981), p. 28.
39. *Ibid.*, p. 173.
40. *Ibid.*, p. 123.
41. *Ibid.*, p. 192.
42. *Ibid.*
43. *Ibid.*, p. 194.
44. *Ibid.*, p. 198.
45. *Ibid.*, p. 14.
46. *Ibid.*, p. 200.
47. *Ibid.*, pp. 199–200.
48. *Ibid.*, p. 199.

Chapter 6 Academic and detective novels

1. Dorothy L. Sayers, *Gaudy Night* (1936; New York: Avon, 1968), p. 249.
2. A.S. Byatt, *Still Life* (1985; New York: Penguin, 1988), p. 210.
3. *Ibid.*, p. 184.
4. *Ibid.*, p. 289.
5. Sayers, *Gaudy Night*, pp. 25–6.
6. *Ibid.*, p. 25.
7. *Ibid.*, p. 194.
8. *Ibid.*, p. 377.
9. *Ibid.*, p. 378.
10. Byatt, *Still Life*, p. 110.
11. *Ibid.*, p. 118.
12. *Ibid.*, p. 128.
13. *Ibid.*, p. 258.
14. A.S. Byatt, *Babel Tower* (London: Chatto & Windus, 1996), p. 444.
15. Byatt, *Still Life*, p. 283.
16. Byatt, *Babel Tower*, p. 80.
17. *Ibid.*, p. 155.

18. Byatt, *Still Life*, p. 306.
19. *Ibid.*, p. 151.
20. Byatt, *Possession*, p. 468.
21. *Ibid.*, p. 459.
22. *Ibid.*, p. 276.
23. *Ibid.*
24. *Ibid.*, p. 276.
25. *Ibid.*, pp. 458–9.
26. Dorothy L. Sayers, *Strong Poison* (1930; New York: Avon, 1967), p. 7.
27. Sayers, *Gaudy Night*, p. 33; *Five Red Herrings* (1931; New York: Avon, 1968), p. 243.
28. Dorothy L. Sayers, *Have His Carcase* (1932; New York: Avon, 1968), p. 351.
29. *Ibid.*, p. 239.
30. Dorothy L. Sayers, *Murder Must Advertise* (1933; London: Landsborough Publications Ltd, 1959), p. 54.
31. Sayers, *Have His Carcase*, pp. 121–2.
32. Dorothy L. Sayers, *The Unpleasantness at the Bellona Club* (1928; New York: Avon, 1963), pp. 80–1.
33. *Ibid.*, pp. 172, 179–80.
34. Sayers, *Strong Poison*, p. 38.
35. *Ibid.*, p. 18.
36. *Ibid.*, p. 38.
37. Sayers, *Busman's Honeymoon*, p. 21.
38. Byatt, *Still Life*, p. 215.
39. A.S. Byatt, *The Virgin in the Garden*, p. 348.
40. A.S. Byatt, *Passions of the Mind: Selected Writtings* (New York: Random House, 1992), p. 239.
41. Byatt, *The Virgin in the Garden*, pp. 34–5.
42. Georgette Heyer, *The Unknown Ajax* (1959; New York: Ace Books, 1972), p. 237.

Chapter 7 'The Higher Common Sense'

1. Elizabeth Bowen, *English Novelists*, 'Britain in Pictures' Series (London: Collins, 1947), p. 46.
2. With Greek tragedy, and Shakespeare, it is different; the rareness of this artistic achievement speaks for itself about the difficulty of achieving it (or the special circumstances which are required to produce it).
3. A.S. Byatt, *Iris Murdoch* (Essex: Longman Group Ltd, 1976), pp. 24–5.
4. Elizabeth Bowen, 'Notes on Writing a Novel,' reprinted in Hermione Lee, ed., *The Mulberry Tree: Writings of Elizabeth Bowen* (London: Virago, 1986), pp. 34, 46.
5. A.S. Byatt, *Still Life* (1985; New York: Penguin, 1988), p. 344.
6. George Eliot, *Middlemarch* (1872; New York: New American Library, 1964), pp. 811, 809. A.S. Byatt has also edited this novel.
7. A.S. Byatt, *Passions of the Mind: Selected Writings* (New York: Random House, 1992), p. 243.

8. Iris Murdoch, *A Severed Head* (1961; London: Chatto & Windus, 1972), pp. 248, 252.
9. Dorothy L. Sayers, *The Unpleasantness at the Bellona Club* (1928; New York: Avon, 1963), pp. 80, 179.
10. Susan Howatch, *Ultimate Prizes* (Glasgow: William Collins Sons & Co., Ltd, 1989), pp. 241, 458.
11. *Ibid.*, p. 475.
12. Elizabeth Bowen, *A World of Love* (1954; New York: Avon, 1978), p. 188; *Eva Trout: or Changing Scenes* (1968; New York: Avon, 1978), p. 276.
13. Barbara Pym, *No Fond Return of Love* (1961; New York: E.P. Dutton, 1979), p. 286.
14. Stella Gibbons, *Miss Linsey and Pa* (London: Longmans, Green & Co., 1936), pp. 86, 136, 69.
15. Stella Gibbons, *Cold Comfort Farm* (1932; New York: Penguin, 1994), p. 102.
16. Lee, 'Preface,' *The Mulberry Tree*, p. 1.
17. Gibbons, *Cold Comfort Farm*, pp. 20–1.
18. Georgette Heyer, *The Grand Sophy* (London: The Book Club, 1951), pp. 78–9.
19. *Ibid.*, p. 275.
20. *Ibid.*, p. 119.
21. Gibbons, *Cold Comfort Farm*, p. 47. On the train journey to the farm, she carries with her a copy of Abbé's *Pensées*, 'surely the wisest book ever compiled for the guidance of a truly civilized person' (p. 47).
22. *Ibid.*, pp. 130, 136.
23. *Ibid.*, pp. 136–7.
24. *Ibid.*, p. 180.
25. *Ibid.*, p. 221.
26. *Ibid.*, pp. 201–2.
27. Barbara Pym, *Excellent Women* (1952; New York: Harper & Row, 1978), p. 7; Elizabeth Bowen, *English Novelists*, p. 34.

Index

KING ALFRED'S COLLEGE
LIBRARY